THE
PRESIDENT'S
MAN

Also published in Large Print
from G.K. Hall by Elliott Roosevelt:

A First Class Murder
Murder in the Blue Room
Murder in the Rose Garden
Murder at the Palace
The White House Pantry Murder
Murder at Hobcaw Barony
The Hyde Park Murder
Murder and the First Lady

THE PRESIDENT'S MAN

A "Blackjack" Endicott Novel

Elliott Roosevelt

G.K.HALL &CO.

Boston, Massachusetts

1992

This Large Print Book carries the
Seal of Approval of N.A.V.H.

Published in Large Print by arrangement with
St. Martin's Press.

G.K. Hall Large Print Book Series.

British Commonwealth rights courtesy of
Scott Meredith Literacy Agency.

Printed on acid free paper in the
United States of America.

Set in 18 pt. Plantin.

Library of Congress Cataloging-in-Publication Data

Roosevelt, Elliott, 1910-
    The president's man : A "Blackjack" endicott Novel / Elliott
Roosevelt
        p.   cm. — (G.K. Hall large print book series)
    ISBN 0-8161-5396-5 (hc). — ISBN 0-8161-5397-3 (pb)
    1. Roosevelt, Franklin D. (Franklin Delano), 1882-1945—Fiction.
2. Large type books.   I. Title.
PS3535.0549P7 1992
813′ .54—dc20   92-17879

CHICAGO

July 2, 1932

It was triumph and bedlam all mixed together in one great, gaudy, noisy night; and for a time it seemed the applause would never die down, the tumult never quieted.

Just before he moved out to the lectern, the Governor of New York waited patiently while the steel braces on his legs were locked. Then he lurched forward, supported by his son James on one side, a bodyguard on the other—until they reached the lectern. The Governor gripped the lectern with both hands, and the two others moved back. He stood there, erect, grinning, nodding. He wore a gray, double-breasted suit and a bow tie. The bright lights of the auditoriurn glittered on his pincenez. From time to time he loosed one hands grip on the lectern and waved at the cheering thousands.

He had flown from Albany to Chicago in a Ford Tri-Motor, a nine-hour flight in rough weather, to accept the presidential nomination of the Democratic National Convention. In doing that he had broken precedent in a most dramatic way. Tradition dictated that the candidate should remain at home and not launch the campaign until an official delegation from the party should wait on him and formally notify him of the nomination—usually not until after several weeks. Not only had Governor Roosevelt come to the convention to accept the nomination; he had flown!

He had a flair for drama. He knew how to make news. Everything he did was suddenly fascinating, the subject of attention and comment. And . . . some estimates had it that as many as ten million people would tune their radios to the address he was about to make. No political speech ever made had been heard by even a fraction of that many people.

When at last the auditorium fell silent—reasonably silent—Franklin D. Roosevelt began his acceptance speech:

I have started out on the tasks that lie ahead by breaking the absurd tradition that the candidate should remain in professional ignorance of what has happened for weeks until he is formally notified of that event many weeks later. You have nominated me and I know it, and I am here to thank you for the honor. Let it also be symbolic that in doing so I broke traditions. Let it from now on be the task of our party to break foolish traditions.

In a box not far from the front of the hall, a woman in dark hat and veil sat alone to watch and listen. It was in a section reserved for the wives and children of prominent politicians. This one had in fact been reserved for Mrs. Alfred Smith; but Smith had left the convention and returned to New York City without waiting to hear the Governor accept the nomination he had so desperately wanted for himself, and of course his wife had gone with him.

Reporters could not get near the rigidly guarded box. That, plus the woman's veil, had inspired intemperate curiosity among the press corps. From across the hall, two reporters from New York papers stared at her through powerful binoculars.

"Damned if I can make it out," said one. "It's not his mother."

"Don't necessarily have to be anything to do with Roosevelt," said the other. "Could be Mrs. Al Smith sneaked back to watch."

"Could be Al himself, dressed like a woman," laughed the first reporter.

"Naw, she don't have a cigar."

The woman seemed nervous and from time to time glanced behind her as if she were looking for someone to come and occupy the vacant chair beside her.

The Governor continued:

Work and security—these are more than words. They are more than facts. They are spiritual values, the true goal toward which our efforts at reconstruction should lead.

A man pushed his way through to the guards behind the woman's box. They stood aside and let him in. He sat down, spoke quietly to her, and turned to listen to Governor Roosevelt.

"Oh-ho!" said the reporter with the binoculars. He handed the glasses to the second reporter. "Who's that?"

The second reporter studied the man. He was tall, erect, probably in his forties—more likely late than early forties. His black hair was parted just off the middle. He wore a thin black mustache. He was well dressed, and displayed a red flower in his lapel. He looked comfortable and self-confident.

"Okay, I got it," said the second reporter, returning the binoculars. "The guy's a Boston fella named Jack Endicott. Rich as Rockefeller. Flies a plane, sails a boat, races cars. Plays a hell of a game of blackjack and is sometimes called Blackjack. Ladies man, too, for damned sure. So the woman in the veil is his date for tonight. And she's wearing the veil 'cause she's either a high-price hooker or she's some other guy's wife."

"So what's he doing here in a box seat?"

"Friend of Governor Roosevelt. They went to Harvard together. Just a few weeks ago he took the Governor for a cruise on his sailboat. No big deal. He's probably gonna make a big campaign contribution, or maybe he already has. Just a guy with more money than brains. No big deal."

I pledge you, I pledge myself, to a new deal for the American people. Let all of us here assembled constitute ourselves prophets of a new order of competence and courage. This is more than a political campaign; it is a call to arms. Give me

ix

your help, not to win votes alone, but to win in this crusade to restore America to its own greatness.

The veiled woman turned to John Lowell Endicott and said, "That's very good. Not just what he is saying but the way he says it. I'm really very proud of Frank."

Jack Endicott nodded and leaned closer to her, so she could hear him over the cheering. "I'm glad I could bring you to see it, Lucy. He knows you're here. He's happy that you are."

Lucy Mercer Rutherfurd reached up under her veil and wiped tears from her eyes.

1

"Thank you, Drake," said John Lowell Endicott one evening in the late spring of 1932. He was speaking to his man, who had just finished pinning his boutonniere in the lapel of his cutaway coat. He had held his head up and to the right as Drake brandished the pin near his throat, and now he stared down over his cheek to be sure the white flower was securely in place. He shrugged, to be sure his coat and waistcoat were properly settled on his shoulders. "Have I gained a pound or two, Drake?" he asked as he placed his high silk hat carefully on his head.

"That appears possible, Sir," said his manservant dryly.

"Well, I've a choice, have I not? I can try to sweat off the pound or two, or I can have the tailors adjust my suits. P'raps you'd better make me an appointment for steam and a rub in the morning."

Drake nodded in approval.

"Well . . . then. You need not wait up, for me. I shall be rather late, I imagine."

"A taxi, Sir?"

"I'm going to the club first. I'll walk."

John Lowell Endicott did not often take dinner at the Common Club. It was too . . . too *Boston,* too *Harvard;* and though his life was firmly moored to Boston and Harvard, he did not habitually seek out its foundation stones for his dinner companions. Au contraire, he had sought out— some said he had founded—a lighter circle in Boston society. He was of course entirely at home and entirely welcome in whichever group he wished to favor. He was, after all, a Lowell *and* an Endicott.

This evening he meant to favor both circles. He had a dinner appointment at eight. Before that he would pass an hour at the club, see who was there, and be seen.

He walked down the worn stone steps from his door to the brick sidewalk, tapped his stick once on the bricks, and strode off jauntily toward the Common Club.

It was a fragrant spring evening. Jack Endicott could not identify the fragrances he smelled—botany, or whatever you explored to find out things like that, had eluded him as a study—but he identified what he

2

smelled with a pleasant spring evening, and that was enough for him. The leaves were out, and some of the trees were white or pink with blossom. Another, astringent sort of odor rose from the damp bricks of the walk. It was, he believed, the odor of the moss that had long since stained the bricks a kind of greenish black, so that the original red showed through only where the soles of shoes scrubbed off the green. He could smell, too, carried to him on a light evening breeze, the distinctive odor of a fine Havana cigar.

"Uncle Henry!"

The cigar smoker was Jack's uncle, Henry Endicott, the younger brother of Jack's late father. He, too, was on his way to the Common Club, where he went every evening after he left the bank; but, unlike his nephew, he'd not yet had time to change into evening clothes. He would drink his usual two Scotches in the wrinkled dark-blue business suit he had worn all day. He was not quite twenty years older than Jack and wore a thick, bristly, white mustache. He looked, as he often did at the end of the day, weary, and his veteran gray fedora was smashed carelessly down over his white hair.

Uncle Henry was a big man, heavyset—
he had once played rugby and had broken
his nose three times. "An evening ahead of
you, I surmise," he said, taking note of
Jack's clothes.

"Dressed for dinner," said Jack.

"Oh, yes. Yes . . . Well, I'll get into my
boiled shirt a little later. On you way to the
club barroom, are you?"

"I had thought of sipping a drink or three
before being off to dinner," said Jack.

They lived in the twelfth year of Prohibition, and they had never missed a drink:
of whiskey, gin, champagne, beer . . . whatever they fancied. Jack Endicott was quoted
occasionally at parties for something he had
said ten years ago: that Prohibition was for
the yahoos in parts of the country where
yahoos lived, which was . . . well, wherever
they were to be found, certainly not within
the smell of Atlantic saltwater.

Though Uncle Henry could be scornful
of his nephew, he accorded him a grudging
respect; and the two men, senior and ju-
nior, mounted the steps of the Common
Club and entered its gaslit precincts as
though they were brothers, not uncle and
nephew.

They left their hats and sticks with the

attendant in the cloakroom and mounted the long, broad, curving staircase to the second floor, the stairs creaking as they climbed. That the barroom should be on the second floor was the club's only concession to Prohibition. Although clearly no policeman would think of entering the Common Club to inconvenience its members at their libations, if some cretin of a federal agent should happen on the premises he would have to climb these creaking stairs to reach the barroom, where he would be confronted only by indignant members sipping ginger ale and lemonade.

Although the foyer and stairway of the club were lighted by gas mantels inside round globes, the barroom was electrically lighted by clear bulbs with glowing filaments, in the old style the Germans called *Glühbirne*—glow pears. The bar was an ornate structure of carved oak, some thirty feet long. It had been purchased from a saloon closed in 1920, carted here, and lovingly installed. Gentlemen stood at it now as generations of men, not all of them gentlemen, had: each with one foot resting on a polished brass rail, with one arm on the bar, glass in clenched hand.

The two Endicotts stepped up and ordered Scotch. A bottle of Black Label was pushed across the bar to them, with glasses. Ice, if they wanted it, was in a silver bucket, water in a crystal pitcher.

They nodded at the other men at the bar— Charles Gardner, John Cabot, George Saltonstall, William Holmes, John Whitney, Richard Emerson, Charles Adams . . . Everyone but Henry Endicott was dressed for dinner.

"Well, Jack," said Uncle Henry as he used the tongs to put one chip of ice in each glass. "Are the Democrats going to nominate your friend?"

"Unless they come up with someone better," said Jack. "I see in today's papers that another state delegation—Tennessee, I believe it was—has declared for him."

Uncle Henry poured Scotch into their glasses. "So long as they don't nominate that damned Al Smith again," he said. "Of course, it makes little difference who the Democrats choose. It is inconceivable to me that the country would elect a Democrat in the midst of this economic downturn."

"All the political pundits see it otherwise, I am afraid," said Jack as he raised his glass. "Everyone au courant seems to think the Democrats will unseat President Hoover."

"Humphh. Well, what sort of man is your old school chum Roosevelt?"

"Not a bad sort of fellow, actually," said Jack. "We met at Harvard. He'd come from Groton. He'd have been a Republican by natural inclination, I think. That's how his sentiments lay. But his father was a Democrat for some odd reason."

"Pushy sort, I've heard," said Uncle Henry.

"I s'pose he is," said Jack.

"Well, so was his Uncle Teddy," said Henry Endicott.

"His *Cousin* Teddy," said Jack. "And third or fourth cousin at that."

"Never could imagine what Henry Cabot Lodge saw in Theodore Roosevelt," said Uncle Henry. "If he'd kept calm in 1912, instead of running as a damned-fool Bull Moose, we'd have got Big Bill Taft for another term, instead of that insane Wilson."

"I can think of worse men for the presidency than Frank Roosevelt," said Jack.

"Oh? Name *one,*" said his uncle loftily.

"You just did. Al Smith. And how about Cactus Jack Garner? Would you like him?"

7

"William Gibbs McAdoo," said Uncle Henry. "Newton D. Baker."

"Huey Long," laughed Jack.

"Take my word for it," said Uncle Henry. "When the oath of office is given on the steps of the Capitol next March, the man with his hand on the Bible is going to be Herbert Hoover. Every American with a damned *grain* of sense is going to vote for Hoover."

He had raised his voice, and John Cabot had heard him. "Hear, hear," he said quietly.

Jack turned slightly so as to include Cabot in the conversation. "Well, gentlemen," he said, "I suspect you are right. But if it has to be a Democrat, then the country could do worse than Frank Roosevelt."

"Is he sound on money?" asked the slight, gray-haired Cabot. "You know what I mean. No escapades in economics."

"He's for economy in government and a balanced budget," said Jack. "He told me so himself. And by the way, speaking of economy and budget, I may be asked for a bit of investment advice this evening. Any suggestions?"

"Don't put money in the stock market unless you can afford to lose it," said Uncle

Henry. "If you do invest, diversify. Don't establish too big a position in anything."

"I think Radio will be all right in the long run," said John Cabot. "And New York Central. If I were buying right now, I'd probably pick up a few shares of those."

"Thank you, gentlemen," said Jack, raising his glass in salute. Your advice will make me sound like an expert."

Jack ordered the taxi driver to circle the Common and drive to an address on Beacon Street. There, while the taxi waited, Jack went to the door of a red-brick house much like his own.

He knocked, using the heavy brass knocker: A maid answered and welcomed him into the foyer. And in a moment, Felicia Bowdoin Cushing hurried down the stairs and extended both hands to him.

"Felicia," he said. "You are beautiful always but extraordinarily so tonight."

"And you are the suave rogue, ever," she said. "The most debonair man in Boston."

They laughed, and he took her arm and led her out to the taxi.

Felicia Bowdoin Cushing was roughly fifteen years younger than Jack. Her late husband had been Jack's age, and he had left her enough Cushing money to live on quite comfortably in the style to which a Cushing was entitled. She was a stunning beauty: elegant, poised, and self-confident. Her eyes were perhaps her best feature: deep blue twinkling, showing her ready sense of humor. But a discerning observer saw in them, too, a dreamy, suggestive wistfulness. Her eyebrows were plucked into thin arches. Her mouth was wide and her lips thin. She wore her blonde hair softly styled, turning just under her ears. A white silk dress clung to her figure, and a fur hung around her shoulders.

The driver crossed the bridge into Cambridge and drove north.

"Have you heard from Marietta?" Felicia asked.

She referred to his eighteen-year-old daughter, Marietta Biddle Endicott, who had gone south by train to spend a week with her mother in Philadelphia. Cynthia Biddle Endicott had not remarried, repeatedly declared herself lonely, and constantly importuned her daughter to spend more time with her. Marietta had spent only as much as the decree required, and now that she was eighteen she was no longer subject to the decree and had cut the time in half.

"A wire from New York," he said. "She

got off the train and checked into the Waldorf for one night, so she could take in some Broadway show she wants to see. Then of course I got a frantic wire from Cynthia, wanting to know where Marietta was. Felicia—"

"The girl is independent. Would you want her to be anything else?"

"Maybe just a touch less independent," he said.

"Are you sure everything's okay with Maury?" she asked.

He nodded. "Everything is just fine with Maury. I talked with him on the phone this afternoon."

"I guess Maury's only problem," she said, "is that this time a year or so from now, he's going to be out of business. When we can simply walk into the Copley dining room and have drinks and wine with dinner, Maury will go out of business. All the speaks will."

"Maybe not," said Jack. "Not Maury, anyway."

The speakeasy was called Leedo— named and reputation established before the reasonably literate Maury acquired it. It was in a big old house on a residential street, and patrons were required to come in taxis or park their cars at least a block away, to avoid annoying the neighbors. Most arrived by taxi; and when they were ready to leave, taxis were always available, the drivers knowing full well that tips paid by Leedo customers were always much better than any others in Boston.

The sky was still gray-red when Jack and Felicia walked up to the great, old, pine-shaded house. The twin doors had big windows of frosted glass, and they were not locked. They led only into a vestibule, from which access to the house was available only through a single heavy oak door. Jack pressed the bell button. The characteristic speakeasy spy door opened, and a face stared out.

"'Lo, Teddy," said Jack.

A noisy lock was released, and the door swung back.

No matter how many times he came there, no matter how much money he spent, Jack was never welcome to Teddy, who treated everyone equally: as a possible fed. He nodded gravely and with a short gesture suggested to Jack that he take his lady inside.

They walked through another door and entered the main dining room and barroom of the speakeasy. The redoubtable Maury had been warned they were entering, likely by telephone from Teddy; and he bustled across the big room, arms spread, grin wide.

"Mr. Endicott! Welcome! Sally! Mr. Endicott's hat and stick! Mrs. Cushing's fur!"

A tubercular girl wearing a red corselet, with stockings held up by black garters, took the hat, stick, and fur.

"I've a choice of two tables for you," said Maury. "Near the stage, near the band. Or back enough that you can talk without being drowned out."

He looked first to Jack, to hear the choice, but it was Felicia who made it. She gestured toward the rear. "Music tonight?" she asked.

"Jazz," said Maury.

"Of course," she said. "Put us where we can hear it but will not be overwhelmed by it."

Maury nodded obsequiously and led them to a table five ranks from the stage. "Champagne?" he asked.

Jack looked to Felicia. She shook her head. "No, I think a double shot of gin, on the rocks. Real gin, Maury. Real gin."

"Mrs. Cushing!" Maury protested. "Would I serve *you* anything but real gin?"

"Right off the boat, hey?"

He raised his hand. "As God is my witness," he said solemnly. "Walker Black, Mr. Endicott?"

Jack nodded, and Maury hurried away, snapping his fingers at a waiter across the room.

They glanced around the room, to see who was there.

The walls had been taken out, making one room of what had been a big parlor, a dining room, and maybe a library or sitting room. The light was from flame-shaped orange bulbs in sconces around the walls. Except for the small stage where the musicians would play and the small cleared area where people danced, the main room of the Leedo had the aspect of a rather ordinary restaurant.

That it was a speakeasy was proved by one inconspicuous feature. Beneath each table, hidden by the long tablecloth, was a galvanized bucket. On a signal, the ringing of a bell, everyone poured whatever was being drunk in the bucket, and the waiters would rush those buckets in the bathroom and flush the contents down—while the pa-

14

trons at the tables poured seltzer or ginger ale into their glasses to rinse away the vestiges of alcohol and to be seen drinking these innocent elixirs when the feds arrived. Everyone knew what to do, but no one had ever had to do it.

The kitchen had been converted into two bathrooms, with signs on the door reading POINTERS and SETTERS. Cooking was done in the cellar.

A poker game or two, plus a game of craps, were probably already in progress upstairs. Two bedrooms on the back were the cribs for two hookers Maury kept available for the occasional gentleman who wanted one.

"Did you buy those parachutes, Jack?" Felicia asked.

"I haven't, actually, but I suppose I will."

"I enjoy flying with you, darling," she said, "but I won't go anymore without a 'chute. After all, we don't go sailing without life preservers."

"I was going to suggest a hop out to Nantucket," he said. "But I won't have the 'chutes yet."

"Can't you borrow some?"

"There's a thought. Maybe Billy has some."

A man at a table nearer the stage lifted a hand in greeting. Jack nodded and smiled. The man with whom he had exchanged salutations was Peter O'Malley, known as "Hammer Pete." Maury worked for him. Everybody who had a speakeasy in Boston worked for O'Malley one way or another. He was a big, beefy, florid-faced man with white hair cut bristly short. He was wearing what was called an eighty-dollar tuxedo. His shirt studs were large diamonds.

Sitting with O'Malley was a dark-visaged, nervous man who kept glancing around the room as if he feared some threat. He glanced at Jack and Felicia for a moment but did not show any sign of recognition. His name was Luigi Loparco.

Felicia quietly asked Jack who that was.

"A bad sort, I'm afraid," said Jack. "The story is that he has committed a number of murders."

"Ooh!"

Jack shrugged. "He's no threat to *us,* of course. Their kind only kill each other."

"O'Malley keeps glancing at you. Do you suppose—?"

"I imagine he'd like an invitation to join us for a drink," said Jack.

16

"Do you know him on a social basis?"

"Not exactly. On a business basis. But . . . Do you mind?"

"I hope Loparco comes, too," she said.

With a gesture, Jack suggested to O'Malley that he join them at their table. The big man rose immediately, jerked his head to order Loparco to join him, and walked over.

"Hello, Pete," said Jack, rising and extending his hand. "You've met Mrs. Cushing. But I don't think Mr. Loparco has."

"An honor to see you, Mrs. Cushing," said O'Malley smoothly. "This is Luigi Loparco. He's a business associate of mine."

O'Malley and Loparco sat down.

The two mob men were genuinely deferential to Jack and Felicia. Jack had discovered that men like O'Malley and Maury idolized old money and the power they suspected it bought. Totally cynical, totally ruthless in their own milieu, they lived in superstitious awe of the mysterious powers a man like John Lowell Endicott might possess.

Maury was at their side in a moment, when he saw O'Malley and Loparco join Jack and Felicia. At the same time the

17

waiter brought Jack's Scotch and Felicia's gin.

"Gin?" asked O'Malley. "Put a bottle of Beefeaters on the table, Maury. And a bottle of Black Label."

Luigi Loparco stared at Felicia, failing utterly to conceal the mixed emotions she raised in him: ingenuous veneration and irrepressible lubricity.

"I read about your automobile race," O'Malley said to Jack. He referred to a story in the Sunday newspapers about a road race driven by Jack in his 1928 Bugatti Type 44. "Comin' in second wasn't so bad, if you didn't have money on bein' first."

Jack grinned. "No, not so bad," he agreed.

The jazz band had taken its place on the little stage by now, and the music began. The five Negro musicians began with a Scott Joplin rag, and six chorus girls trotted onto the little dance floor and began to kick and wiggle. Dressed like the hat-check girl in red corselets and dark stockings held up by black garters, they brought far more energy than talent to their performance.

"I'm still looking for legitimate ways to invest," said O'Malley. "The banks . . . Well, you know."

18

"With the banks," said Jack, "things are going to get worse before they get better."

"What are you investin' in, Jack?" asked O'Malley.

"A few high-grade stocks," said Jack. "A little in real estate."

"I bought the stocks you told me," said O'Malley. "But, I . . . Well, you know."

"You haven't lost anything on them," said Jack. "The way things are today, if you can invest without losing anything, you're doing well. But give those stocks time, Pete. Give them time."

"Yeah . . ."

"That's the trouble with what ya call investments," said Loparco. "You gotta wait for yer dough."

"That's *businesses*," said O'Malley sharply to the dark little man. "Makin' money takes time."

"Who's got time?" asked Loparco.

Jack was amused by the little Italian, a weasely fellow whose black hair was shiny with the brilliantine, maybe even Macassar oil, he had used to slick it down. He would be entertaining to Felicia, no doubt.

"If you don't keep your money in banks, where you keepin' it?" asked O'Malley.

19

"Some banks will survive," said Jack. "Put some of your money in State Street."

O'Malley's eyebrows rose. "That's not *your* bank," he said skeptically.

"My bank is going to be all right, too," said Jack. "But suppose I told you to put your money in my bank and it failed. You wouldn't think me so good a friend then, would you?"

Loparco began to laugh, a first a restrained snicker, then a hearty laugh. "The guy's got brains, Pete," he said. "That's what I call brains."

Hammer Pete O'Malley was not amused, and his hard glance demolished the broad grin on the face of Luigi Loparco.

Maury returned with the bottles of Beefeaters and Black Label and set them on the table.

"Send a case of that to Mrs. Gushing, my compliments, said O'Malley, nodding at the bottle of gin. Then he faced Jack and asked, "You have a business of your own that I could invest in?"

Jack smiled and shook his head. "I'm afraid not, Pete. You see, I got most of what I have the hard way: by inheriting it. I do own a piece of the bank but not enough to control it. Other than that, I have investments, some of them of many years standing, in two score companies, plus some real estate; and a part of what I have is in Europe, England mostly. I'm diversified, Pete. I recommend that to you."

"Don't put all your eggs in one basket," said O'Malley.

"Exactly."

As the band moved on to its second number, the girls of the chorus pulled down their corselets and began to dance with their breasts bare. Of the six, four blushed bright red.

"I was thinkin' ten thousand shares of Woolworth," said O'Malley. He was thinking of an investment of well over half a million dollars. "Whatta ya think? After all, when folks can't afford to shop at Saks Fifth Avenue no more, Woolworths—"

"Two thousand," Jack interrupted. "Put some in Radio. Some in New York Central. Diversify."

Hammer Pete grinned. "How many guys in my line of business got an Endicott for a financial adviser? Your evenin' here's on me. On me, Jack . . . an' my pleasure. Me and Luigi—"

"I'd like to ask you something, Mr. O'Malley," said Felicia.

21

"Sure, Mrs. Cushing. Anything."

"Well . . ." she said. "Jack and I were talking. What happens to a place like this, what happens to this kind of business, if they repeal Prohibition?"

O'Malley tipped his head to one side. "Why you think I'm worryin' about investments? We're gonna be put outa business. Y' know what I mean?"

"If we could have drinks and wine at the Copley tonight, we might not be here," she said.

"You said it." Jack laughed. "We won't abandon you, Pete."

"Maybe you won't," said O'Malley somberly. "And there's other guys that won't. But you gotta figure something, Jack . . . Mrs. Cushing. Place like this—" He glanced around. "It does okay, makes a livin' for Maury. But the real money's in beer! Beer . . . An' if six months from now they can just open a brewery and make it anywhere Well. You see the point."

Felicia giggled, her silvery voice cutting through the music and attracting the attention of people at other tables. "Then you are . . ." She stopped to giggle some more. "You are *drys!* No?"

Luigi Loparco nodded. "You got it figured out, lady."

She laughed harder. "That's funny! I don't know why that's so very funny! You're on the same side with what Jack calls the yahoos."

"God bless the yahoos, whoever they are," said O'Malley emphatically.

"Wha' they call 'em . . . ?" Loparco pondered. "Lessee, there's what they call, uh, *Baptists* . . . an uh . . . uh—They come from places like, uh, Kansas an Ar-kansas an Misippi. Like that." He giggled, too—only gutturally, deep in his throat. "Like that."

"What if the Democrats nominate Al Smith and elect him President?" Jack asked. "He'll support Repeal, and—"

"Naw," said O'Malley. "The New York guys got Ol' Al in their pockets. He won't do anything to hurt the brothers."

"What about Roosevelt?"

Hammer Pete's face reddened. "Ain't nobody can trust that son of a bitch," he said.

"He's a close personal friend of Jack's," said Felicia—and instantly blushed, realizing she had said something she shouldn't have. "That is, they went to school together."

O'Malley frowned hard as he spoke to Jack. "Lots of 'em talk Repeal," he said. "Roosevelt would do it."

Jack nodded thoughtfully. He pretended his attention was distracted by a young brunette in the chorus line.

"You know him, you tell him it ain't a good idea," said Hammer Pete O'Malley darkly. "A gentleman like you—like Franklin D. Roosevelt, for that matter—gets what drinks he wants. Prohibition don't make no difference to you. But it makes a whole lot of difference to a whole lot of guys. You tell him, if you know him. Jack . . . We're friends, aren't we? I'm honored to call a man like you a friend. How would Pete O'Malley ever have got to be friends with a man like John Lowell Endicott if we didn't have Prohibition? We can do good stuff for each other. Can't we? You know we can. But if this man Roosevelt gets in the White House and repeals . . ." He shook his head. "It's gonna spoil a lot of good things."

Jack grinned. "Well, Frank Roosevelt hardly takes political advice from *me*. You ask me to suggest a stock. Frank asks me to suggest a horse to put some money on. That's the way it is between Frank and me."

"Tell ya what," said O'Malley. "Bet he

likes Château Lafite Rothschild, hey? Ten cases! From Pete O'Malley, delivered to the Governor's Mansion in Albany. No strings. Gesture of good will. Right? You explain to him, okay? And where ten cases of wine came from can come one hell of a big contribution to his campaign. I mean, hey, Jack, let's look at it this way—Everybody can be happy. Why not everybody be happy? No reason guys should work against each other, is there? Maybe he listens to you, since you're old school chums. He don't wanna bust up somebody's business, does he? I bet he doesn't. We can work together, ya know? Huh? Why not?"

Jack looked first into the eyes of Felicia, where he saw nothing approaching understanding, then into the eyes of Hammer Pete O'Malley. He shrugged. "As I told you, he does not ask me for political advice. I'll be glad to tell you what you suggest, though. Happy to tell him. Why not?"

"Mr. O'Malley . . ." said Felicia. "Does Maury have a good game going on tonight?"

"Dunno," said Hammer Pete.

"Like to get into a good game of blackjack?" she said. "Or craps? Even craps. I shoot a mean game."

25

Hammer Pete shrugged. "Let's see."

Felicia exited the cab with Jack, at his house. He let them in with a key, Drake having long since gone to bed as Jack had told him to do. Both of them—and either of them would have admitted it— were more than a little tipsy. They stopped just inside the door, both to regain balance and to clutch each other in passionate embrace.

"Hmm . . . Jesus!" Felicia gasped. "Say one thing for you, you depraved fella. You do provide an interesting evening."

"'T's an art," said he insouciantly.

"Bet you can't even do it," she said.

"You've made a bad bet."

He tossed his stick and hat aside. Drake would recover them and put them where they belonged in the morning—together with her fur, which she let fall to the floor.

"You got a message," she said, pointing to the silver tray on the table in the entrance hall. "You return a phone call tonight, I'll kill you!"

He picked up the note left for him by Drake. "Ha!" he said. "Coincidence, b'God." He handed her the note.

It read:

Please telephone ASAP Governor Roosevelt Executive Mansion in Albany.

2

"Can you imagine how my Missus proposed to deal with ten cases of Château Lafite?" asked the Governor of New York. The
question was rhetorical; he meant to answer
it himself. "By flushing them down the toi-
lets! A violation of the Volstead Act! Illegal!
Ten cases of . . . Jack! What you see—that
I can't get up out of this chair—is not my
heaviest burden."

"I'll be glad to beat her for you, Frank,"
Jack said.

Franklin D. Roosevelt leaned back in
his chair behind the governor's desk and
laughed loudly and heartily. "Good!
Good! But, no thanks. She's got a good
heart, as they say. A good heart, *really!*
And I owe her more than I can ever repay.
But, in some respects, she was born . . .
Not yesterday, Jack. Not yesterday. But
maybe Friday."

"Ah," said Jack, joining in his friend's
laughter.

"God bless Louie," said the Governor. "He saved my *ten* cases of *glorious* wine!"

He meant Louis McHenry Howe, the wizened, asthmatic chain-smoking one-time newspaperman who was his chief political confidant and mentor.

Jack sat across the desk from FDR, the leading candidate for the Democratic nomination for President of the United States. They'd known each other at Harvard, when Jack had doubted that Frank would ever amount to much of anything. He was a mama's boy. He had been then, and he still was—dependent on his mother, the redoubtable Sara Delano Roosevelt, who expected everything of him and reared him to expect everything of (and for) himself.

Only two bad things—three, in Jack's estimate—had ever happened to Frank since they had known each other as schoolboys. First, Frank had allowed himself to be nominated for vice-president in 1920, a year when Democrats hadn't a chance; and second, the assault of poliomyelitis that had cost him the use of his legs a year or so later. The third misfortune—strictly in Jack's judgment had been Frank's marriage. But the man had used his advantages well and had overcome his disadvantages opportunistically, and he sat in this shabby office in Albany, likely to move into the mystic office in the West Wing of the White House in Washington.

Frank's personality had changed little since the turn of the century. He was still ebullient, charming, forceful. People who hadn't known him before he lost the ability to stand eleven years ago didn't realize what a big man he was; and that he was so big a man in part explained the power and vigor of his personality. His legs were useless, and that imposed extra duty on his arms and shoulders, which were muscular and strong. He was smoking a Camel as they talked, in the long holder that was something of a trademark with him.

The Governor had always been a little careless about his clothes. His gray suit was wrinkled and even a bit shabby. He wore a gold watch in his breast pocket, and its chain descended from his lapel buttonhole.

He was an effective governor, everyone said. Still, in Jack's judgment, he was out of place in this somber office, and Jack wondered if he wouldn't be in the presidency, too. An aggressive executive coping with the repeated crises of the Depression was not Jack's image of his old friend—that of an athletic young man, a sailor, a swimmer, a competitor, ready even for a boyish tussle if no other game offered itself. He remembered perilous ice-boat racing on the frozen Hudson—made more perilous because Frank Roosevelt was more than a little reckless. Obviously he was not that brash young man anymore. Still . . . President of the United States?

"Peter O'Malley . . ." the Governor mused. "I suppose that's 'Hammer Pete.' A friend of yours, is he?"

"He owns my favorite speakeasy," said Jack. He paused to light a Tareyton. "In fact, he owns every speak in Boston."

"Plus a lot of other things, I should imagine," said Frank Roosevelt. "Breweries, houses of ill-repute .

"Loan sharks," Jack added.

"You do have contacts with these people, don't you, Jack?"

Jack turned up the palms of his hands, shrugged slightly, and smiled. "Not really," he said. "Hammer Pete owns my speakeasy. He supplies my liquor. He supplies the Common Club. He controls the trade, so

I suppose anyone who buys genuine stuff in Boston buys it from him, directly or indirectly—most of them indirectly."

"Would Hammer Pete introduce you to some other fellows in his line of business, if you asked him to?"

"Why do you ask?"

The Governor caught the sudden look of apprehension on Jack's face. He grinned, leaned back in his chair, and said, "I'm seeking an ambassador."

"To *the mobs*, you mean?"

"Right. They're an element of American society, and I'm looking for someone who can talk to them for me—in utter, total, complete, and absolute confidentiality."

Jack smiled weakly. He was not certain Frank Roosevelt was serious. He'd find out. He shrugged and said, "Well, you can't appoint me to anything. I'm not a citizen of the State of New York."

The Governor's smiled disappeared. He lowered his head, regarded Jack for a moment over the rims of his pince-nez, and said, "I'm going to call in Louie Howe to talk to you."

The conversation was taking a definitely serious turn, and Jack wondered if he weren't sorry he had come to Albany. But

Frank had picked up the telephone, and shortly Howe appeared in the door.

"Come in, Louie. Sit down. You know Jack Endicott."

Howe gravely shook Jack's hand, then sat in a chair beside him.

Howe was a gnome. Though racked with emphysema, he smoked four or five packs of Sweet Caporals every day. The ash was all over his ill-fitting blue suit, which drooped from thin shoulders, down over his cavernous chest. His hair was gray. His skin was gray. He was said to be Roosevelt's éminence grise, but from what Jack knew of him he was nothing of the kind; he was self-effacingly loyal to Frank and had been his political mentor for almost twenty years.

"I've just broached with Jack the subject we discussed last week," said the Governor to Howe. "I don't think he's much impressed with the idea."

"He doesn't understand the implications," said Howe.

"Now wait a minute," said Jack. "Are you two seriously suggesting that your campaign should have a . . . a go-between with the *mob?*"

"Something like that," said the Governor.

"My God, no wonder it has to be confidential! What do you want of them, campaign funds?"

"Hardly," said Howe. "What we are looking for is some way to discourage them from attempting to assassinate the Governor."

It was like being hit with a club. For a moment Jack could not comprehend what he'd just heard. He began to shake his head.

"We've had threats," said Howe. "We've increased the police guard. I don't suppose I have to explain to you who wants to assassinate the Governor, and why."

"I know," Jack admitted.

"Politics makes strange bedfellows," said the Governor. "Imagine! Henry Ford and Al Capone. Bishop Cannon and Lucky Luciano. Allies in the crusade to keep the country dry."

"I'm afraid it's not coincidence that makes this conversation take the same turn as one I heard one night last week," said Jack.

"Repeal of Prohibition," said the Governor, "will eliminate the mobs' chief source of revenue. They know that, and they'll do anything they can to prevent it."

"Including assassinate—"

"Me."

"And you're suggesting I could—"

"Carry the word to them, Jack. You have contacts. You might be able to set up meetings with the right men."

"Who would I see and what would I say?"

"Try to see Dutch Schultz, or a representative of his," said Howe. "The threat has been conveyed indirectly, but we think that's who it's coming from."

"Tell them Prohibition is dead," said the Governor. "Tell them it's going to be repealed, no matter who is elected President in 1932. Even if Hoover is re-elected, which is all but impossible, Prohibition is going to be modified if not repealed. There's nothing they can do to save it."

"And if they try to murder a candidate for President, it will only make Repeal more certain," added Louis Howe.

Jack shifted uncomfortably in his chair. "Frank . . . Louie. I'm not the man you need. I—"

"You're a man I can trust, and that's the point," said the Governor.

"I probably don't have the courage to—"

"Don't tell me you lack courage, *Major* Endicott," said Frank Roosevelt.

"I don't—"

He was interrupted again, this time by

a faint rap on the door, after which it opened and Eleanor Roosevelt stood there, looking expectantly into the room. She wore a floppy black hat, a light beige-colored coat over a mint-green dress fussy with decoration, and she carried a stuffed leather bag. "Am I interrupting anything?" she asked in that melodious voice that grated on Jack's ear. She glanced at Jack then went on—"I'm about to catch the train for the city, Franklin. As usual. I shall see you Thursday."

"Well . . . good-bye then, Babs," said the Governor. "And you might say good-bye to Louie and Jack, too."

The comment was not without its barb. Eleanor Roosevelt did not like John Lowell Endicott, and she had never been at any pains to conceal it. Probably every married man has a friend his wife does not like— typically, as she sees it, a rogue, a malign influence from her husband's younger days, when he was immature and irresponsible. The friend comes along from time to time to remind the husband of the youth he has lost, and the wife sees him as a threat. In this marriage, Jack Endicott was that friend. Eleanor did not welcome his occasional visits.

Jack frankly didn't give a damn—which she knew, and that didn't help matters.

Eleanor Roosevelt had a reputation for being perhaps the ugliest woman in America. Unfriendly editorialists said she was. Jack knew better. The truth was, he had never known a woman to whom the camera was less kind, less fair. In person, she was actually a rather attractive woman, in a distinctive way. Frank had known that when he married her. The handsome Frank would not have married an ugly woman, Jack thought—nor have had five children with her.

For a woman she was extraordinarily tall, almost as tall as Frank himself. She carried herself with grace and dignity. Her clothes seemed to have been chosen with the same carelessness that went into selecting Frank's suits, but when occasionally she wore something becoming, she could attract admiring glances. She was no radiant beauty, certainly, but she was a singular woman, once seen in person not soon forgotten.

Jack's sense of justice, and perhaps his sense of loyalty to 'her husband, had led him to defend Eleanor against slanders to her appearance. As for the rest of her, he liked her no better than she liked him. She was the sort of woman who could flush ten cases of Château Lafite down the toilet. Far worse, she was the sort of woman who could tell herself her husband wouldn't care.

Jack had read an interview in which she had told a reporter the Governor cared nothing about what he ate, that she could serve him scrambled eggs three times a day and he wouldn't even notice. Jack knew it wasn't true. Frank cared about a lot of things that Eleanor didn't; and either she tormented him by pretending she didn't know, or she had rationalized to herself so long that she really had lost touch with what he cared about.

In important ways, Frank was her prisoner—and his mother's. Jack remembered vividly the day when Frank had said to him, almost tearfully, "You know when you're in my condition and have to ask someone else to bring you what you want, and you want orange juice and they bring you milk, about all you can do is smile and say that's fine and drink it."

"Hello, Jack," she said. "And good-bye. I didn't know you were in the house. I really do have to go, or I'll miss my train."

"It's good to see you, Eleanor. Another time . . ."

"Yes. Let us hope so. Shall I buy you some neckties, Franklin? That one is really atrocious."

"Please," said the Governor.

"Good-bye, Louie. Take good care of things."

And as quickly as she had appeared she was gone. That was something else about her that Jack didn't like. She *bustled.*

The Governor's smile was small and measured as he watched her stride across the outer office and into the hall.

"Well, then. You'll stay for dinner, of course. And you, too, Louie."

"Be my guest for dinner at my hotel, Frank."

"What, and not be here to share that Château Lafite? We shall crack two or three bottles. Have you checked into that hotel? If not, unpack here. Enjoy the threadbare elegance of *le château du gouveurneur.*"

"Scotch for Jack," said the Governor an hour and a half later, when the dinner party assembled in the library of the mansion for their predinner cocktails. "I'm going to make Old Fashioneds."

"I thought you favored martinis," said Jack.

"I'm beginning to," said Frank Roosevelt. "There's a certain clean freshness about them, and after a while you begin to find cocktails like Manhattans and Old Fashioneds cloyingly sweet. But—tonight . . .

The dinner party consisted of the Governor, Jack, and Louis Howe, plus the Governor's personal assistant Marguerite "Missy" Lehand. Jack had accepted the Governor's invitation to put up overnight in the mansion and had telephoned a flower shop to deliver boutonnieres for the men and a corsage for Missy.

The men were in black tie. Missy wore a wine-colored silk crepe dress that flowed over her figure like a stream of water, with a simple short strand of pearls around her neck. Her blonde hair was cut short, showing her ears. While she was much more the conventional beauty than was Eleanor, she was not nearly as exceptional a woman. She had worked for Frank Roosevelt since about 1920 and was as committed to him as Louie Howe.

Jack had been with Frank and Missy aboard *Larooco,* the houseboat-yacht on which Frank had spent lazy months cruising and swimming in warm Florida waters while he struggled to recover some use of his legs. Jack understood that the relationship between Frank and Missy was man-and-woman and more than friendly. He knew, from things he had heard her say, that she was uncritically admiring of Frank. She offered him a kind of companionship the independent, hyperactive Eleanor could not—just as Eleanor supplied astute observations and shrewd judgments that Missy could not. It was as difficult to imagine Missy returning from a political meeting with cunning insights as to imagine Eleanor in a bathing suit cuddling on Frank's lap.

Missy poured Scotch for Jack and watched the Governor mix Old Fashioneds.

"To the next President of the United States," said Jack solemnly when their drinks were ready and they could lift their glasses.

"Amen," said Louis McHenry Howe.

"Thank you, Jack. And to good friends. Without them no such thing would be possible. And without them it wouldn't be worth doing, anyway."

They relaxed. One thing to be said for the old governor's mansion was that people could be comfortable in it—though Jack wondered if the Governor actually was. He sat in a plain wooden wheelchair, with no arms; and he whirled it around and dashed here and there in it, actually rushing ahead of people striding to keep up with him. He sat now with a cocktail glass in his right hand and his cigarette holder in his left, drinking, smoking, and apparently genuinely pleased with the company and the evening.

"You play polo, don't you, Mr. Endicott?" Missy asked.

He smiled at her. "I do if you call me Jack."

"Or Blackjack," the Governor laughed. "That's what he's called by people who've lost money to him at the card table."

"And bridge," she said. "I understand you are a bridge master."

"I am a wastrel, is what I am," said Jack. "I have made a career of spending what my father and grandfather earned."

"He might want to make the Internal Revenue Bureau think that," said Governor Roosevelt. "I happen to know that in spite of the Depression he is worth a hundred

fifty percent of what he was when he in-
herited his fortune."

Jack shrugged. "I am constantly harassed
by men who know how to make money
grow and insist I must do this and that.
When I wanted to take full advantage of the
bull market of 1929, my Uncle Henry all
but sat on me and forced me to sell stocks
and accumulate cash. I mean, please,
Frank. I am a Lowell, an Endicott, and am
married into the Biddle family; I am related
one way or another to the Vanderbilts and
even distantly to J. P. Morgan. If I lost
money, they would make dolls of me and
stick pins in. I have nothing to do with making money, only with spending it."

"He lies," said the Governor with an
amused smile.

"Constantly," agreed Jack. "But—I am
constantly asked what you will do after you
become President, Frank. I tell people you
believe in a balanced budget and economy
in government. But so does Herbert Hoover. So what are you going to do?"

The Governor smiled, glanced at Howe,
then at Missy, and shrugged. "To tell the
truth, Jack, I haven't the remotest notion.
All I can tell you is, we will do *something*.
The Hoover administration is paralyzed by

caution, or timidity, or by obsessive devotion to old verities. I really don't know what has to be done to recover prosperity, but clearly it is something different from what has been done so far. People are actually starving in the United States of America. That can't continue, no matter what we have to do."

"If we don't do something," said Jack grimly, "there will be a Marxist revolution."

"I think that is not beyond the realm of possibility," said the Governor. "What are we talking about? Something like thirty percent of our people, maybe one-third, don't have enough to eat, don't have proper clothing, don't live in decent housing. We have got to do something to change that."

"You're not a socialist, are you, Frank?"

"I'm not an *ist*," he said. "Not a socialist, not a communist, not an anarchist, not a prohibitionist, not a Baptist nor a Methodist nor an atheist—" He chuckled. "Not even a 'vegetarianist.' I—Well, what I am, I'm a *pragmatist*. I'm for anything that will work to save this country's people from starvation, and that's my whole campaign."

"Hoover is satisfied he will be re-elected. He doesn't even think he'll have to campaign much."

The Governor shook his head. "Twelve years ago I wished Herbert Hoover were a Democrat, so we could have him on the ticket. The relief administrator, the great humanitarian. Now he sits in the White House, eats his seven-course dinners, reviews the troops like the old mad King of Bavaria, and doesn't seem to see what's going on around him."

"Al Smith thinks he's going to take the nomination away from you."

The Governor's face clouded. "I've put up with a lot from Al," he said.

Missy had stiffened and sat erect, shoulders back. "Eff Dee," she said crisply. "You can't say it, maybe; and maybe Louie can't; but I can. Jack . . . Al Smith is a sleazy crook!"

"Missy . . ."

She shook her head and shook off the Governor's objection. "Al Smith is everything that stinks about Tammany Hall. He won't be beat just because he's a Catholic. I'm a Catholic, and I can say it. He wasn't beat in 1928 because of his religion—*my* religion. He was beat because the odor of garbage clings to the man. And that's because he is garbage!"

The Governor had turned his attention determinedly to the stirring together of another pitcher of Old Fashioneds. Howe stared at a Sweet Caporal as he lit it with a big wooden match. Missy looked at Jack and smiled defiantly. He nodded and grinned. He agreed with her. Like Frank and Louie, he'd rather *she* had said it.

Jack spoke to the Governor. "Will you have time for a weekend's sailing before the convention?" he asked.

"A weekend as a passenger on your boat," said the Governor. Rarely, but still occasionally, a hint of bitterness escaped him, as it did then.

"We'll sail where the fishing is good," said Jack. "Out where the water rushes over the sandbar between the Cape and Nantucket."

"It sounds like heaven," said the Governor. "You know, I can still work the tiller."

"The wheel is yours, Frank," said Jack. "All of us, huh? A nice weekend of salt air."

"Well . . . Louie is going on out to Chicago," said the Governor. "But, Missy and

I will join you. I'll say to the Missus that she's invited, too. She won't come."

"Sounds like a fun weekend," said Missy. "It does, really. We'll have a lot of *fun!*"

The kitchen staff of the governor's mansion was capable of setting a good table, when Eleanor Roosevelt was not there to impose her peculiar limitations on them. ("The Governor," she would tell them, "doesn't have time to dawdle for an hour over a meal. Prepare things we can eat quickly. The Governor likes simple, nutritious food, nothing fancy.") When she was in the city, the Governor ate better. Friends who knew him brought him braces of mallards, that were allowed to hang and ripen. Others brought fish they had caught or shellfish they had found in Maine or Maryland waterfront markets. And he and his friends dawdled over dinner.

This night they dawdled over standing ribs of rare roast beef, preceded by large artichokes, accompanied by broiled potatoes, and followed by strawberry shortcake with coffee.

Afterward, the steward brought in a tray of liqueurs and brandies. Louis Howe, who was by now coughing painfully, said he would excuse himself. Missy, sensing that Eff Dee probably wanted to talk with his friend alone, excused herself, too, leaving Jack and the Governor at the table.

Frank Roosevelt did something almost no one ever saw him do. He accepted from Jack a fine Havana cigar. Fat brown cigars seen shoved in the yaps of politicians like Al Smith and John Nance Garner were an element of the image of everything that was worst in politicians, he believed, so he was never seen in public smoking a cigar. Tonight, he was comfortable after his before-dinner Old Fashioneds, the excellent wine they drank with dinner, and now his brandy; and he lit the cigar and leaned back to enjoy it,

"I want to return to what we were talking about in the office this afternoon," he said to Jack.

"I was afraid you might."

"I have no right to ask a man to risk his life."

"Would I be risking it, really?" Jack asked. "Is what we were talking about actually that serious? Is *your* life at risk?"

The Governor turned down the corners of his mouth. "I don't know, for sure. It might be."

"Jesus . . ." Jack whispered.

"It's a risk that can be headed off, I think," said the Governor. "It's a matter of their understanding that Prohibition is dead, no matter who's elected President."

"They think they can control Al Smith. At least that's what Hammer Pete told me."

Frank Roosevelt shook his head. "Al can't stop it. Hoover can't. The repeal resolution will be passed by Congress, and it doesn't require the signature of the President. He can't veto it. After the resolution passes, the proposition goes to the states. Have you seen the latest poll? Repeal is inevitable. No politician can stop it now."

"Neither a candidate for President nor the President himself can stop it."

"A Republican Congress," said the Governor. "That might stop it. Let them try to get a Republican Congress elected in 1932."

"Frank . . . Why me?"

"First reason. You are not politically identified with me. The word is, you vote Republican—"

"I won't if you're the candidate, Frank."

The Governor smiled faintly. "Thank you. Anyway, if word got out that a representative of mine was talking to the likes of Capone, Luciano, Schultz, Anastasia . . . whoever. Any contact at all with them—"

"You'd be a gone goose, politically."

"I'd be a gone goose. Who can I trust? It's got to be somebody who isn't obviously my emissary. I could send Louie, but the first reporter that got wind of the idea that Louis Howe was talking to Dutch Schultz . . . You see the point."

"I don't know if I can make the contacts."

"You can try. You have as good a chance as anybody."

Jack sighed and nodded. "I could wind up on the bottom of the Atlantic, wearing cement shoes."

"Not likely. But you've got the guts. Where was it I found you in France when I came over as Assistant Secretary of the Navy?"

"Not any place I'd volunteered to be," said Jack.

"I'm not convinced of that," said Governor Roosevelt. He put his cigar aside. "I'm not so sure you're the frivolous playboy you make such a point of being. I—"

"I crawled around on my belly in the French mud—not in mud, actually: in

50

muddy water—for six months, Frank. I know what gas smells like, and cordite, and I know what shell shock is. I got my Purple Heart—"

"And a Croix de Guerre," the Governor added.

"And a Croix de Guerre. And I haven't yet been frivolous long enough, Frank. I think I'm entitled to ten more years of it, maybe more."

"Jack . . . Why'd you do what you did in the War? Don't answer. You can't. Or won't. You'll deny the answer. But I'll answer for you. You did it to serve your country. Maudlin, huh? But that's why you did it. You were in your thirties and didn't have to. But you did. Says something about what kind of man you are, Jack, whether you want to admit it or not."

"Are you trying to call this idea of yours the same kind of deal?" Jack asked coldly.

The Governor picked up his brandy snifter and took a sip. "You put me in a tough position," he said. "Is trying to fend off an attempt to murder me the same thing as serving your country?"

Jack pushed back his chair and rose to his feet. He walked to the windows, parted the curtains, and looked out. "Yeah," he muttered. "Yeah. Sure it is. A decent man, trying to do something good. Whether he's going to be the grand exalted savior of America or not is doubtful. But . . . but he's trying. And because of that, some people want to kill him."

"Something like that," said the Governor.

"Besides, we're friends," said Jack.

"I'm counting on that," said the Governor.

Jack turned and faced Franklin Roosevelt. He shook his head. "You're putting your trust in the wrong man," he said gravely.

"I don't think so," said the Governor. "Neither does Louie, who is a good judge of men, as good as any I've ever known."

"What do you want me to do? Go back to Hammer Pete and . . ."

"See if you can get him to introduce you to some of the others. Try to find out what they really want. Tell them I can't save Prohibition for them, nor can anyone else."

Jack nodded, but his expression was bleak. "I don't think it'll work, Frank. I'll try, but I really don't think it'll work."

3

Five o'clock. John Lowell Endicott stood on the brick sidewalk in front of the Common Club, looking up and down the street. He wore a dark-blue pin-striped suit, with a black homburg, and he leaned lightly against a thin black stick, its point planted firmly in a crack between two bricks. A small red carnation adorned his lapel.

A man approached. "Mr. Endicott . . ." he said timidly.

"Johnson! How good to see you! How is it with you, old fellow?"

Johnson—Johnson? Jack remembered his last name confidently but could not for the moment think of a Christian name. The man stopped and smiled faintly. He stood there, as if suspended for a moment, regarding Jack with watery blue eyes. He was unsteady on his feet. Jack did not remember him as a man who drank.

"Johnson?"

"Thank you. Thank you, Mr. Endicott . . . for remembering me."

Still unable to recall any name but Johnson, Jack smiled at the man and recalled that the fellow had sold him a car—a royal blue 1931 Le Baron–bodied Marmon V-16, the automobile that was his basic chauffeured car. It was an impressive piece of machinery, with six nickel-plated wire wheels with white sidewall tires—six because a wheel was mounted on each front fender as a spare—and oversize nickel headlights. The huge engine was modeled on Ettore Bugatti's aircraft engines; and when Jack himself occasionally drove it, he could outrun, over a long course at sustained speed, nearly anything on the road. Johnson had pointed out all this and more a year ago when he sold him the car. He had been one of the most persuasive automobile salesmen Jack had ever encountered.

"Of course! You sold me that damned piece of junk! I'll never forget you."

"Oh, Mr. Endicott, I am terribly sorry! The Marmon—"

"Johnson! It's a *wonderful* car! A beautiful car! I'm grateful to you. So, how is your business?"

Johnson shook his head. "I am afraid, sir, that yours was the second . . . actually, the third to last car I ever sold."

"Really!"

"I was laid off, Mr. Endicott, as business went from bad to worse. I held hopes of returning, but—In point of fact, Mr. Endicott, the automobile agency no longer exists."

"Ah," said Jack. "And what business are you in now, Johnson?"

"None, sir. I'm unemployed. I'm one of those veterans who will be entitled to a bonus in 1945, and I'm thinking of joining the march to Washington to demand our money be paid now, when we need it."

"M' God, Johnson! Are things really that bad with you?"

"Mr. Endicott . . . I have sold cars since 1921. And I invested my earnings, my savings—as we were told to do, were we not?—in the stock market. I bought my share of 'Coolidge prosperity.' I owned American Can, which fell by sixty percent in six weeks; General Electric, that dropped fifty-eight percent; Westinghouse, that dropped sixty-six percent . . . and so on. I'd bought on margin, of course. When my margin loans were called in November of 1929, I was suddenly a poor man. Bankrupt, in point of fact. But, of course, I could still sell cars. I am not a bad salesman—"

"I will testify to that," Jack interrupted.

"But you can't sell cars when nobody can afford to buy them," said Johnson. "Or ladies' garments, or vacuum cleaners, which I've tried to sell since.

"So you are . . . ?"

"The object of public charity, sir," said the man despondently.

"Seriously, Johnson? I knew things were bad. But you are—You are *destitute?*"

"I am, sir. And, believe me, Mr. Endicott, I did not come here looking for you, hoping to, as they say, 'put the touch' on you. This is—"

"Coincidence, Johnson . . . coincidence. I—I cannot offer you employment. I don't employ people, except for a few on my household staff. But—" He reached inside his coat and took out his wallet. "Here, old fellow . . . Here is twenty dollars. When it is gone, apply to me again. I—"

"Ho, Jack . . ."

Jack turned away to see Peter O'Malley, who had walked up to them while Jack's attention was so firmly fixed on Johnson that he did not notice.

"Not late, am I?" said Hammer Pete. He glanced around at the facade of the Common Club. "Don't usually come here and wasn't exactly sure where it was.

O'Malley was looking dapper. He had dressed for this venture into a neighborhood he did not often visit. His double-breasted gray suit was a bit overstyled, but his intent had been correct. He had no stick or flower, but he wore a handsome gray homburg. He looked skeptically at Johnson, his expression betraying his suspicion that he had come upon Jack just as he was being touched by a panhandler.

"Allow me to introduce my friend," said Jack. "Mr. Johnson, this is Mr. Peter O'Malley."

Johnson started and instinctively stepped back a pace. O'Malley laughed.

"Mr. Johnson sold me a very fine car last year," said Jack to Hammer Pete. "Now he finds himself unemployed, through no fault of his own. I've just given him twenty dollars. Why don't you do the same?"

O'Malley grinned. He reached into his pants pocket and pulled out a fat wad of bills. He pulled off two fifties and handed them to the apprehensive man. "There y' go, buddy," he said. "Any friend of Jack's is a friend of mine. And if you need a job, come see me. I can always use an honest man."

Stunned, Johnson mumbled, "Why, thank you, Mr. O'Malley. Thank you very much. And thank you, too, Mr. Endicott. I won't trouble you gents anymore. I know you have business. I . . . Thank you both again."

He walked away, visibly trembling.

Jack gestured toward the steps to the door of the Common Club.

"I don't need to tell ya I've lived in Boston forty-four years and have never been in this place," said O'Malley when they were inside.

"To be frank, membership is mostly by inheritance," said Jack. "If your grandfather was a member, then you are almost automatically a member."

"'No Irish need apply,'" O'Malley laughed. "They may throw *you* out when they find out you've brought *me* in."

They left their hats at the checkroom and climbed the steps to the barroom. O'Malley stared like a tourist at the old wood and the antique lights. "It's class . . ." he muttered quietly to Jack. "What ya call class."

They stood at the bar, and Jack ordered Scotch for both of them.

"I've got a proposition, Pete," he said.

"Figured you did."

"I went to Albany and met with Governor Roosevelt."

"Yeah?"

Jack nodded. "He was very grateful for the wine. He told me to tell you so. We talked about Prohibition. About Repeal."

"Yeah?"

"He asked me to talk to you about it. He says you have to understand that Prohibition is going to be repealed, or if it's not repealed it's going to be modified. Modification means bringing back beer, so the breweries are going to reopen. And the point is, there's nothing he can do about it. It's what the people of this country want, and it's what they're going to get. Even if Hoover is re-elected, beer is coming back, at the very least."

"The yahoos are goin' to have some say about that."

"Of course they are. But there aren't enough of them anymore," said Jack. "Pete . . . Listen. Every year *Literary Digest* takes a nationwide poll on Prohibition. Every year more people vote wet. More than two-thirds of the people voting say they want Prohibition either repeated or modified. Seventy new wets were elected to Congress at the last election, plus four new wet Senators. It's just a matter of time now. That's all it is: a matter of time."

"That's the Governor's message to me?"

Jack nodded. "That's the Governor's message. It's not up to him. He couldn't keep Prohibition alive if he wanted to."

"If he's right, I'm goin' out of business," said O'Malley unhappily.

"Out of the beer business," said Jack. "I'm sure you have other interests. Anyway, this can't be news to you."

"I suppose it isn't, really. I did kinda think your pal in Albany could help out if he wanted to. Maybe I oughta read the newspapers more.

O'Malley sucked his lips in between his teeth and turned his brows into the shallow *v* of a dark frown. He glanced along the bar as he sighed.

Tall, toothy George Saltonstall noticed, smiled at Jack, and walked along the bar with his hand out. "Hello, Jack!" he said cheerfully. He shook Jack's hand, then turned and extended his hand to Hammer Pete. "I don't recall having met this gentleman."

"Then let me introduce Mr. Peter O'Malley," said Jack. And to O'Malley he said, "George Saltonstall."

Saltonstall flushed. "O' . . . Malley," he stuttered. He shook hands limply. "Yes . . . Well! It, uh . . . It's a pleasure." And so saying he retreated.

"He's heard the name," said O'Malley dryly.

"Evidently," said Jack quietly.

"Like I said, you'll get tossed out of the club."

"Not really," said Jack. "Anyway, Governor Roosevelt—"

"What would it take to get him to change his mind?" O'Malley interrupted.

"Nothing. It's not a matter of his changing his mind. That wouldn't make any difference."

O'Malley lifted his glass of Scotch and drained it. "Liked the wine, though, did he?"

"Pete—There's more to this conversation. The Governor has been threatened."

"Threatened with what?"

61

"Assassination," said Jack.

O'Malley drew a deep breath. "That's too bad," he said.

"It would be the worst thing that could possibly happen to men in your kind of business," said Jack. "You know what I mean.

As Hammer Pete pondered for a moment, Jack signaled for two more drinks.

"If the Governor's worried, you can tell him it won't happen. There's a rule about things like that."

"Apparently not everybody knows the rule," said Jack.

"Like who? Who threatened?"

"The word comes indirectly. But apparently it's from Dutch Schultz."

O'Malley frowned again, more deeply. "Dutch Schultz is a crazy man.

"Maybe Anastasia, too."

"The Sicilians. They're movin' in on everything. But they got tighter control over their guys than anybody else has got."

Glancing at the bartender, who was pouring Scotch, Jack finished his drink. "Maybe Schultz thinks what you thought: that Governor Roosevelt is going to make Repeal happen. Maybe he thinks he can save the beer business by getting rid of the

Governor. You believe me, don't you, Pete. You believe what I told you?"

O'Malley nodded. "I suppose so. Sure. There's no percentage for you in steerin' me wrong."

Jack paused while the bartender brought their fresh drinks and moved back out of earshot. "What the Governor would like for me to do—what in fact, *I'd* like to do—is carry the same word to some other men. Maybe to Dutch Schultz himself."

Hammer Pete shook his head. "Those guys won't talk to you. If they did, they'd laugh at you."

"Maybe they'd listen if you introduced me," said Jack. He let that soak in for a moment, then said, "Maybe they wouldn't laugh at me if you were there with me."

O'Malley looked at him grimly for a moment, and then a grudging smile came to his lips. "What percentage is there in that for me?" he asked.

"The percentage for you is that you won't lose what you're going to lose if one of those fellows kills the Governor of New York. You know as well as I do that the murder of a governor and a candidate for President would produce a crackdown like nobody ever saw before, all across the country."

Hammer Pete O'Malley nodded, and his smile spread into a grin. "I never figured you for a dummy," he said. "Just a rich guy with a good education and all, but no what-ya-might-call practical sense. But it's pretty damned tough bargainin' you're doin'. So . . . Okay. Let's see who'll talk to ya."

Four days later Endicott and O'Malley arrived in Grand Central Station, New York, on an early-evening train. They checked in at the Waldorf and dressed for dinner, then let the doorman hail them a cab and gave the driver the address of the Stork Club, the city's most fashionable and expensive speakeasy.

Back in Boston, Felicia sulked at home. She had wanted to come with Jack to New York. More than that, she had wanted to see the notorious gangster he was supposed to meet. She had promised Jack she would go out with someone else while he was away. She would probably bring him home to bed, just to teach Jack a lesson.

"I don't know what kinda break this is, for sure," O'Malley had said on the train between Boston and New York. "It sounds like the best in the world, but it may be a bad break. It could be the worst. I don't know what kind of impression the guy'll make on you. I only met him once. But the word I get is, he's the guy who'll talk to ya, and he's the guy you should see."

Jack had frowned and repeated the name O'Malley had mentioned on the telephone when he called to say he'd made a contact. "Charlie Lucky."

Jack had telephoned a newspaper reporter in New York—once a lieutenant who served under him in France—and had asked for a rundown on this Charlie Lucky. The man, it seemed, went by various names. He was a Sicilian. No one knew what his real name was, but besides Charlie Lucky he was called Charles Luciano, Salvatore Luciano, and sometimes Lucky Luciano. He was a new kind of mobster, the reporter said: an organizer who had been brought to the States to try to whip the old semifeudal and semiautonomous Italian gangs into one disciplined organization. He was also, the reporter said, reputedly quite capable of killing.

They were on their way to the Stork Club because it was the meeting place specified by Charlie Lucky when Hammer Pete called him from the Waldorf. Charlie Lucky said he had given the host, Sherman

Billingsley, word that they were coming and were to be admitted as his guests.

A greater contrast could hardly have existed than that between the quiet solemn precincts of the Common Club and the garish and tacky Stork Club. Prohibition agents had taken axes to the furnishings of the Stork Club, which apparently had inspired Billingsley to be closefisted in his investment in this one. He must have been obsessed with mirrors and pink light. Cigarette smoke hung so heavily in the air that the customers could hardly see across the main room. The place was doing a bustling, noisy business. Without the word from Charlie Lucky, Jack and Hammer Pete might not have found a table.

That they were going to meet a prominent man was confirmed as soon as they were inside the door. Sherman Billingsley hurried to welcome them and personally ushered them to a high-backed booth a little apart from the tables and traffic in the club, where they could have private conversation. With all the obsequiousness of Maury at the Leedo, he offered drinks and hors d'oeuvres and snapped his fingers at the club personnel to alert them to be attentive to this table.

"Sherman Billingsley . . ." Jack mused when the man had gone. "Something of a name. What's he called, 'king of café society'? Something like that."

"He oughtn't to put on airs," said Hammer Pete scornfully. "A guy that works for me was his cellmate in the federal pokey at Leavenworth. Billingsley did fifteen months there, and that ain't the only time he's done. He was a bootlegger *before* Prohibition. Comes from Oklahoma, which went dry before the rest of the country did, an' he and his brothers started cookin' alky before it got fashionable. He's been run out of half a dozen towns. 'Café society' my achin' backside. Any society that makes Sherman Billingsley a big man couldn't amount to much."

Maybe so, Jack reflected, but his Stork Club seemed to amount to something. Glancing around the room, he saw people he recognized. One or two recognized him. Rudy Vallee nodded as Jack's eyes passed over his table. F. Scott Fitzgerald returned Jack's restrained greeting: a short nod and a quick lift of his hand. Not everyone wanted to be recognized while drinking in a speakeasy.

He recognized a couple who would have

had no way of recognizing him: Noel Coward and Gertrude Lawrence.

The Stork Club attracted an interesting clientele.

"He'll want something," said O'Malley.

"Hmm?"

"Charlie Lucky. He does nothin' for nobody without there's a percentage for him."

"There's the same percentage there is for you, Pete."

O'Malley shook his head. "I don't think he'll buy that. You can try it on him, but I don't think he'll buy it."

They hadn't long to wait to find out. Three men strode across the room toward them: Charles or Salvatore or Lucky Luciano, better known as Charlie Lucky, and two bodyguards. People jumped aside to make way for them.

Jack rose to shake the man's hand. Hammer Pete did not. Jack, rising to his feet and extending his hand, seemed to make the bodyguards tense; but Charlie Lucky smiled and took Jack's hand and clasped it firmly.

Charlie Lucky was a compact young Sicilian of dark complexion, with wavy black hair. He might have been called handsome, and in fact probably was; but in the outer corner of his right eye he bore a thin scar, very likely evidence of a knife wound, and the wound had caused his eyelid to droop. That lazy eyelid, half covering his right eye, gave him a cynical, even sinister look—probably unintentional. He wore a tuxedo, with a white handkerchief in his breast pocket.

"Mr. Endicott," he said with a deep nod that was almost a bow. "I'm happy to meet you." He spoke with an Italian accent that he had well under control.

"Well, I'm glad to meet you," said Jack, unsure as to whether he should call the man Mr. Lucky or Mr. Luciano, or what. "I appreciate your agreeing to see me."

Charlie Lucky joined Jack and O'Malley in the booth, sitting beside Hammer Pete and facing Jack. The two bodyguards took chairs at a nearby table.

Billingsley half trotted across the room, urging a tray-balancing waiter along ahead of him. On it was a bottle of Italian red wine and a glass. With sweeping gestures Billingsley snatched the wine and glass from the waiter's tray, put them before Charlie Lucky; and stepped back to see if he was pleased.

Charlie Lucky ignored Sherman Billingsley. He took a sip of the wine, put the glass aside, and reached into his pocket for a silver cigarette case.

"The way I understand this," he said to Jack, "you are a—How shall we call it? You are an emissary from Governor Roosevelt."

"Strictly unofficially," said Jack.

Charlie Lucky smiled as he lit his cigarette. "I had not expected to meet with an official representative of the Governor of New York," he said.

Jack took interest in the way the man spoke English: with an interesting trace of accent, yet with vocabulary and grammar that surpassed Hammer Pete's. He seemed to be, as Pete had suggested, a new kind of mobster, though Jack could not yet guess what kind that might be.

"What does the Governor want to say?" asked Charlie Lucky, with surprising directness.

Jack spoke for a few minutes, explaining what he had already explained to Hammer Pete O'Malley. He concluded—I am sure you understand as well as I do, if Dutch Schultz or anybody else assassinates a man as prominent as the Governor of New York, the public reaction will be so hysterical as to cause a police crackdown like we've never before seen in this country. That's the word I'm trying to convey. I'm hoping you'll help by passing that word."

"Simple as that, huh?" said Charlie Lucky.

"The Governor is not afraid,"Jack said. "On the other hand, he is not ignoring the threat, and that is why I am here. In trying to protect Governor Roosevelt, p'raps I'll be serving your interests too, indirectly. As a matter of fact, in this particular matter, our interests may not be too far apart."

Charlie Lucky took a sip of wine and picked up a caviar-laden cracker from the plate between them. "I don't think our interests are very different at all," he said.

"I'm glad to hear it," said Jack.

"Right . . ." mumbled Charlie Lucky through his cracker and caviar. "The Governor doesn't want some dummy trying to murder him. I don't want some dummy trying to murder him. The Governor wants Repeal. I want Repeal. And the sooner the better."

"You *want* Repeal?" asked O'Malley skeptically.

"The sooner the better," said Charlie Lucky. "Put the bootleggers out of business."

"Dammit, Charlie, *I'm* a bootlegger. Why you wanta put me outa business?"

A small, half-scornful smile came to the face of Charlie Lucky. "Pete . . . You know what's wrong with bootlegging as well as I do. Anybody that can afford to rent a warehouse or garage can bootleg beer. All a man needs is the place to brew it and a few trucks to haul it. He doesn't even need the trucks. He can steal them. Madden did. After he got out of jail, he hijacked five trucks and was in business. Anybody that's got a kitchen can cook alky: make whiskey or gin. Ten thousand guys do it in New York. Every time you turn around, a new man has set himself up as a bootlegger, and either the old hands put up with him or they have to put him out of business—and you know what that leads to." He shook his head. "It's not good. It's what you call anarchy. What we've got to have is organization."

O'Malley sighed. "But a lot of guys have made big dough from beer, and a lot of guys are going to have a hard time when they can't bootleg beer anymore."

"That's right," said Charlie Lucky. "A lot of guys. There aren't going to be as many guys anymore." He tipped his head to one side and fastened appraising eyes on Hammer Pete. He stared for a long moment, then said, "A man like you, though. Pete . . . You'll be bigger than ever."

"In what business?"

Charlie Lucky shrugged. "Well—You've got trucks. That's how you haul your beer. You go in the trucking business."

"In Boston, there's more truckers than there is business," said O'Malley.

"But maybe there won't be. Suppose there was only one trucking company in Boston. Suppose there were only two or three. The men who had those companies would make a lot of money. In a legitimate business.

"What's going to happen to the other trucking companies?" Jack asked.

Charlie Lucky fixed a curious stare on Jack, as if he could not quite decide if this John Lowell Endicott was serious or making a little joke. "A man like Pete O'Malley has a lot of friends," he said. "A lot of contacts. Some businesses will want to give him all their hauling. He's got friends in the unions, so it's going to be easier for him to hire drivers and roustabouts. And he's got political friends who can take care of the licenses and things like that, He'll compete better than the other men. And he'll buy some of them out. And some will just go out of business."

"I see."

Charlie Lucky grinned. "What'd you think he was going to do, go out and kill all the other truckers? That's what's *not* going to happen. That's what Prohibition and bootlegging got started, and that's what's coming to an end. Men like us—and you know what kind of men we are; you asked for this meeting—are going to organize and run our businesses without the kind of stuff that happens in Chicago."

"Used to happen," said O'Malley. "Chicago's a lot quieter now."

"Dutch Schultz is a bootlegger," said Jack.

"And Waxey Gordon," said O'Malley. "The biggest in New York."

Charlie Lucky rubbed his hands together. "So the Governor figures it's Dutch Schultz that sent him the threat, huh?"

Jack nodded. "He didn't make any threat directly. But the Governor feels certain that's who made it. And it's not just one threat but several. They may not all come from the same source."

"The Dutchman's crazy," said Charlie Lucky.

"That's the most frightening part," said Jack.

"There's rules against this kinda thing," said Hammer Pete.

"And there are men who do not follow the rules," said Charlie Lucky. "That's what I'm talking about: organizing so that everybody follows the rules. There's no room for the Dutchman in the new scheme of things," he added with grim menace. "No room."

"I'm not asking you to—" Jack began, meaning to say he was not asking Charlie Lucky to kill Dutch Schultz.

"No, and I'm not going to," said Charlie Lucky. "But I'll help put out the word, like you asked. Maybe I can arrange for you to talk to Dixie Davis."

"Dixie . . . Davis?"

"The Dutchman's lawyer," said Charlie Lucky. Abruptly he slid out of the booth and extended his hand for another handshake with Jack. "I'll be in touch with you gentlemen soon."

There was of course no check to pay. Billingsley smiled unctuously and suggested they might stay and enjoy dinner. But Pete O'Malley emphatically did not like the Stork Club, and Jack was not much pleased with it either.

They decided not to take a taxi but to walk the short distance to the Waldorf.

The night was warm, and neither man wore an overcoat. Both sported high silk hats. Because their destination for the evening had been a speakeasy, Jack did not carry the stick he might otherwise have brought. As they walked across Fifty-third Street, O'Malley told Jack he had been completely surprised by Charlie Lucky, that he'd not dreamed the Sicilian would be so cooperative.

Park Avenue was ahead. They would walk down Park to the Waldorf. The pavement was wet from a light rain that had fallen earlier, and lights gleamed off puddles. Two policemen drove by in a Chevrolet coupe painted green and white.

A black Packard turned into Fifty-third, off Park Avenue; and suddenly its engine roared as the driver accelerated.

"Watch it!" snapped Hammer Pete.

Jack saw the men in the back seat thrust gun barrels through the open window. His instinct, born of months of combat experience in the trenches of the World War, was to take cover—in this instance that of a parked Chrysler. He dropped to a crouch on the sidewalk, where the heavy body of the Chrysler shielded him from the gunfire that exploded from the Packard. O'Malley's instinct was different. It was to jerk a revolver from inside his jacket and begin to fire back.

The Boston mobster actually fired three shots as a stream of submachine gun fire at first missed him, then caught him in the legs, and then two booming shotgun blasts threw him on his back on the sidewalk. The gunmen in the Packard fired a second long burst; but they did not know for sure where their second target had gone, and they were not willing to wait around to look for him.

Hammer Pete O'Malley was dead. From where Jack crouched, he could see the shattered body and the blood glistening on the pavement.

The Packard roared away and Jack cautiously stood up. He had read of attacks like this, where a second car came along in a moment to finish the work.

No second car came. The street was quiet, unnaturally quiet. Lights went out in windows. No one ventured onto the street.

Jack made a judgment. He would not be serving Frank Roosevelt very well if he had to go to police headquarters, answer questions, and get the Governor's name in the newspapers. Anyway, what could he contribute to the investigation? What could he tell? He didn't even know if the gunmen in the Packard had come to kill him or O'Malley. He settled his hat more squarely on his head and walked rapidly to Park Avenue.

NEW YORK CITY—A TENEMENT ON THE LOWER EAST SIDE

The building was dirty and dingy. A barber shop operated in the basement, a second-hand store on the first floor, selling everything from castoff clothing to battered musical instruments. Above, some of the windows were boarded over. Sagging green blinds covered others. The windowsills and the sidewalk were fouled with droppings from the pigeons that flew out of coops on the roof.

A shiny green Cadillac was parked in front of the building. A black Packard was parked across the street. The Packard was attended by two men: one obviously a chauffeur, who walked around the car, flicking off dust or rubbing away small spots with a rag, the other apparently a guard, who lounged against a front fender and appeared to be reading a newspaper while keeping a sharp eye on the tenement. Only one man guarded the Cadillac. He sat behind the wheel.

On the fourth floor, three men sat around a table in a room modestly furnished, yet far better decorated than was to be expected in this building—with a couch and chair upholstered in brown plush, a radio, a floor-model windup phonograph, and a round oak table covered with a fringed cloth. This was the living room of a flat. Two other men were in the kitchen, sitting at an enamel-top table and drinking beer.

The men spoke Italian. They were Charlie Lucky, Albert Anastasia, and Frank Costello.

"Chi? Chi?" Who? Who? *"Perchè?"* Why?

Charlie Lucky was talking, and he was angry. "We don't know who," said Frank Costello. "We don't know why."

Charlie Lucky tapped the table firmly with one finger. "This kind of thing . . . has got to stop. If it was Schultz—"

"I don't think it was Schultz," said Anastasia. "More likely it came down from Boston. Think about it. *Il Martello*—" The Hammer, he meant Hammer Pete. "—comes to New York. He thinks he's safe. Even Loparco doesn't come with him. But somebody in Boston heard him talking to you, Charlie, and knew where you two were going to meet. He thought nobody knew. But somebody did. And somebody got rid of Signor O'Malley. Maybe Patriarca, hmm?"

Albert Anastasia was a somber-looking young man, with a mouth not quite horizontal across his face but tipped noticeably toward the right. He had wavy black hair well plastered down, an oversize nose, and a receding chin.

"Makes sense," said Costello. "Besides, the O'Malley crowd in Boston are supposed to think somebody down here did it."

Costello was a nondescript man of uncertain age, with only two distinguishing characteristics: thick black hair slicked straight back, and a mole on his chin.

"If Patriarca sent men down here to kill O'Malley, he's gonna answer for it," said Charlie Lucky. "That's exactly the kind of stuff the new organization is not going to stand for."

"Got a question, though, Charlie," said Anastasia. "Is is possible somebody was gunning for the other guy, the dude you met that night?"

Charlie Lucky rubbed his chin and pondered that for a moment. "What's your idea, Al?" he asked.

"Suppose the Dutchman really is trying to send a message to the Governor. It'd be a pretty damned spectacular message if he knocked off the Governor's dude buddy."

"And the Dutchman is just crazy enough to do it," said Costello.

"What kinda guy is the dude?" Anastasia asked.

Charlie Lucky sneered. "He's a playboy. No crumb, he's got a lotta dough. But all he's doing is playing a game. He's got no idea what he's mixed up in. And neither does the Governor, you wanta know the truth."

"Then maybe what he said is a lotta baloney," said Costello.

"Where's his percentage in feeding me baloney?" asked Charlie Lucky. "Where's the Governor's percentage in it? No. Somebody's sent the threat to Albany all right, and this Endicott character is the Governor's errand boy."

"He's smart about one thing," said Anastasia.

"What?"

"He walked away the other night. The cops don't even know he was there. You sure Billingsley won't talk?"

Charlie Lucky fixed a cynical smile on Anastasia.

"Okay," said Costello. "You think Dixie Davis is gonna show?"

"He'll show," said Charlie Lucky. "Don't forget we own twenty-five percent of the Dutchman's beer action. Dick thinks that's what we're gonna talk about. What he's gonna hear is the word. The word, guys. From this meet, the Dutchman gets the word."

4

"A certain Mr. Loparco wishes to speak with you, sir," said Drake, Jack's manservant. "I told him you were engaged, but he insists."

Jack pulled his watch from his vest pocket and checked the time. He and Felicia Cushing were about to leave for dinner and were dressed for it. He shrugged. "I'm afraid we've really got no choice," he said to her. "Luigi Loparco is not the sort of man you just tell to go away."

"Particularly in the circumstances," said Felicia.

"Show him in, then."

A moment later the saturnine little man they had last seen at the Leedo with Hammer Pete O'Malley walked in. "No, I'll keep it," he said to the manservant, who had for the second time offered to take his hat. He kept it on his head as he stood just inside the door and stared around the two-hundred-year-old room, his eyes stopping on the heavy, leather-upholstered chairs and the horsehair-upholstered sofa, on the crystal decanters of wine and liquor sitting between lighted candles on a sideboard, on the blackened, time-softened brick of the big fireplace and on its stately oak mantel, on the pegged oak floor and oriental rugs, and finally on the painting above the fireplace: the John Singleton Copley portrait of the Reverend Josiah Endicott.

"A drink, Mr. Loparco?" Jack asked.

Loparco shook his head. "I just come to ask a question," he said. He ceased his scrutiny of the room and fixed skeptical eyes on Jack and Felicia. "I just got one question," he said. "You didn't set Pete up, did you? You can swear to that?"

Jack stepped to the sideboard. He remembered Loparco drinking gin at the Leedo, and he poured him a generous shot of it and put in some ice. "To use one of Pete's favorite expressions, what percentage would there have been for me in that?" he asked.

"I can't see one," Loparco admitted. "But then maybe I wouldn't."

"Look at it another way," said Jack as he handed him the glass of gin. "Pete made the calls and set up the meeting in New York. I didn't."

"Yeah . . ."

"And if you want me to swear I didn't set him up, then very well. I swear."

Loparco tipped his glass and drank most of the gin at a gulp. "You met with Charlie Lucky," he said. "Lucky leaves. A minute or two later, you guys leave. Then—maybe Charlie Lucky set him up."

Jack poured a small Scotch for himself, a small gin for Felicia. "What's the percentage for Charlie Lucky?" he asked.

"You ever hear of the Unione Siciliana?" asked Loparco. With the thumb and index finger of his right hand he began to pinch the crease in the wide lapel of his beige double-breasted suit. "You ever hear of the Black Hand, sometimes called the Mafia? Unione Siciliana is the American piece of it. The head of it in New York, until about a year ago, was a guy named Joe the Boss Masseria. He was knocked off about a year ago, and Charlie Lucky took over his businesses—his businesses but not the Unione. The new head of the Unione was a guy called Salvatore Maranzano. Then *he* got killed last November. Now Charlie Lucky is head of the Unione Siciliana, and his idea is to make every Sicilian in the rackets answer to the Unione. His other idea is for the Unione to take over all the rackets."

For Jack, this was new information about the man he had met at the Stork Club, enough to make him wonder if Charlie Lucky hadn't ordered the deaths of both him and Hammer Pete. "Did Charlie Lucky kill Masseria and Maranzano—or have them killed?" he asked.

"Masseria probably," said Loparco. "Maranzano, no. Maranzano was knocked off by a guy named Bo Weinberg, who works for Dutch Schultz."

"Then . . . Then Charlie Lucky and Dutch Schultz must be pretty good friends."

Loparco shook his head. "The Dutchman is a crazy man, like Pete always said. He didn't do anything for Charlie Lucky. He did it for some other reason, of his own. So he's marked. The Unione will get him, sooner or later."

Felicia sat on the horsehair sofa, wearing a tea-colored satin dress with bold décolletage front and back. She had listened to the conversation with profound interest. "How does this man come to be called Charlie Lucky?" she asked.

Loparco smiled for the first time. "Some guys took him for a ride. Dumped him, thinkin' he was dead. When he come walkin' in, all bloody but alive, he got the name Lucky."

"My question," said Jack, "is how far can I trust him?"

Loparco chuckled. "About as far as you could throw him."

"He's supposed to be setting up a meeting for me, with Dixie Davis."

"Well, carry a biscuit," said Loparco.

"Carry what?"

"A biscuit. A gun."

Jack frowned. "I . . . I'll think about that."

The dark little man nodded emphatically and tossed back the last of his gin. "What Charlie Lucky's doin' for you makes it look like you and him are buddies. You may not be close enough to Lucky to make his friends your friends, but you don't have to get very close to him to make his enemies your enemies. I'd keep a biscuit under my coat if I was you. And keep your eye out, especially behind your back."

They dined with George and Abigail Saltonstall, and on the way to Felicia's home on Beacon Street, in Jack's Marmon

V-16, which tonight he drove himself, without the chauffeur, Jack told her he was going to New York again in the morning and so would not stay with her that night.

He did accompany her into her house and then into her living room, where she insisted he must have a cigarette and one final small Scotch.

"You haven't been much fun tonight, you know," she complained. "You've been obviously preoccupied. Are you thinking about where you're going to get a 'biscuit' between now and train time in the morning?"

"I've got a 'biscuit' if I need one," he said.

"Then, sit down," she said.

"Well . . . Just for a minute," he said. "I don't want to be discourteous, but . . . But I seem to have gotten myself involved in more than I agreed to."

"Sit, for God's sake! Between Loparco and the Saltonstalls I've hardly had a moment to talk with you all evening."

Her living room was furnished in an English-country-house style, with overstuffed chairs and a couch upholstered in floral fabrics. Sprays of flowers filled vases around the room and scented the air. The room was small, and Jack had always found it a little cloying.

"As I said, I'm catching an early . . . train."

He had hesitated because as he spoke she had put her cigarette between her lips to free both her hands to pull apart her décolletage, exposing her small, firm breasts.

"If I can't get your attention any other way—"

"Felicia . . ."

She pulled her dress over her head and tossed it on a chair. Naked except for her black patent-leather shoes, stockings rolled just below her knees, and a pair of black lace panties, she stalked across the room and opened her liquor cabinet. Quickly she poured two drinks, then carried the glasses back to where he was standing. She pointed peremptorily at the couch. He sat down. She sat beside him; and, seizing his hand, she pressed it to her right breast.

"Train . . . train, hell," she whispered. "Relax. You can sleep between Boston and New York."

He relaxed.

They sat in silence for a while, smoking,

sipping their drinks. He fondled her breast, and she sighed and closed her eyes.

But then she stirred and uncrossed her legs and said, "Jack . . . Can I go to New York with you?"

"No."

"No? Why not?"

"Because I'm going down there to meet with mobsters. I think in Hammer Pete O'Malley and Luigi Loparco you've met all the men of that type you need to meet in a whole lifetime. As, in fact, have I."

"I'd like to meet the one they call Charlie Lucky," she said. "Are you going to see him on this trip?"

"Yes. He set up the meeting with this lawyer they call Dixie Davis. Maybe he's going to meet Davis, too. I don't know."

"Where are you meeting Davis?"

"I don't know. I have to see Charlie Lucky to find out."

"Where are you meeting Lucky?"

"A restaurant on Mulberry Street. For lunch. Then after I see Davis, I'm supposed to be guest of honor, so to speak, at a party he's having at a hotel."

"What hotel would let *him* have a party?"

"Just about any hotel in town. Don't kid yourself about that."

"What hotel?"

"It's in Brooklyn. Called the Metropolitan Hotel."

"You confident you'll come out of this party without a loathsome disease?" she asked playfully. Then, more seriously, she asked, "You sure he isn't setting you up to kill you?"

Jack smiled. "As that type likes to say, what's the percentage for him in doing that?"

"Well, you be careful, lover," said Felicia. "I mean it. You be damned careful."

The "biscuit" hung heavy under Jack's double-breasted jacket as he counted off money to pay his taxi driver, outside the restaurant where Charlie Lucky had arranged their second meeting. It was a short-barreled, .38 caliber, five-shot hammerless Smith & Wesson revolver; and he was all but certain it bulged under his left arm, where it hung in a soft leather holster. Odd that he should find himself carrying it. He had found it in the house after his father died and learned only then that his father had habitually carried it under the Prince Albert coat he had worn daily at the bank. Indeed, the old man's coats had been tailored to accommodate it. Jack had bought new ammunition for it and had taken it to a remote beach on the Cape to try firing it at a target. He'd had some experience with pistol shooting in 1917 and '18, and he found the thing frustratingly inaccurate. No doubt, though, it would be deadly at short range, which was what it was for.

This was the first time he had ever worn it under his clothes, and he was acutely self-conscious, sure someone on the train would notice it. It was of course a concealed weapon, and illegal—though that didn't worry him as much as the embarrassment of being seen carrying a pistol on the streets.

Mulberry Street was in the Manhattan neighborhood called Little Italy and was known for good restaurants. The Ristorante Siracusa, where Charlie Lucky had told Jack to meet him, was distinguished by a broad green canvas awning over the sidewalk, shading the plate-glass windows that afforded diners in the shady interior a clear view of the sunlit street but passers-by a very restricted look into the restaurant. As Jack handed money to the driver, he stared at the windows and saw tables set with heavy silver, crystal, and china, on long white cloths. Only one of the window tables was occupied; and as he watched, a waiter poured wine, wholly visible from the street, in open defiance in Prohibition.

"Good luck," said the driver.

"Thanks. But, what do you mean? Do I need it?"

"You ain't from this neighborhood," said the driver. "You ain't even from N' Yawk. I can tell from your accent. Ever been in this place before?"

Jack shook his head.

"There've been three murders in that joint in the last year," said the driver. "So good luck. Duck if the lead starts flyin'."

Jack went in. A person who seemed to be the proprietor, a short, swarthy, bald man, wearing an ankle-length white apron tied around his waist, hurried forward and asked if he were Mr. Endicott. When Jack said he was, the man gestured toward a table, where Charlie Lucky sat waiting for him.

The proprietor took his hat, and Jack sat down.

Charlie Lucky wore an outlandish white bib, and an enormous lobster, already half eaten, lay in wreckage on a platter before him. "Like one of these?" he asked. "They get 'em live, straight down from Maine." He lifted the bottle from an ice bucket and filled the glass before Jack with cold white wine. "And try that," he said. "From Italy. Bet you didn't know we make white wine in Italy. But we do. Best in the world."

Jack tried the wine. It was dry, with a subtle fruitiness that was not at all heavy. He said he would have a lobster. Charlie Lucky gave the proprietor the word, in Italian.

Very few people in the room had not by now checked out the tall man in the tan double-breasted suit, who had sat down with Charlie Lucky. Only two women sat at the tables. The rest were occupied exclusively by men, most of them engaged in hushed, earnest conversations punctuated with gentle, fraternal squeezing of hands and arms and light slaps on shoulders. They were determinedly solemn, except for one heavy older man with a great gray walrus mustache, who ate and drank with evident pleasure and smiled broadly and happily, constantly nodding and chuckling at the talk of the others around his table.

Jack sensed that he was not just in a

neighborhood restaurant but in a fraternity meeting room—and that he was not an initiate.

"There's another guy who might have sent the threat to the Governor," said Charlie Lucky. "Waxey Gordon."

"Public Enemy Number One," said Jack.

Charlie Lucky sneered. "Listen, the guy's got—The Jews have a word for what Waxey's got. Chutzpah. Ever hear of it? Brass. Balls—"

"Hubris," said Jack.

Charlie Lucky frowned. "Whatever . . . Lemme tell ya what he did. This little fellow Tom Dewey—You heard of him? The Assistant U.S. Attorney? Anyway, he sends federal agents over to Hoboken to pick up some records of Waxey's that Dewey had subpoenaed. So the Hoboken cops, which are in Waxey's pocket, arrested the feds and charged them with impersonating federal officers. During the time it took these feds to get loose, the records they'd come for disappeared. That's the kind of chutzpah Waxey's got."

"And his chief source of revenue is beer," said Jack.

Charlie Lucky nodded. "So he feels no friendship for Governor Roosevelt."

"Can we give the word to him that we're giving to Dutch Schultz?"

"I've done it," said Charlie Lucky. "But he may be the one who sent the threat. Dixie Davis swears the Dutchman didn't do it. Anyway, I figure the trouble is over. Everybody's got the word. Waxey's a cocky guy, but he's not stupid. The Dutchman's stupid, but he knows which way the wind blows. I figure the Governor's got no problem."

"We appreciate your help," said Jack.

"It's good politics," said Charlie Lucky. "I'm a businessman. My friends are businessmen. A good businessman always keeps his political fences mended. Isn't that the way they put it: keeping your fences mended?"

Jack smiled. "That's how they put it. But, say—Is there any point in my meeting Dixie Davis, if everything is fixed?"

"Yeah. You meet him. That's keeping *your* fences mended."

The taxi driver who dropped Jack at the Empire Chop House on Broadway south of Union Square, a little after seven, had no comment to make about it. The place lacked the style of Ristorante Siracusa. The floor was black-and-white tile. Ceiling fans turned slowly, stirring the air. Skimpy and darned tablecloths covered the small round tables where people sat on wire-back chairs. The mimeographed menus were small, but a board behind the counter offered special dinners for 25¢, 35¢, and 50¢. Charlie Lucky had warned that dressing for dinner would make a man absurdly conspicuous in the Empire Chop House, so Jack was still in the suit he had worn all day—and even so he stood out.

No headwaiter stood ready to lead a customer to a table; the drill was to take whatever table was free. Jack went to the cashier, who seemed likely to be the proprietor, and said he was meeting Dixie Davis. The man nodded, came out from behind his cash register, and led Jack to the back of the restaurant and through a door into a short hallway. Another door opened to the right, onto a small private dining room.

Two men sat at a table in the private dining room, where they had a clutter of papers spread out on the table. One rose and extended his hand. "I'm Dick," he said. "And this is Arthur." He shook Jack's hand, and then Arthur rose to shake it.

Jack was surprised at how young Dixie

Davis was. He had supposed the lawyer for a man like Dutch Schultz would be at least forty, but Davis did not look over thirty. His puffy, lazy eyes gave him a look of insolent self-confidence. His lips were fat and seemed pursed to whistle. He was carefully dressed, in a light gray double-breasted suit with wide lapels. His starched white shirt was fresh, his tie knotted with precision.

"We have some beer and a bottle of rye," he said. "I can order something more to your taste."

"I usually drink Scotch," said Jack. He could have accepted rye or beer but suspected it might be well not to seem too easily pleased. "If it's no great inconvenience."

"I'll get it," said Arthur. He pushed back his chair and went out.

"Let me suggest you taste something," said David. He picked a brown bottle of beer out of a bucket of ice. "This is what the boss sells. Try a sip. You'll see why we're successful."

Jack nodded, and Davis pried off the cap with an opener. He didn't offer a glass, so Jack tipped the bottle and took a swig. He was surprised. The beer was good. It wasn't home brew or the unpalatable swill pushed by the typical beer baron. It was as good as the old beer that you got before Prohibition, as good as the Canadian beer he kept at home.

"You can understand," said Davis, "why we don't want every amateur who knows how to make home brew breaking into the business. To make beer like that, you have to run a quality operation. One of our guys brought a *braumeister* here from Bavaria, believe it or not. We've got a big investment in it."

"I understand that," said Jack. "All I'm asking you to understand is that the Governor cannot prevent Repeal. It's not a question of wants to or doesn't want to. It's a question of *can't.*"

"But he wants Repeal," said Davis. "You won't deny that, will you?"

"No, I won't deny that. My point is that what Governor Roosevelt wants or doesn't want is not the decisive factor. If you could change his mind and make him a dry, he couldn't prevent repeal. Herbert Hoover can't prevent it. It's coming. It's a popular movement."

Dixie Davis tapped the beer bottle with one finger. "Can we get a license to brew this legally, you think? I mean, after Repeal?"

Jack shrugged. "I don't see why not."

Davis frowned. "Hmm . . . ," he murmured. "Interesting."

Arthur returned carrying a bottle of Black & White. He put it down on the table and sat down without a word.

"Mr. Endicott likes our beer," said Davis. "He thinks we can get a license to brew legally, after Repeal."

Arthur turned down the corners of his mouth and tipped his head to one side. He was unprepossessing in every respect. His hair had been inexpertly cut, probably by a cheap barber who had run the clippers as high as the top of his ears; and his gray, single-breasted suit fit him ill. He sat with his jacket and vest unbuttoned, showing how his shirt bloused out over his belt. He smiled oddly, with his lips kept down over his teeth. His nose had been broken, and his complexion was sallow. Overall, he looked like a vacuum cleaner salesman having a bad year.

"Actually," said Jack, "I have no idea whether or not you can get a license. All I said was, I don't see why not."

"What would get in our way?" asked Arthur.

"Two things, maybe," said Jack. "One

thing is, when legal brewing comes back, there'll be big corporations in it—big corporations with lots of money. Tough competition. The other thing you might have to worry about is, your boss has a bad reputation."

Dixie Davis flushed. "A bad—"

Arthur began to laugh, at first quietly and then with more gusto until it was a thin cackle—though still managing somehow to keep his teeth hidden behind his lips.

Davis glanced back and forth between Jack and Arthur, his expression brittle. After a moment, he eased, and a small smile came to his face. "I guess you don't know who Arthur is," he said to Jack. "I should have given you his full name . . . Arthur Flegenheimer."

Jack had never heard the name, but he began to suspect—

Arthur guffawed and reached over to slap him on the shoulder. "Arthur Flegenheimer," he laughed. "More often called Dutch Schultz."

"Jesus Christ," said Jack glumly.

The Dutchman slapped his shoulder again. "And you're right. I do have a bad reputation. That is, in some quarters."

"I feel like an idiot," said Jack.

Schultz laughed on. "You stepped on your cock," he chortled. "But it's okay. I like it. It's interesting to see an educated guy, a rich guy, do somethin' stupid. Proves a point of mine. But think nothin' of it. It's okay."

"Thanks."

"The point it proves," said Schultz, "is that a guy like me can compete with a guy like you—I mean a guy with money and education. It's like it was with Napoleon, you know. Dixie did me a big favor, gave me a biography of Napoleon Bonaparte, and I've learned a lot from it. Like, Napoleon was a little guy and not good-lookin', and he came from a poor family, and he didn't get much education; but he got to the top by climbin' over guys that, on the odds, were better'n him; and next thing you know, guys that came from good schools and had lots of money were workin' for Napoleon. Right? Like, take Dixie here. Dixie's a lawyer, which means he's got a college degree and all that, but he works for me. I got a guy named Biederman who works for me. We call him Abba Dabba, 'cause he's a genius at numbers. He can figure up in his head in ten seconds what it'd take a guy with an adding machine five minutes to do. But he works for the Dutchman. Talleyrand was the smartest man in the world in his day, but he worked for Napoleon. Bernadotte was the best general, but he worked for Napoleon. Marie-Louise was the daughter of an emperor, but she married Napoleon. Right? An' you know what brought him down in the end? Little guys. Little guys ganged up on him. Little guys betrayed him. Man, I think a lot about Napoleon!"

Jack was wholly unsure how to react to that, and Dixie Davis seemed to understand and broke the awkward moment by saying, "Anyway, have a drink."

Schultz opened the bottle of Scotch he'd brought for Jack and poured a water glass half full. He didn't have water or soda or ice to offer. Jack picked up the glass and took a drink.

"I'll get Pete to bring some ice," said Davis, and he got up and went out.

"So you're a pal of the Governor, huh?" said Schultz.

Jack nodded. "That's exactly what I am, his friend. I don't work for him."

"Yeah. That's the word we got from Charlie Lucky. You're a friend of his, too, huh?"

"Not really. Governor Roosevelt asked me to contact some people and convey a message to them. Because I'm from Boston, I asked Pete O'Malley to make my first contact for me, and that's who he contacted."

Schultz's head bobbed in a jerky, nervous nod. "Y' see why I'm so much interested in Napoleon? I'm tryin' to run a business and make it bigger, and I've got all these damned guineas tryin' to gang up on me.

"Do you understand what the Governor is trying to tell you?" Jack asked.

"That he couldn't stop Repeal if he wanted to? I understand it. I'm not sure it's right, but I understand it."

"Someone sent the Governor an assassination threat," said Jack. "Whoever it was tried to make it look like it came from you."

Schultz laughed, and this time Jack saw why he kept his lips nearly closed even when he cackled—the Dutchman had a small chew of tobacco in his mouth. "Sneaky, sneaky! *You* think it came from me. The Gov thinks it came from me. But I like the way you put it. What you call diplomacy, hey?"

Jack fixed an unblinking eye on the Dutchman and asked, "Well? *Was* it you?"

"No. You're right. Somebody tried to make it look like I did it." He grinned. "Cheap tactic. Kind of thing the guineas'd do."

"Can I assure the Governor that the threat didn't come from you?"

The Dutchman shrugged. "'Course," he said.

Dixie Davis returned with a water pitcher filled with ice. As he put ice in Jack's glass and in his own, Schultz talked about the threat to the Governor.

"Look," he said. "If anybody takes a shot at Roosevelt, it's gonna be a nut. It's not gonna be a businessman, not a business-man of any kind. In the first place, that kind of thing is not allowed. I mean, there are some rules. Y' know?

"Listen," he went on, obviously mesmer-ized by the sound of his own words, for he was by no means drunk. "What I'd watch out for is guys in silk shirts. Only two kinds of guys wear silk shirts, in my judgment, and that's queers and guinea greaseballs. It's guys like Charlie Lucky and Anastasia and Profaci that you oughta worry about. And guys like Capone, only you don't have to worry about Big Al 'cause he's locked up in the federal pen. Listen, a guy like me never had an ambition to take over the country. All I want is to run my business and be left alone. If you wanta take word back to the Governor, tell him to speak out against Repeal. He can do that much. That'd be good politics and good policy."

Jack had nothing more to say. He was careful, though, not to seem too anxious to leave; and he affected thoughtful interest while Schultz rambled over such subjects as the Depression and how to end it, why a man was a fool to invest in stocks, and how much he paid for his hats. Jack accepted and drank another Scotch before he suggested he had probably better go back to his hotel.

Dutch Schultz stood when Jack did. He took Jack's hand in a firm grip and looked up solemnly into his face. "Look, Endicott," he said. "You're an okay guy. You ever have any trouble, need some money or anything, you just call on the Dutchman. I'll always be ready to take care of you. You ask Dixie. Dutch Schultz makes friends easy and is always loyal to his friends. Isn't that right, Dixie?"

Davis nodded and smiled. "Arthur is always good to his friends."

Schultz slapped Jack's shoulder again.

"Provided they don't try to screw me," he laughed. "That's the only condition. Provided they don't try to screw me."

When Jack walked out onto Broadway, traffic on the street was light, and there was no taxi in sight. He stepped between two parked cars and scanned the street. Two ancient, rattling cabs sped by, both hauling passengers. He stood there, faintly annoyed, wondering if he should go back inside the Empire Chop House and ask Schultz for a ride uptown and not sure he wanted to get in a car with the man. He decided to stand on the street a few minutes. Probably a taxi would show up.

A young woman in a too-tight flowered cotton dress walked past him. "Lotsa fun, two dollars," she murmured quietly. Jack did not turn to look at her, and she ambled on.

When a black Packard turned into the street and came toward him, Jack stepped back between the parked cars, remembering what had happened on Fifty-third Street. But the Packard sped past, driven by a chauffeur and carrying a man and woman in the back seat.

An empty cab appeared at last, and Jack

got in and gave the driver the address of the Metropolitan Hotel in Brooklyn.

The hotel was a small, square building of soot-stained brick, on a dark and quiet street in Williamsburg. The lobby was shabby and attended by an inebriated desk clerk. The hard-looking men who sat in chairs and watched Jack come in were not drunk and were alert. Jack walked to the desk and told the clerk his name.

The clerk looked past him, to one of the men.

"He's expected," the man grunted.

The clerk pointed to the stairway and said, "Third floor front."

Jack climbed the stairs, reached the third floor, found himself in a dingy hallway, and turned toward the front of the hotel.

The door to "third floor front" was wide open, and the party had spilled into the hall, where a man and a girl were locked in an erotic embrace—she with her back to the wall, he shoved up against her—rubbing their bodies together as he kissed her fervidly.

Jack slipped past them and into the living room of a suite that didn't seem to belong in the Metropolitan Hotel. If it was tastelessly furnished, it was nevertheless *well* furnished, with new chairs and couches, rugs that were not threadbare, and a floor-model radio that stood on legs and blared dance music into the room through a horn on top. Somewhere in New York the Paul Whiteman Band was playing a song Jack recognized and wished he didn't, called "Ragamuffin Romeo."

The room was filled with heat and with cigarette smoke that all but overcame the stench of perfume mixed with copious sweat. Four couples were dancing, the young men in their shirtsleeves, their pants hanging from mustard-colored suspenders, two of them with hats on their heads. The girls wore garish red makeup. Two of them were garbed in kimonos, not dresses, and one danced barefoot.

"Mr. Endicott."

Jack turned and faced a burly man who had come out of one of the rooms to the sides of this parlor.

"Welcome. My name is Joe Profaci."

Profaci was a bulky man, no more than five-feet-six but carrying the weight of a man three or four inches taller, not in loose fat but in plain bulk, some of it muscle. He appeared to be in his early thirties. His facial features were hard and a little exaggerated but otherwise not remarkable. His upper lip on the right was marked with what may have been acne scars. A wisp of his dark hair lay across his forehead.

"Thank you," said Jack. "I am Jack Endicott. I am pleased to meet you."

"Charlie's in the bedroom," said Profaci, nodding toward a door. "Wants to see ya."

In the small bedroom, Charlie Lucky was stretched out on the bed, propped up against wadded pillows. He was drinking red wine, but there were bottles of liquor on the dresser. A woman occupied a chair beside his bed. Another, much younger, sat on the foot of the bed.

"Pour Mr. Endicott some Scotch," said Charlie Lucky to the woman in the chair. "And remember him. Don't forget his face."

The woman rose obediently and went to the dresser to pour Jack a drink. She was of middle age, had an olive complexion, and was memorable only for her prominent hooked nose.

"Sit down," said Charlie Lucky, pointing to the chair the woman had vacated. "Sit here beside me."

Jack was reluctant to take the woman's place but knew she would not sit there again when Charlie Lucky had given her chair to someone else. He sat down.

"You met Joe Profaci," said Charlie Lucky. "He's boss of things in Brooklyn. Aren't many guys with more say-so than Joe. Aren't *any* in Brooklyn. He agrees with you about the Governor. The word's gettin' around."

"I appreciate that," said Jack. He accepted a glass of straight Scotch from the woman. "The Governor will appreciate it."

"How'd it go with the Dixie Davis? He buy the deal?"

"I think he did," said Jack. "But Dutch Schultz himself also came to the meeting, and I'm not sure he did. He is a hard man to judge."

"The Dutchman . . ." Charlie Lucky shook his head. "He doesn't live in this world."

"What he lives in," said Profaci, "is the world like it was ten years ago."

"Anyway," said Charlie Lucky, "I talked to Joe here and to all my guys. I'm still workin' on a sit-down with Waxey Gordon. So I'm doin' all I can for the Governor. Now I want the Governor to do somethin' for me."

Jack nodded and waited to hear what

Charlie Lucky would demand. Hammer Pete had warned him there would have to be a quid pro quo. Guys like Charlie Lucky, Pete had said, would expect a percentage.

"It's easy enough," said Charlie Lucky. "I won't be askin' the Governor—the President, I mean—to make an appointment. I'm askin' him *not* to make an appointment. Okay?"

Jack tried to keep his face bland as he waited for the rest of it.

"It's the U.S. District Attorney. When a new President takes over, I suppose he'll appoint a new DA. Okay? All I ask of Governor Roosevelt is, when he gets to be President, don't appoint this Dewey the new DA. In fact, I'd like him to appoint somebody who won't keep Dewey on as assistant. Okay?"

Jack frowned and nodded and took a moment to think through what the man was saying to him. He'd heard of Dewey, of course. The district attorney was a Republican, appointed by Hoover, and his assistants were all Republicans. Was it possible that men like Charlie Lucky and Joe Profaci were so naive about politics they didn't understand that very early in his administration any Democratic President would appoint a complete new set of district attorneys, all Democrats, and that those Democrats would appoint Democrats as their assistants?

"You, uh, understand I can't make promises for the Governor," Jack said. "But I don't see any problem. I'll take the word to Governor Roosevelt."

"And you'll let me know what he says, right?"

"Yes."

Charlie Lucky smiled. "Okay. We got a deal. So . . . Listen, uh, you're a guest. Anything we can do for ya. You're welcome to stay for the party."

The words said one thing. The awkwardness with which they were spoken said another, and Jack understood he had in effect been dismissed.

"Tell ya what," said Charlie Lucky with a grin. "Why don't you let Polly take ya to her place?" He winked. "There's no place in New York you can have a better time than at Polly's."

Jack glanced at the woman, then said to Charlie Lucky, "Thanks, but I got up before dawn this morning to catch the train from Boston. I think I'll just go back to the hotel."

"Okay. Tell the guy at the desk to call you a cab. They don't cruise around here."

In the lobby, he told the desk clerk to order a taxi. Then; annoyed by the stares of the guards in the lobby, he stepped out on the street to wait.

Music from a radio in third floor front came down to the sidewalk, as did the noise of harsh laughter. The street was dark except for the lights from the hotel and the streetlights at the two corners. It was a street of small stores, and they were all closed this time of night. Jack lit a Tareyton and began to walk back and forth.

When a man spends months in combat, in close contact with a skilled and malevolent enemy, he acquires certain instincts that remain with him for the rest of his life. He sees shadows within shadows, hears sound beneath sound—usually to no effect at all, now that the perils of combat are long and far behind him. But the intensified senses remain. He cannot get rid of them if he would.

So it was that Jack had a brief moment of warning before two men stepped out of the shadow of the hotel on its northeast corner and fired at him with pistols.

He was still carrying the "biscuit," the

114

Smith & Wesson in the soft leather holster under his left arm, and as he threw himself against the wall of the hotel he fired a shot. It was not aimed at all, but it would let them know they, too, could get hurt, which would slow them down.

He moved backward, toward the stone steps that led up to the door to the hotel. His first impulse was to run up those steps and through that door. He suppressed that impulse as it dawned on him that the two gunmen might be two of the guards from the lobby, come out a side door. Instead, he dropped to a crouch and aimed the Smith & Wesson with two hands.

The pair had hesitated, as he had known they would, when they saw a muzzle flash and heard the crack of a pistol. But they weren't cowards, and they stood legs apart on the sidewalk and fired again. Their slugs whacked hard against the brick wall, blasting out eruptions of brick dust that fell over Jack.

The Smith & Wesson had a short barrel, and he had never been able to hit anything much with it. But he leveled it on one of the gunmen, steadied, and squeezed the trigger. The man shrieked and staggered back, dropping his pistol and clutching his hands to his belly. He fell to the pavement, screaming.

The second man turned and ran.

Jack rose slowly from his crouch, holding his revolver ready. The music had stopped in third floor front. Men yelled. Jack glanced all around, looking for another threat.

"Endicott!"

It was a whisper, a hiss. The woman called Polly had come out the door. She beckoned to him, and when he hesitated, she beckoned again, insistently.

"My car's out back!"

Not at all sure he wanted to get in a car with this woman, he looked around for the taxi. As likely as not, the clerk had not called for one. Conscious that he might be walking into a trap, Jack walked up the steps and followed the woman into and through the lobby. They went out a back door; and, as she had said, she had a car parked in a small unpaved lot behind the hotel.

It was a Cadillac coupe. Polly slid behind the wheel and started the engine.

"You don't wanta see the cops," she said. "They might be Profaci's cops, and then again they might not be. Besides which, the new guys are gonna show up."

Jack shoved the Smith & Wesson back inside his jacket. "Who were they?" he asked.

She shrugged. "Who knows? And was it you they wanted to kill, or somebody else? Who knows? Charlie Lucky told me to get you out of the neighborhood before the cops come."

Jack sighed and settled back on the leather seat. Gradually the high tension subsided.

"Where to?" she asked.

"I'm staying at the Waldorf."

"I can give you a hell of a lot better time at my place than you can get at the Waldorf," she said.

He looked at the woman. He had been telling the truth when he said he was tired. Anyway, she did not appeal to him. Her anxiety to have him come to her place was unappealing. "I've had a difficult day," he said.

She smiled and nodded. "Exactly," she said.

"I'm sorry. I'm grateful to you, but I think I'd better just go to the Waldorf."

"Your choice," she shrugged. "Anyway—" She reached into her purse and handed him a card. "Anyway, that's my card. Come by anytime. Or give me a call. A friend of Charlie Lucky's is a friend of mine."

He pushed the card down into his jacket pocket and did not look at it until he was in his room in the Waldorf and had called for room service to bring him some dinner—since he'd had none that evening. Only after he had made that call did he pull out the card and look at it.

The woman was—My God, she was Polly *Adler!* He had been rescued by Polly Adler, the most famous madam and procuress in New York; and she hadn't been inviting him to have fun with her personally; rather she had been inviting him to partake of the legendary pleasures of her world-famous brothel.

As he'd said to her in the car, he'd had a hell of a day.

5

Missy Lehand knelt on the floor in front of Franklin D. Roosevelt and unbuckled the braces that gripped his legs, kept them rigid, and prevented his falling when he stood. If anyone supposed those braces did not hurt, watching him grimace as they were removed would have eliminated the error. Jack knew. Missy knew. Very few others did—including, for the most part, the Governor's wife, who only rarely saw them put on or taken off. As much as the Governor hated the complete uselessness of his legs when they were not in the tight grip of steel and leather, he had to hate the braces more; and as Missy carried them to a bedroom, to put them out of sight, the relief was visible on his face. He used his hands to place his legs in a natural sitting position. If anyone had come in now, they would hardly have been aware that he could not stand or walk.

He sat on a salmon-colored plush couch

in a suite in the Waldorf-Astoria Hotel. After spending three days in Boston, Jack had returned to New York and the Waldorf. Frank had come down from Albany because he was making a speech tonight at Madison Square Garden.

"It has been an experience," said Jack. He was responding to the Governor's question of a moment ago, about what had happened while carrying the word to the mob leaders. "Those fellows are a rough crowd."

"Do you know who killed Pete O'Malley, and why?"

"I've begun to think Pete just happened to get in the way when they were shooting at me."

"Who was shooting at you?"

"If I knew the answer to that, I'd know how to get out of the way," said Jack.

"What makes you think they were shooting at you?" Missy asked.

Jack picked up a newspaper from the coffee table. "Look at that," he said. Part of the story read:

NO CLUES TO IDENTITY
OF BROOKLYN KILLER

Police acknowledge that they have no

clues that seem likely to lead them to identify the killer who shot down a man on the street in front of the Metropolitan Hotel Tuesday night. The dead man has been identified as Louis Feinman, also known as Fine Louie, an acknowledged mobster with a long criminal record. He died in St. Catherine's Hospital three hours after the shooting, without giving police any statement.

Guests in the hotel could give detectives no assistance. They said they heard shots fired outside the hotel and looked down from their windows to observe Feinman lying on the sidewalk. No one else was in sight, they insist.

Such known gang leaders as Charles "Lucky" Luciano and Joseph Profaci were in the hotel at the time of the shooting, attending a party. A dozen witnesses vouch for their story that they were in a third-floor suite at the time of the shooting.

Governor Roosevelt scanned the story, then pulled off his pince-nez and said, "Another gang killing. Is there anything especially significant in it?"

"Only that I am the missing killer," said Jack.

"You?"

"This Feinman and another man tried to kill me. I was carrying a gun and shot back. I seem to have been a little better marksman than either of them."

"Who and why?" asked the Governor.

Jack lit a Tareyton. "The explanation I'd like to believe is that when you associate with gangsters you are apt to get in the way when they start shooting at each other. An explanation I don't like is that whoever made the assassination threat is trying to put some emphasis on it by killing the man you sent to make peace.

"I don't like that explanation either," said the Governor. "In fact, I like it so little that I relieve you of your commitment to do this job. I had no idea what I was asking of you, Jack."

Jack shook his head. "Thank you, but I'll keep at it."

"I don't want you to get hurt, my friend."

"I'm not a professional hero, Frank. But I've got two reasons for sticking with this little job. In the first place, I'm convinced now the threat is real, that somebody actually has it in mind to assassinate you, however stupid that might be. My second reason is that I don't think I could back

122

away if I wanted to. In some people's minds I'm Governor Roosevelt's contact man for the mobs, and to change their minds the very least I'd have to do is go around and see each of them again and say I've quit. Even if I did that, I doubt most of them would believe me."

The Governor frowned. "I should never have asked you to get involved," he said.

Jack stood up and stepped to his friend's side. He put a hand on Frank Roosevelt's shoulder. "What are friends for?" he asked. "If I can do anything to prevent an attempt to murder you, it's worth the risk. Well worth it."

The Governor put his hand on Jack's hand. "Thank you," he said quietly, solemnly.

Missy stood at the window, looking down on Park Avenue, The light shone through her simple white cotton dress, silhouetting the sleek shape of her legs. She turned around and said, "You still haven't said who you think might have tried to kill you. Do you have any idea?"

Jack shrugged. "It could be Charlie Lucky. He's clever. He could be playing me along. It could be Dutch Schultz, It could be somebody else: Waxey Gordon . . . or

123

somebody I haven't even heard of. One thing does argue that Charlie Lucky has something to do with it."

"What's that?"

"He knew I'd be at the Metropolitan Hotel. Dutch Schultz didn't know. Schultz is crazy, and I'd call him the man most likely to have sent those two hoodlums; but unless he had me followed, how could he have known where I'd be?"

"On the other hand," said the Governor, "if this man they call Charlie Lucky wanted to have you killed, why would he do it right outside a hotel where he was having a party? That would have identified the murder with him, at least to an extent. That doesn't make sense to me."

"Besides," said Jack, "if he wanted to kill me, why didn't he do it while I was inside the hotel, where he had probably twenty gunmen, instead of on the street, with only two? Besides, I was driven away from the hotel by a woman. Charlie Lucky sent her to help me get away from there before the police came. Anyway, that's what she said."

"It is, of course, possible," said the Governor, "that Pete O'Malley was in fact the target on Fifty-third Street and that you were the victim of mistaken identity Tuesday night."

"I've told myself that over and over," said Jack. "I'd certainly like to believe it."

Missy went to a cabinet and opened it. From among the four bottles on a shelf inside she chose a bottle of rye. "Eff Dee?" she asked.

The Governor smiled at her but shook his head. "After the speech tonight," he said.

"Jack?"

"A splash of Scotch, please. And, Frank . . . Charlie Lucky gave me the price for his cooperation."

"Uh-oh."

"Not really. It's easy. He wants your word that you will not appoint Thomas E. Dewey the new United States District Attorney."

Missy joined the Governor in laughing.

"I told him I couldn't speak for you but thought I could promise you wouldn't go for Dewey. I'm supposed to report back to him."

Franklin Roosevelt laughed again. "You can assure him I will not appoint Dewey," he said.

"I'll give him the word. He'll be most pleased to have it."

The Governor sucked smoke through his holder, then held it aside between two fingers. "Do I need to make a campaign statement about crime?" he asked. "What's going on? The bigger picture? Anything I need to know?"

Jack paused for a moment and watched Missy pour him a short drink. "Many of us have supposed that Prohibition created gangsterism and that Repeal will destroy it." He shook his head. "It's not going to work that way, Frank. We'll have mobs and gangs after Repeal. Maybe worse."

"Living on what capital, when they no longer have bootleg dollars?"

"They're moving in on a lot of things. Since I've gotten involved in this, I've been doing some reading, trying to find out who these people are that I've been talking to and hearing about. I've got a girl working in the Harvard library for me, pulling out newspaper and magazine articles. What I'm reading confirms what I'm hearing."

"Which is?"

Jack accepted his drink from Missy and took a small sip. "Criminals . . . criminal gangs . . . are nothing new. There have always been a certain number of men, plus a few women, who chose to live outside the rules of civilized society. But Prohibition brought a whole new dimension. Before the Eighteenth Amendment, crime was risky, and the profits were not often great. With passage of the Eighteenth Amendment and the Volstead Act, suddenly there were immense profits to be made, with reasonable risk. So suddenly you've got bootleggers, and not just bootleggers but big bootleggers, making fabulous fortunes. Big Jim Colosimo, Johnny Torrio, Bill Dwyer, Dion O'Banion, Al Capone, and—" He stopped for a moment, and his lips stiffened. Then he went on—"and Joseph P. Kennedy."

The Governor laughed. "You Boston Brahmins can always find an unkind word for the Boston Irish."

Jack's face softened. Then he smiled. "Well . . . His name doesn't belong in company with the others. But he is a bootlegger. Maybe I should say a smuggler. He brings the stuff in on a Cape Cod beach."

"A rum runner," Missy chuckled.

"Anyway," Jack went on, "the yahoos who brought us Prohibition also brought us big-time gang crime. The original mobsters are mostly gone. Colosimo and O'Banion are dead, murdered. Torrio is retired, at least ostensibly. Dwyer spent time in a federal penitentiary and is out on parole. Capone is in the penitentiary. But none of that makes any difference. A new, smarter group has taken over. Here in New York we have this man Charlie Lucky, whose real name is probably Luciano, plus Costello, Profaci, and Anastasia, and two leaders called Bugsy Siegel and Meyer Lansky. In Chicago Frank Nitti and a man called Greasy Thumb Guzik have taken over the Capone operations. A man named Raymond Patriarca seems to be taking over Boston. And so on, all over the country. The new crowd is trying to set up a nationwide organization."

"Seriously?"

Jack nodded and continued. "They held a meeting in Cleveland in 1928. They did it again in 1929, in Atlantic City. Gang leaders from all over the country. The Atlantic City meeting sent a message to Al Capone—your Valentine's Day Massacre is giving everybody a bad name, and we don't want any more of that kind of thing. Enough of them joined in the message to scare Capone."

"What we need then," said Missy, "is a message saying, 'Don't try to kill the Governor of New York.'"

"Exactly," said Jack. "That's what I think I've managed to do, by talking to Charlie Lucky. The word seems to be out."

"Then who tried to kill you Tuesday night?" asked the Governor.

"There are some people who aren't listening to the organization," said Jack. "Notably, Dutch Schultz. Probably also, Waxey Gordon. Plus others. Independents. Schultz, for example, sees parallels between himself and Napoleon. Not a very rational man.

"Well," said the Governor, "the original threat came from Schultz. Or so we think."

"So Louie Howe thinks," said Missy.

"Louie knows as much about these things as anybody," said Governor Roosevelt. "You ought to sit down with him, Jack. Louie the Howe is a very bright guy."

Felicia Cushing lay on her back on the salmon-colored couch where Franklin D. Roosevelt had sat earlier. She pointed her toes at the ceiling and let her skirt fall back to her hips, showing Jack that she had not today rolled her sheer dark stockings but wore them hip-high and attached to a garter belt. She had been shopping while the Governor was with Jack, and she had drunk thirstily from the gin on her return, so she was thoroughly relaxed. She had insisted on coming to New York with Jack this time. It had been too long since she had been in Saks or Tiffany, she said.

"I'm not sure you are going to like Louis McHenry Howe much," Jack said. "He is not a fun man."

"Then get rid of him as quickly as you can," she said. "There will still be time for . . . Well, for the Stork Club. I want to see it, too, you know. Or we can go for a midnight cruise. This is New York, Jack! Not Boston."

He laughed. "All right. Don't drink so much gin that you can't go out."

Jack had invited him for dinner, and Howe arrived at seven—a wizened old man in a rumpled dark-blue suit smeared with gray cigarette ash. His ears were big, his eyes large and bulgy, his chin jutted out, and his cheeks had long since collapsed.

Felicia was curious about him and was on good behavior, eschewing additional gin and successfully concealing most evidence of what she had already had. She wore a tight red silk dress, adorned with beads and sequins.

"How long have you been with the Governor, Mr. Howe?" she asked as she handed him a glass of rye over ice.

"Since his first political job, just about," said Howe, sucking hard on his cigarette and allowing a thick blob of white smoke to trickle out through his nose as well as from the corners of his mouth. "He was elected to the state senate in 1910. I was a capitol reporter in Albany. When President Wilson appointed him Assistant Secretary of the Navy in 1913, I went to Washington with him. I've been with him ever since."

"When did you first decide he'd make a good President?" she asked.

Howe smiled. His smile, though genuine, was that of a man who had to be careful not to dislodge false teeth. "Oh, I'd say sometime in January, 1911. I was a little late. His mother had figured it out about 1882."

"Jack . . ." said Felicia with a wicked grin. "When did you decide he'd make a good President?"

"About two weeks ago," said Jack dryly.

Howe laughed. "You two have been such good friends for so many years, I suspect you saw a President in him years before I did."

A warm reminiscent smile came to Jack's face. "I saw in him a fun fellow," he said. "Before the disease . . . Frank loved to sail, swim, hunt, fish . . . play any kind of game. He loved to laugh."

"He still loves to laugh," said Howe. "He likes the company of good friends. He likes to play poker. He'll sit up till dawn, playing poker and drinking beer."

"So long as the Missus isn't home," said Jack.

Howe's chin rose sharply, but before he spoke he took a moment to drag smoke through thin, hard lips and draw it down into his lungs. He coughed, then said, "Eleanor is a brilliant woman. She is underappreciated. Because of the quirks in her personality. But she has ability, and a conscience."

"I never doubted it," said Jack.

Howe sipped rye. "Well," he said. "Frank tells me you've had remarkable success in establishing contact with the mobs."

"Louie . . . What made you think the threat came from Schultz? Are we really sure that's the source? Schultz denies it. He says whoever did it wanted it to look that way. He says we should worry more about the Sicilians. And it occurs to me that maybe the Sicilians are playing a game with us."

"Pretending to cooperate while . . ." Howe mused, frowning. Then he shook his head. "No. The threat came from Tammany Hall. It came from Jimmy Hines."

"Jimmy . . . ?"

"James J. Hines. Democrat district leader, Tammany man. He and Dutch Schultz are partners. He provides political protection for Schultz. He makes sure that honest cops get transferred to precincts where they can't interfere with mob operations. He owns some of the prosecutors and sees to it that they don't harass Schultz and his men. He even has judges in his pocket. Magistrates dismiss charges against bootleggers and numbers runners, or let them go on bail so low they can and do disappear. Schultz pays him big money, much of which Hines uses to buy more political influence. Jimmy Hines hates Frank, and Frank has been an outspoken enemy of Tammany since he entered the state senate more than twenty years ago."

"Another motive," said Jack. "More than just the beer."

Howe nodded. "Governor Roosevelt has

cut off Tammany's patronage, so far as state offices are concerned. When he becomes President, he'll cut if off for federal appointments."

"Are you saying this Hines had the temerity actually to threaten to assassinate the Governor?" Felicia asked.

"Not to his face, not directly," said Howe. "The word came in the form of a friendly warning, brought to Albany by one of the assemblymen from Tammany. He said the Governor should be careful, because Dutch Schultz was talking about eliminating him. The assemblyman who brought that friendly warning crawled right out of Jimmy Hines's pocket."

"When he said 'be careful,' just what did he mean?" Jack asked.

"Oh, he was specific," said Howe. "He said if Frank ran for President, he'd be constantly exposed to big crowds, which could be dangerous if anybody had it in for him. He said he hoped Frank would consider running for another term as governor and staying away from the dangers."

"And he said Schultz wanted to kill him?" Felicia asked. "Why would he bring a warning like that if Hines and Schultz really meant to try it?"

"It would be far better for them if Frank could be scared off," said Howe.

"So far he hasn't scared," said Jack, "so they've decided to try to kill me to make the warning more emphatic."

"I think that's very possible," said Howe. "You'd make an ideal victim. You're a close friend of Frank's, and he'd hate to have anything happen to you. But you're not a public fellow. Frank would get the message, but the press probably wouldn't, the public wouldn't, and it wouldn't cause the big outcry they want to avoid."

"How very nice," said Jack grimly.

Felicia had begun to shake her head and kept shaking it. "You're missing something, both of you," she said. "In fact, you're missing two things. You think somebody working for Schultz killed Hammer Pete by mistake while trying to kill you, Jack, and that Schultz sent Feinman and his accomplice to the Metropolitan Hotel. But how could Schultz have known where you were, either night? And what about Fine Louie Feinman? Was he ever associated with Schultz? Who was he associated with? It'd be worthwhile to find out, don't you think?"

Jack nodded agreement. "Yes, but how do I find out?"

"I have a suggestion on that," said Howe. "This fellow Dewey is a Republican—I should say an ambitious Republican: But so far as I can tell, he's honest. I'll give him a call, introduce you. You go see him, Jack. He may know a lot."

"All right," said Jack.

"And another suggestion. We're leaving for Chicago shortly. You could do worse than go down to Atlanta Penitentiary and pay respects to Al Capone. He may be locked up, but he's got influence. A word from Big Al could make a difference in Chicago."

Thomas E. Dewey ostentatiously pulled his watch from his vest pocket and noted the time as Jack Endicott sat down after shaking his hand. He was all but unbelievable: short, tight-lipped, cold of manner, wearing a black mustache he might have grown for something to hide behind. It was odd to hear coming out of this little man the meticulously modulated bass voice of the Episcopalian choirboy he had once been. It was odd, too, to see what

136

looked like utter self-confidence, justified by nothing apparent.

"I will be happy to assist the Governor," he said. "I understand I am to do it in an unofficial way."

"For the moment," said Jack.

"Very well. What can I do? Mr. Howe didn't explain much, only asked me to see you.

Jack took a moment to light a cigarette, noting as he did that Dewey took that moment to glance over a paper before him on his desk. The man did count his minutes.

"The Governor," said Jack, "has been threatened with assassination. The threat probably came from Dutch Schultz. But maybe not. The Governor has asked me to look into the matter a little, as a friend and on a strictly unofficial basis."

Dewey shook his head. "Flegenheimer would not attempt to assassinate the Governor," he said. "Not on his own. Not as his own idea. If the threat is real, real enough to be taken seriously, it has to have come from the likes of Jimmy Hines and Mayor Jimmy Walker—anyway, the Tammany crowd."

"What about Waxey Gordon?" Jack

asked. "What about the Sicilians? What about the bootleggers?"

"The smart ones are going to use the capitol they accumulated during the Prohibition years to establish new businesses," said Dewey. "They are infiltrating the labor unions, particularly on the waterfront and in the construction trades. They have gambling: the numbers racket, also called policy. They are heavily into extortion, the so-called protection racket. They dominate the prostitution racket. And I am afraid they are going into still another racket: the importation of dope into America." He shook his head. "Repeal won't hurt them. Not much, anyway."

Dewey shoved his chair back to the steam radiator that stood just behind it. Behind that was a streaked window covered by a venetian blind. His desk was surprisingly modest for a man supposed to be exercising important power; it had the look of a cheap wooden crate turned on its side. It was also much too tidy for someone engaged in meaningful work. In fact, that was the word for Thomas Dewey: tidy—he was tidy of appearance, mind, and personality. And maybe frugal, too, since Jack observed that he smoked his cigarettes down till they almost burned his fingers.

"Government can run them out of business," said Jack. "Government can—"

"That's exactly what I have in mind," said Dewey. "Prosecutions."

"Not what I mean," said Jack. "By legalizing beer and liquor—and perhaps making it a state monopoly the way some states are talking about doing—you drive the bootleggers out of business. And you can do the same thing with the policy books. Like, set up a state lottery . . ."

"You mean, make crime a state-sanctioned business?" Dewey asked. "A state lottery? The policy racket a state business?" He shook his head. "Never!"

Jack grinned. "A thought," he said. "I'm sure you have compelling arguments against it. Let's be specific, Mr. Prosecutor. Who was Fine Louie? Louis Feinman?"

Dewey focused a cutting gaze on Jack—cutting coupled with what he couldn't hide: a gleam of triumph. "Hmm . . ." he said. "Let's see now. The handsome, well-dressed man with the neat black mustache. A shot effectively aimed and effective in its result. An army officer who knows how to use a pistol. And now an inquiry: who was

139

Louis Feinman?" He smiled and shook his head. "Mr. Endicott, really . . ."

Jack let Tom Dewey see a scornful smile. "Want to press that case, Mr. Prosecutor?"

Dewey shook his head. "Not interested," he said. "Louis Feinman worked for the late Legs Diamond. When Diamond was killed—and that, incidentally, was almost certainly done by the Schultz mob—Feinman went independent. He was a contract killer. He worked for whoever paid him. Which tells us nothing about who may have paid him to come after you."

"So who do you suppose is threatening to kill the Governor, Mr. Dewey?"

"I don't know. You can tell the Governor he will have every kind of cooperation I can give him to prevent any attempt on his life. If any information comes to me—"

"I'm sure the Governor will appreciate that."

"I'd take the threat seriously," said Dewey. "What I would take very seriously is the unholy alliance between politics and crime. Aside from the two Jimmys, Hines and Walker, I don't want to name names. I'm sure the Governor knows, or his advisers know, that his nomination would be a significant defeat for certain people.

Some of them—By no means all, but some of them, are closely affiliated with the worst elements our country has to contend with. The threat is not something to ignore."

6

Jack was surprised by "Scarface" Al Capone. The scars on his left cheek were nothing grotesque, just some lines that looked as if he had been hit with a broken beer bottle. Also, the notorious gangster was hardly more than thirty years old.

The room where they met was a small conference room, with a big yellow-oak table in the center and cases of books along one wall. Six heavy wooden armchairs sat around the table, on a maroon rug scarred by scuff marks where these chairs had been pushed under the table and pulled out again, for many years. The place was like any of a hundred drab little meeting rooms he had seen; only the heavy steel bars on the two windows reminded Jack that he was within the walls of a federal penitentiary.

Nothing about Capone reminded anyone that he was a convict. He wore a silk dress shirt, open at the collar, and a pair of dark-blue pin-striped trousers. He smoked a big cigar, and another one—the one he had offered Jack—was in his shirt pocket. He was an undistinguished young man. He looked like a street tough. His eyebrows were thick and black, his lips were thick. His features were in fact distinctly coarse.

"The last thing in the world I'd want would be for the Governor of New York to get hurt in Chicago," he said to Jack. "Somebody'd find some way to pin it on me, even with me locked up in this joint. I got no control over anything, you know. I got almost no influence. I'll be glad to send word to my old friends to look out for the Governor while he's in our town, but—"

"That's all I want from you, Mr. Capone," said Jack. "All I'm asking."

Capone nodded. He leaned back in his chair and blew cigar smoke toward the ceiling. "I'm not at all the guy they say I am, Mr. Endicott. Never was. Hell, they blame me for everything but the Chicago Fire. You know what I was, all I ever was? I was a businessman. I was just a supplier of things people want: beer and liquor, plus a little fun. All that talk about how I killed guys—" He paused and shook his head. "If I killed guys, how come they never charged me with murder? Here I am because my stupid bookkeepers messed up my taxes. But all I am is a businessman, and all I want is to be allowed to live in peace when I get out of here. You can tell the Governor he has my best wishes, and I'll be glad to do what little I can do to help him."

The speech was obviously rehearsed and phony. Looking at Capone, and listening to him, Jack could not judge if he were capable of beating a man to death with a baseball bat, which he was accused of doing in one of the most widely circulated stories about him; but it was apparent that imprisonment had not excised his swagger or infected him with sincerity.

"Do I understand that a Mr. Nitti is handling your affairs while you are away from Chicago?" Jack asked.

Capone nodded. "Him and my brother Ralph. Also Jake Guzik."

"Can you get me an introduction to them?" Jack asked.

Capone shrugged. "Easiest thing in the world. I'll also send 'em word that you and the Governor are my pals."

"I'd appreciate that."

"And maybe when the Governor gets to be President he can do something for me sometime," said Capone. He fixed a cynical stare on Jack, and when he didn't get a smile or wink in return, he said, "I don't mean a pardon. Hell, they'd eat him alive if he pardoned Al Capone. But there is something—There's talk around here that the feds are going to open a new joint in San Francisco, on an island out in the bay. There's talk about transferring certain guys, like maybe me, to this new joint. Now, all I'm doing time for is not paying my taxes, right? I don't wanta go where all the guys are killers and sex fiends and like that. Maybe the Governor could give the order that keeps me *here*—that is, when he's Prez."

"I'll mention it to him," said Jack.

Capone's thick lips curled into a lazy smile. "You do that," he said. "You tell the Governor, I'm just a businessman, a little guy, a little guy that had some success in business but still a little guy. Maybe I can do some things for the Governor. Anything. All he has to do is send the word. Whatever I can do. Whatever. You tell him. I got friends. Sometimes we can get things done, like things that are hard to get done. Glad to help Mr. Roosevelt. I always did admire him. You tell him that, too. You tell him

145

Al Capone has always admired him a whole lot."

On Tuesday, Jack would leave for Chicago. Not before. He could not expect that word from the Atlanta Penitentiary would reach the likes of Frank Nitti and Greasy Thumb Guzik in less than a week. So he had returned to Boston from Atlanta, had played in a bridge tournament at the Common Club on Thursday and Friday evenings, and now on the weekend was racing his ketch.

The course was from Point Gammon on Cape Cod, just south of Hyannisport, to Cape Poge on the northernmost tip of Chappaquiddick Island, to East Chop on the northeast tip of Martha's Vineyard, and back to Point Gammon. It was an all-day race in the blustery waters of Nantucket Sound, and at noon Jack's ketch, Marietta, was a hundred yards ahead of its closest rival.

In addition to himself and Felicia, Jack's crew consisted of his eighteen-year-old daughter Marietta, for whom the boat was named, and George and Abigail Saltonstall. The competition was called the Yarmouth Club Challenge Cup Race; and in the term used forty years before when it was established, it was a "Corinthian" competition—meaning everyone involved was strictly amateur.

One reason why Blackjack Endicott often won was that his crew was skilled and experienced. George Saltonstall had sailed all his life and owned a sleek cutter that he never raced but used for comfortable sailing on long cruises up and down the coast. Felicia had learned to sail as a girl, before she married Cushing, but had learned only what were then supposed to be "women's jobs" aboard boats. Cushing had taught her to function as an active crewman. Abigail Saltonstall did the "women's work" aboard *Marietta*. She was chief of the galley. The crew never wanted for hot tea or coffee, or a bracing shot of grog.

Then there was Marietta. An impetuous dark-haired, dark-eyed beauty, she was the only one aboard who defied the Yarmouth yachting convention that men wear white duck trousers and dark-blue blazers with club emblems, the women pleated white flannel skirts and the same blazers, and everyone must sport white yachting caps. Marietta conformed as to the blazer and cap, but she wore a pair of white duck slacks, tight across her hips but tapering out until they were very wide at the cuffs.

Marietta was sailing close-hauled on a port tack. "Stand by to tack!" yelled Jack. Then, "Lee-oh!" as he spun the wheel. George and Felicia worked the main sheets, Marietta the mizzen sheets; and, skilled and practiced, they cranked the winches to loose the old sheets and sheet the sails for the new course. Marietta loved the strenuous work. Felicia was not so sure. For George Saltonstall, it was simply something a gentleman knew how to do, and did.

With the ketch established on its new tack, the crew could relax. "I am not going to forgive you," Marietta said to Jack. "Not very easily, anyway."

"For what?" he asked as he turned the wheel to make a fine adjustment.

"For not taking me with you and letting me meet those deliciously evil men you're dealing with," she said.

"They are not 'deliciously' evil, Marietta," said Jack. "They are simply evil, just evil. Prosaic, what's more. Crude. There's nothing romantic about them."

"Even so, I—"

"It wouldn't be the adventure you think," he said firmly.

"Well, am I expected to spend the summer reposing languidly around the pool at the Yarmouth Yacht Club while you go off to Chicago to the Democratic National Convention?"

"Precisely," he said. "You are not to come within two hundred miles of Chicago."

"I believe you are serious!" she laughed. "I think you're playing daddy!"

He nodded. "Entirely serious."

She cupped her hands against the wind and lit a Pall Mall. "You have no idea how much evil lurks in the hearts of the Harvardians around the Yarmouth Yacht Club," she said.

"Well, take it easy on the gin, and maybe you'll be able to resist them."

The wind shifted slightly, and almost before Jack could call out the command his crew was at the winches, easing the sheets. Looking back at the next boat in line, Jack could see that the distance was opening.

"How many times do you have to win the cup before it's yours permanently?" Marietta asked.

"You can't win it permanently. That wouldn't be Corinthian," he laughed.

Felicia stepped aft a few paces and asked, "Who's that back there, Jack?"

"Adams," he said. "His life would be whole if he could win the cup just once."

"Then why don't we let him?" she asked. "Who wants to go chasing the wind to East Crop when we could turn into Edgartown, drop anchor, and run up a party pennant? Jack, the damned cup has gotten all rusty and looks like hell on your mantel. C'mon! God knows who's on the Vineyard. Some of the funnest people in the East, likely! Likely somebody's got a game or two going, too! Chemin de fer! Blackjack! Hey!"

"Well, what would we tell the committee?" Jack asked. "And Adams wouldn't want the cup if he thought we just dropped out to let him have it."

"Tell 'em we split a seam," Felicia laughed. "Tell 'em we discovered a rusty scupper."

"Say we severed a pin in the rudder linkage," Marietta suggested. "That put Greenie Peabody out of the Poponnesset last year."

Jack glanced at George Saltonsrall, who had come back to see what was being discussed. "Well, I don't really see how we can do—" His thoughtful frown softened, and

150

then he grinned. "We'll take a vote of the crew. George?"

George shook his head. "No, I don't think it would be right."

"It'll be all right if you keep you mouth shut about it," said Felicia sharply.

"Marietta?" Jack asked.

"Par-ty, par-ty!" she chanted, giggling.

"Abigail!" Jack yelled down the companionway. Abigail Saltonstall appeared. "We're taking a vote. Do you want to sail on and try to win the race, or turn into Edgartown and run up the party flag?"

Abigail, a timid blonde, looked to George.

"I've got two votes for partying and one for racing," Jack said to her. "I haven't voted yet, myself."

"George . . . ?"

Felicia turned on Abigail. "If we lie convincingly, we can let poor Adams have the cup for a year, which will make him happy. And we can turn this muscle-tearing athletic contest into a fun weekend. All we have to is tell our lie and never, never betray each other afterward."

Abigail smiled weakly. "Well . . ." She shrugged. "What the hell?"

Jack laughed and spun the wheel, turning

the bow directly into the wind. The sails began to flap, and *Marietta* lost headway. As the Adams boat overtook and passed, all but George mimed frustration. George didn't have to. He *was* frustrated. But the party was glorious.

The word Jack left with his daughter and Felicia Cushing was that he was on his way to Chicago, with a stopover in New York. When he left on Tuesday he promised them he would telephone from Chicago when he was settled in the Palmer House.

The truth was, he was stopping in New York only long enough to change trains. His actual destination was an elegant estate in rural northern New Jersey, named Tranquillity. It was on a branch of the Erie Railroad, near a small station called Allamuchy. His reason for going there was far more secret than his meetings with the bosses of organized crime.

A big dark-blue Packard waited for him at the Allamuchy station. The chauffeur put his luggage in the rear and set out for Tranquillity—almost without a word, since his employer imposed a hard discipline on his staff. Winthrop Rutherfurd knew the dignity and restraint of English servants,

152

and that was what he wanted from his own. He was a flinty old man, enormously wealthy and accustomed to having his way with people, with everyone, family and servants much the same.

He was also the husband of Lucy Mercer—now Lucy Mercer Rutherfurd.

"Wintie!" Jack said to the cane-wielding old man.

Winthrop Rutherfurd nodded, smiled wanly, and extended his hand. He was seventy-one years old and vigorous though in failing health. "Jack . . ." he murmured. "Always good to see you." And, having met his guest at the door, he led him toward the library, jamming his cane hard on the floor as if he resented having to use it and thought to punish it.

The house was sumptuous. It was one of two estates kept by Rutherfurd. The other, where he and Lucy spent the winter months, was near Aiken, South Carolina. Bent, as though playing the role of elderly man, Rutherfurd wore striped morning trousers but a short black alpaca jacket instead of a cutaway, no waistcoat, and a black bow tie with an ordinary dress shirt. He led Jack into a library filled with glass-front bookcases and furnished with leather couches and chairs. His butler pursued them and only inside the library had his first opportunity to take Jack's gray homburg, gray suede gloves, and stick.

The elegance of Tranquillity House was oppressive, as Jack remembered. The books behind glass, uniformly bound and stamped in gold with the Rutherfurd crest, were not likely—as Jack supposed—even to have been opened. He doubted that Wintie could read all the languages in which they were printed. The vast oriental rug seemed to have been chosen for gloomy colors. The drapes were dark and were kept half closed over the leaded windows.

"What word from Boston?" Rutherfurd asked.

Jack had made a point for years of coming to these visits with a list of investments his most trusted banking friends recommended. He knew Wintie Rutherfurd otherwise than as an investor, simply because men in their station of life tended to become acquainted whether they wanted to or not; but Wintie had come more and more in recent years to accept and esteem the recommendations Jack brought him, and bringing them gave him the excuse to pay these visits.

Something else did, too. In his younger years, Winthrop Rutherfurd been a fox hunter. Now he was an obsessive breeder of fox terriers. To facilitate these visits, Jack had purchased fox terriers and had studied them. He sometimes traded dogs with Wintie.

This he had done to gain entrée into the home of one of the most notoriously jealous old husbands in the United States—and in that home to serve as intermediary between Frank Roosevelt and the woman he loved.

For an hour Jack talked investments and dogs with Winthrop Rutherfurd, before Lucy finally walked into the library and extended her hand.

It had never been difficult to understand Frank's fascination with Lucy—indeed, if she hadn't been Frank's love, Jack himself could have fallen in love with her, and would have been willing to stand against the fury of Wintie or whomever else to free her and marry her.

Lucy had not, of course, been married to Wintie Rutherfurd when Frank fell in love with her in 1917 or '18. He had been married to Eleanor and was the father of their children. The love affair had been impossible, simply impossible, especially for a young man whose ambition was to succeed in politics, maybe even someday to run for President of the United States. He could have suffered a divorce from Eleanor, which was what she initially wanted, and married Lucy. But, by the standards of 1918, he would have sacrificed ambition, reputation, name, and even family—for it had been by no means certain what attitude his formidable mother would have taken, at least in the short run.

Each time he encountered her, Jack saw in Lucy Mercer Rutherfurd the woman Franklin D. Roosevelt could not resist. In some ways she was like Eleanor: tall, with light-brown hair and blue eyes, and with an aristocratic background and the education and training that implied. In other ways she could hardly have been more different. Eleanor's high-pitched voice came out squeaky at worst, at best in the quavering tones of bad music. Lucy's was low and throaty. Eleanor was gawkish. Lucy was graceful. Eleanor had a perverse capacity for choosing the least flattering clothes she could possibly wear. Lucy's taste was exquisite. People had to know Eleanor very well to discover and appreciate the fine qualities she in fact had in abundance. Lucy's were immediately apparent.

"You remember Jack Endicott," Rutherfurd said to his wife. It was almost editorial, as if he were suggesting Lucy had insufficient memory to recall the man from Boston.

She smiled graciously and nodded. "It is good to see you, Mr. Endicott," she said.

She was wearing a chic dress of green silk, with a string of pearls at her neck-manifesting the combined simplicity and gentility that characterized her. Jack had never heard that Rutherfurd was tight with his money; but if he was, he was not parsimonious about his wife's furnishings, probably because he was proud of her and wanted to show her off.

"It is very good to see you, Lucy," he said.

"Wintie, have you offered our friend anything to drink?" she asked.

"If you wish, Jack," he said. "You know I don't drink before five."

"Champagne with lunch, perhaps?" said Lucy.

"Marvelous," said Jack.

He was not staying overnight, but it was the middle of the afternoon before he had the opportunity to speak with her alone—

and that only because Rutherfurd had gone to his kennel to bring back a bitch he wanted to show.

"Next weekend," said Jack to Lucy. "If there is any possible way. A cruise on *Marietta*. It may be the last time before he's nominated for President . . . and if he's nominated, he'll be elected."

"And become more remote, more inaccessible to me, than ever," she said sadly.

Jack nodded. "If the choice had been mine, Lucy, I'd have chosen you over the presidency. Frank—"

"We can't hold that against him," she said.

"I don't. Anyway . . . I told him I'd bring the word to you. A cruise around the Cape and up toward Maine, I think. Offshore. No one will see us."

She nodded. "What will I say to Wintie?"

"Let me try something," he said.

Rutherfurd returned, bringing on a leash a fox terrier bitch that Jack recognized as magnificent. They spent half an hour examining her and discussing her points. Then Jack ventured, "Wintie . . . I'd like to ask you a favor."

"If I can do it," said Rutherfurd without enthusiasm.

"You know I have a daughter eighteen years old," said Jack. "I am embarrassed to have to admit it, but she is . . . How shall I say? She is determined to be . . . independent. She is causing me quite a problem, particularly with regard to a certain young man. She will not listen to me, or to her mother, for whom she has no respect. I should be grateful, Wintie, if my daughter Marietta could spend a little time with a woman she could admire, to hear some advice from her."

"You mean Lucy?" Rutherfurd asked dubiously.

Jack nodded. "Lucy, as she seems to me, is exactly the sort of woman Marietta should know—one whose good judgment and good taste, and success in marriage, would earn the girl's respect. I believe Marietta would be most impressed. And then Lucy could engage her in some conversation about such qualities as a sense of responsibility, perspective, and so on."

"Well, send her down here, or bring her."

"I'm not sure I can get her to leave Yarmouth. That's where she is, at our summer house. Yarmouth is also where the boy is. I was wondering if I could ask you and Lucy to do me the very great favor of traveling up to the Cape, say next weekend. You and I can go sailing, Wintie, and Lucy can stay at the house with Marietta and make friends with her."

Rutherfurd shook his head. "I don't feel up to going traveling in this damned hot weather."

"Oh . . ."

"I suppose Lucy could go, if she wants."

"I will be most obliged," said Jack. "I am sorry to hear that you don't feel up to traveling, Wintie; and I'll be sorry you're not there, but—Well, if Lucy can come . . ."

An hour later Lucy bade Jack good-bye, just before he got into the Packard to be driven back to Allamuchy station.

"We have no conscience, you and I," she said quietly.

"Au contraire," said Jack. "It is conscience that motivates me in this matter, entirely."

Settled early in the evening in his suite in the Palmer House, Jack called the telephone number he had been given by Charlie Lucky. His name meant something to the man who answered; and after a moment a hushed voice came on the line, saying he was Frank Nitti.

"I'll be glad to meet you, Mr. Endicott," said Nitti. "Any friend of Big Al is a friend of mine. How would tomorrow morning suit you? My office is in the Loop and convenient to your hotel."

Jack wondered how Nitti knew what hotel he was in but accepted the suggestion that they meet at ten the next morning. He mixed himself a Scotch and soda from his traveling kit and sat down to look at the evening paper. Someone rapped on the door of the suite.

"Mr. Endicott?" asked the young man at the door. "My name is Murray Humphries. I've been sent to invite you out for an evening on the town."

Humphries was dressed for an evening on the town, in tails, with a silk hat and a stick. He was a handsome young man in a studied sort of way: his black hair slicked back with cream, his clothes conspicuously expensive.

"Indeed," said Jack skeptically. "Who sent you?"

"Indirectly, it was our mutual friend in Atlanta. I don't work for him, of course, but I take care of some business for him from time to time, when he asks."

"A night on the town, you say. Where did you have in mind?"

Murray Humphries smiled. "Your choice," he said. "The Cotton Club is hot. The Dill Pickle is more sophisticated. There are other places, a wide variety of them. I happen to like a small place called Hot Pepper. Whichever you choose, you are our friend's guest of course."

"I've enjoyed the Cotton Club in New York," said Jack.

"Ours is rather different," said Humphries. "It was owned by our friend, and I suppose you could say it reflects his tastes."

Humphries's Lincoln V-12 was waiting on the street, and he drove Jack to the South Side. He was a born-and-reared Chicagoan, he told Jack—also a Harvard man, Class of '24.

"Chicago has changed, you know," he said. "Even before the big man went to Atlanta, things changed. What the boys call themselves now is businessmen without the top hats."

Jack responded with little more than a grunt, and Humphries went on: "This town has got to be wide open for the Democratic Convention. The Republicans are a pinched and crabbed lot. They won't enjoy themselves, and they won't spend. This town's economy depends on some hoopla and big spending. I don't know how much of the city you've seen recently, but we've got more than fifty thousand unemployed."

"I saw vacant factories from the train window," said Jack. "Lots of vacant stores from the cab."

Humphries nodded. "You know what Chicago is?" he asked rhetorically. "Skidrow, U.S.A., that's what."

"The conventions won't bail it out," said Jack.

"All that's going to bail it out is the defeat of Hoover and the installation of a Democratic administration in Washington," said Humphries. "I'd like to see Governor Roosevelt nominated and elected."

"I imagine your father disagrees," Jack suggested.

"My father would vote Communist if he thought it would help."

As Humphries had promised, the Chicago version of the Cotton Club was very different from the Cotton Club in New York. Although a band of Negro musicians played loud and lusty music onstage at one end of the room, the attraction obviously was not jazz but something more primal, something in the dim pink light and the heat and smoke-heavy air, something evocative in the special redolence of the human sweat in this room.

The clientele was divided about equally: half the crowd was what the others would call "citizens," out-of-town Rotarians and Kiwanians come to stare and stock up observations and stories that would last them years, the other half Chicago wise guys of shadowy mien, comfortably enjoying a good time and covertly amused by the persistent furtive glances of the citizens.

Most of the citizens wore evening clothes, while the wise guys favored suits with conspicuous stripes. Most of the citizens had come stag, and the wives or girlfriends of the few who hadn't sat uneasily at their tables, as if afraid they might be kidnapped into white slavery before they escaped this place. That the rest of the women and girls in the Cotton Club worked there was apparent at a glance.

"It's understood whose guests we are, so you can tell the girls to buzz off or you can buy them a gallon of champagne," said Humphries. "It's on the house either way."

Jack was not particularly interested in

telling the girl who sat down beside him to buzz off. She was a blonde, with hair cut short and plastered so tight to her head it suggested a cap. Her makeup was dark and heavy: mascara, eye shadow, and red lipstick. Her white dress was shiny satin, skimpy and tight. She pulled her chair closer to Jack's, tipped her head, and gave him a saucy look, then shrugged her breasts out of her dress.

The girl who sat beside Humphries— dark haired with brown eyes, wearing red—tossed her head peevishly: annoyed, apparently, to have been upstaged.

"Your subtlety is extr'ordinary," Jack said to the blonde.

"Aristotle was subtle," she said. "But you can't live on subtlety. My name is Tiffany. That's a lie, but I won't tell you my real name. Call me Tittie-Poo, like in *The Mikado.*"

"Aristotle and Gilbert and Sullivan," Jack said. "I should hardly have expected it—"

"In a Cotton Club hooker?" she interrupted. "I'm a Hoovergirl. A hell of a lot of people aren't what they want to be, what they were born to be, what they were educated to be . . . before the fuckin' country fell apart. Shall we drop the subject, Mr. Endicott?"

Jack had never before heard the word she had used spoken by a respectable man, much less by a woman, respectable or not. If any single word in the vocabulary of English-language vulgarisms remained unspeakable, the word was "fuck." *No one* said that. Most people didn't even know what it meant. He was not unacquainted with the word, from his service in the World War; but it had been thirteen years since he had last heard it.

"If Tiffany is not your name, how'd you come to choose it?" Jack asked.

"'Cause I'm expensive, like things from Tiffany's."

"No more expensive than I am," said the dark-haired girl. "And my name is Elaine. It really is. You wanta see my tits, too?"

"Why not?" said Jack.

The girl opened three buttons on her red dress and pulled out her breasts, which were larger than Tiffany's but more pendulous, less firm.

The goggle-eyed citizens at a nearby table tittered behind their hands.

A waiter appeared, bearing a bottle of

champagne in a bucket of ice. Jack noticed that the man was deferential to Murray Humphries. He had begun to suspect Humphries was something more than an errand boy. And in a few minutes, he found out who the young man really was.

Tiffany suggested they dance. Jack was happy to. He had, once before in his life, danced with a bare-breasted girl in a public place. That was in Paris in 1924, but not since then.

"You've gotta be from out of town," she said. "I can tell by the accent."

"Boston," he said.

For some reason that made her laugh. Then she said, "I can't figure, then, why you're in Chicago. It's none of my business, but somehow you don't seem much like the kind of guy to be hobnobbing with Murray the Camel."

"Murray the Camel?"

"Sure. Don't you know who he is?"

"I guess I don't."

"His name is Murray Lewellyn Humphries," she said. "Murray the Camel. And if you didn't know that, I've probably said too much."

"I am a veritable sphinx," he said. "I'm in town as an advance man for the Democratic National Convention. Tell me who Murray the Camel is."

"Al Capone's right-hand man," she said. "You know what they mean by the word *consigliere?*"

"You tell me."

"It's an advisor. A man like Capone has guts and all, but likely he's not too smart. So he has advisors. Murray the Camel was one of Big Al's closest advisors. Some say he's running things for Capone now."

"I thought Nitti was doing that."

She shook her head. "Actually, the business is sort of divided up now. Murray's smart. So's Nitti. If they're talking to you about supplying liquor for your convention people, believe them. They can supply anything you want. The best. *Really* just off the boat, not fake. And girls. You want girls, they can supply high-quality girls."

"Like you," he said dryly.

"If you want me," she said bluntly.

He did. She aroused him. He hadn't expected to be aroused by a whore in a speakeasy, but this girl excited his manhood. He decided he would accept what she offered, later. He pulled his arms closer around her and drew her to him; and, to his surprise, he felt her exhale and relax.

"Is Murray the Camel dangerous?" he asked.

"Asks Bugs Moran," she said quietly into his shoulder.

"I'm asking you."

"Murray's job was to get rid of the Moran mob," she said. "He did. I don't know if he actually pulled the trigger on anybody, but there's no Moran mob anymore. I . . . I talk too much. You repeat any of this, I'm dead."

"Don't worry, Tiffany," he said. "I'm a sphinx."

Tiffany could not believe he would take her to his suite in the Palmer House.

"A girl like me . . . If they know who I am, they'll—"

"They damn well know who *I* am," said Jack, "and they'll damn well accept any guest I elect to take to my suite."

In the morning she luxuriated in his bathtub, immersed in many gallons of hot, soapy water. Without makeup she was a different girl: no less alluring but alluring in a different way. Absent the dramatic contrasts of her makeup, her face was a blond monotone, almost innocent.

"They won't hurt Governor Roosevelt," she said. During the night he had trusted her, probably too much. "Murray the Camel, Frank Nitti . . . And, hey, you know, don't you, that Al has an older brother named Ralph Capone? All of them, even the brother, are happy that Big Al is locked up. That man is crazy, Jack. But these guys aren't."

"Did you know Capone?"

"Only too well."

"How much control does he still have over things?" Jack asked.

"None," she said. "They let him think he does. He sends orders. They do what they want to do. A few guys are still loyal to him. A few are still afraid of him. He's a vicious man, and some of them remember that, so they'll still take his orders. But nobody important."

"What happens when he's released?"

She shook her head. "He'll never get back to Chicago alive. He may be the last man gunned down in the old way."

Jack put on his robe and went to the door to let the waiter wheel breakfast into the suite. When the table was set and he had tipped the man, he returned to the bath-room. Tiffany was letting the water run out, and he picked up a big white towel and dried her.

"You're a gentleman," she purred.

Over breakfast he returned to the subject of Al Capone. "They've taken over his en-terprises. I suppose that's why they would want to kill him—so they won't have to give anything back."

"Not the reason," she said as she bit a corner from a slice of toast. She wore a pair of Jack's silk pajamas. "The reason is that Capone gives the rackets a bad name."

Jack laughed.

"Seriously," she said.

After they finished breakfast he dressed in a dark-blue single-breasted suit with fine gray pinstripes and settled a black homburg on his head. He took his wallet from his breast pocket and gave Tiffany a hundred dollars.

"If you'd like to stay here, and be here when I come back, I'll be happy to see you," he told her. "I have absolutely no idea how long I'll be."

She was surprised, not just by the amount of money he had given her, but by his giving her any at all; and she frowned over the money, fingering the twenty-dollar bills as if they might crumble and disappear. "I'll be here," she whispered.

The downtown office of Frank Nitti looked like that of a successful accountant, with nothing in it to suggest the real nature of the business transacted there. His desk was a rolltop, with everything neatly shoved into the pigeonholes or arranged in tidy little piles. Half a dozen orange-fronted letter boxes sat on top. In the middle of the writing surface sat a candlestick telephone.

Nitti was a small, graying man. He looked like the accountant or insurance agent appropriate to this kind of office—nothing like a person who had won his situation as one of the principal heirs to Al Capone by ordering the deaths, if not actually himself killing, a score of men. He rose from his wooden swivel chair and gravely shook Jack's hand.

"You have interesting friends, Mr. Endicott," said Nitti. "Besides getting the word from Big Al in Atlanta, I had a call from Lucky Luciano in New York. At first I couldn't understand why a Boston Brahmin would have such friends, but Charlie Lucky explained it. He said you are concerned about the safety of Governor Roosevelt if he comes to Chicago."

"The Governor has been threatened," said Jack. "The threat came from New York, but I am sure there is no geographic limitation on it."

Nitti frowned and nodded. "You understand, I hope, that I do not control the criminal element in Chicago. Whatever you may have heard of me, I am not a mob leader, Mr. Endicott, and never have been. In fact, I have never committed a crime of moral turpitude. I have broken the law by selling liquor and beer. If violating the Volstead Act makes a man a criminal, then you are one, too, since you drink what I sell."

"Fair enough," said Jack.

"All I can do for Governor Roosevelt is put out the word in Chicago that the Governor is a friend of Big Al's and a friend of mine. That will discourage a few men who may resent the Governor's support for Repeal, but I have no control over the hundreds, maybe thousands, of criminals who infest this great city. Actually, Mr. Endicott, the Governor doesn't need to come here. Candidates don't attend national political conventions. President Hoover is not coming for the Republican National Convention."

"Governor Roosevelt may want to come," said Jack.

"Okay. If he does, it'll be understood by all the connected men that he's under my protection. Which does nothing about the independents, who are the great majority."

Puzzled by some aspects of the conversation and far from satisfied, Jack returned to the Palmer House, arriving there a little before noon. Reaching the door to his suite, he was surprised to find it open.

"May I be so bold as to inquire who you are and what you are doing in my suite?" he demanded of a ruddy-faced man who had been sitting on a couch and rose and walked toward him.

"Detective Sergeant Pat Riley," the man said. He extended his right hand to be shaken, and with his left flipped over the broad lapel of his double-breasted jacket to display his badge. "Investigating the attempt to rob your suite, Mr. Endicott."

Jack looked past the big man and saw a broken lamp lying on the floor, an overturned chair, a smashed vase of flowers.

"Your daughter is a plucky girl," said

Riley. "And God must have been watchin'
over her, too. She's busted up a little, but
she'll be all right."

Jack realized he had to mean Tiffany.

"She's in the bedroom with the doctor,"
said Riley, stepping aside to let Jack hurry
across the living room.

Tiffany, dressed in his robe and a pair of
his pajamas, sat on the edge of the bed, sub-
mitting to the ministrations of a doctor,
who was dabbing her face with a stinging
antiseptic.

"Daddy . . ." she sobbed.

Tiffany's nose was broken. A bleeding
cut was open in her left eyebrow. Her lips
were cut and swollen.

Riley had come in behind Jack. "She
fought back," he said. "And she screamed.
It was that scream that saved her. She could
be heard on three floors."

"I'd like to speak with her alone for a moment," said Jack.

"Sure," said Riley, and he beckoned to
the doctor to come outside with him.

Jack closed the bedroom door. "What
happened? Who did this?"

"Two guys," she mumbled through her
damaged lips. "They came here to kill you.
They thought you'd be here. When you

weren't, they decided to wait. They were going to tie me up and gag me. I screamed. I didn't fight them. They just beat me, after I screamed."

Jack put an affectionate hand on her shoulder. "I owe you, Tiffany," he said. "And you're some little actress, making that cop believe you're my daughter."

She managed a small, lopsided smile. "He doesn't think that," she said. "He knows who I am. He's just being diplomatic. He doesn't think those guys came to steal, either. He knows the score."

CHICAGO—AN OFFICE IN A SOUTH SIDE WAREHOUSE— NIGHT

The office was cluttered with piles of paper-invoices, orders, receipts, all the paper an active business generates and that becomes clutter when not laboriously attended to. Some of the rubber-band bound paper was dark with dust. Dead flies lay on some of the piles. Dregs of coffee stank in a dozen cups, some with cigarette butts sunk in little pools of coffee. Ashtrays overflowed. Empty beer bottles sat on the rolltop desk.

Two men were tied to chairs with rope. Their hands were behind their backs, rope circled their chests, more rope bound their legs together. They were blindfolded, and their mouths were covered with heavy white tape. One man's brown hat remained firmly shoved down on his head. The other's hat had been lost somewhere, as had one of his shoes.

Murray Humphries—Murray the Camel—pinched one man's cheek and the edge of the tape painfully between his thumb and index finger. He jerked, tearing off the tape.

"We were authorized! We had orders!" the man shrieked.

"Shaddup," said Frank Nitti. "Ain't no orders valid in this town without they come from the right guys."

The man whose mouth remained taped was sobbing. Tears glistened on his cheeks.

The man who could talk began to sob. "We only took orders. It wasn't our idea. We just did what—"

Nitti slapped him hard with the back of his hand.

"You were ordered to do what, exactly?" asked Murray the Camel, his voice cold and menacing.

"Knock off the dude from Boston," the man wept.

"Son of a *bitch!*" growled Nitti.

"I don't suppose anybody told you *why* you were supposed to knock off the dude from Boston," said Murray the Camel.

The man shook his head.

Jack Endicott would hardly have recognized the Murray Humphries now rocking back and forth on the balls of his feet. In this shabby, cluttered office, he was an aggressive animal, his eyes glittering, his lips curling. He looked like he could not wait to kill.

"Whose idea was it to beat up on the hooker?" Nitti asked.

"She was yellin', screamin'," the bound man said.

"You could have silenced her with one punch to the jaw," said Nitti. "Maybe with less, grabbing her and so on. You know what you did? You cost me one of my most valuable girls. *Cost me!* Not only did you break her up so bad she'd 've been out of action a month. No. Worse than that. The Boston dude took her home with him! Somebody owes me the five or six grand she'd have made for me this year. Maybe twenty, thirty grand over time. Who's gonna pay me that? You got that much to hand over, Lorenzo?"

"Gimme a chance, I can raise it," the man whimpered.

"Yeah," Nitti muttered. "I bet."

The man pleaded. "I can, Mr. Nitti," he sobbed. "I really can. I'll work for you. What's more, I'll tell you anything and everything I know."

"Yeah, and you'd double-cross me the same way the first time you figured it'd do you any good," said Nitti.

"Anyway," said Murray the Camel, "I doubt he has anything we don't already know."

Nitti shook his head. "He don't," he said. "Far as I'm concerned, I got all I need to know. 'Kay, Murray?"

Murray the Camel nodded.

"Wanta take care of it?"

"My pleasure."

"No! No, please!"

The man whose mouth was still taped grunted in terror through the tape.

Murray the Camel drew from inside his jacket a stubby .38 revolver. He shoved its muzzle near to the throat of the man called Lorenzo and fired one shot. Lorenzo choked and vomited blood for half a minute before he slumped. Murray the Camel put the muzzle near the temple of the other man and let him have a quicker, more merciful death.

Frank Nitti drew a silver flask from his inside jacket pocket and took a slug of whiskey. He handed it to Murray, who smiled faintly as he tipped the flask back and took a long pull.

Street sweepers working outside the Palmer House just before dawn found the two bodies lying along the curb.

7

Jack Endicott was one of the first nonprofessional pilots to fly a Lockheed Vega. It was the airplane favored by Amelia Earhart, who would fly it solo across the Atlantic—the first woman to achieve that flight. The Vega was a high-winged aircraft, with a huge radial engine and wheels encased in immense fairings. Jack's, like Amelia Earhart's, was painted bright red, with gold and black trim. It was a *big* airplane, as private planes went—powerful and fast, and it required a skilled pilot.

He kept it in a hangar on the landing field at Hyannis. Lucy Mercer Rutherfurd had flown in it once before, to a rendezvous with the Governor of New York at Kennebunkport, Maine. She was not afraid to fly. He met her train at Boston and would drive her down to the Cape.

"My daughter and a hired crew are sailing *Marietta* out to Nantucket," he told Lucy as they sped through the streets of

Boston in early morning, in his royal-blue Bugatti roadster. "They should be there shortly. Frank's son Elliott is flying him from Albany in a private plane, and we'll meet them on the Nantucket landing field. It is all very discreet."

Lucy nodded, and she said, "You will never know how much it pains me to have to be discreet."

"I *do* know," he said. "I really do. Please understand that it pains me, too, that you and Frank have not been able to pursue happiness."

"I love Eleanor, too," she said soberly. "Can you understand that?"

"No," he said. "I respect Eleanor. But she detests me, and so I—"

"I am a Catholic," said Lucy. "I am committing mortal sin. But—"

"Lucy! Mortal sin—"

"I tell you that only because I want you to know the depth of my commitment," she said.

In anticipation of an airplane flight and a cruise on a sailing yacht, Lucy was dressed as Eleanor would never have: in white slacks, a white blouse, a dark-blue yachting jacket with brass buttons. She had—and Jack had known it from his first meeting with her—a flair that Frank's wife, for all her undeniably fine qualities, could never approach. Lucy was *chic,* but in no shallow way. Nothing about Eleanor was shallow either, but no one would ever suggest she was chic.

Jack had telephoned the flying field to say he was coming and wanted the Vega ready to fly. It was ready, pulled out of the hangar and sitting before it: a handsome airplane. He drove the Bugatti into the hangar and asked the mechanic to have it washed before he returned in a few days.

Lucy sat beside him in the cockpit and watched him go through the start sequence that set the big engine, first to coughing and vibrating, then to roaring with a confidence-inspiring sound of power. He taxied out onto the field, turned into the wind, and shoved in the throttle. The airplane bounced over the ground for two hundred yards, gaining speed. Jack eased the stick forward to raise the tail, and the speed increased. After another two hundred yards or so, he eased the stick back again, and the Vega lifted briskly off the ground and rose into the air.

No chart was necessary for this flight. He swung the nose around to the south, and by the time the airplane was a thousand feet in the air they could see Nantucket. They could also see tall storm clouds building in the distant west, though the skies over the Atlantic to the south and east were clear. He did not climb above a thousand feet. In less than a quarter of an hour they flew over the village of Nantucket and could see *Marietta* lying in the harbor. He made a pass over the landing field to take a look at the wind sock, then knowing the wind he turned and brought the Vega down to a landing made just a little bumpy by gusts off the Atlantic.

A blue-and-yellow Fairchild sat on the field. A high-winged airplane, it was very much like the Vega except that it had no cowling covering its big radial engine and no fairings over its wheels. It had been flown from Albany by Elliott Roosevelt, bringing his father to Nantucket.

The Governor and Elliott were sitting in an open car in front of the hangar, and they waved happily as Jack taxied the Vega to the hangar.

As soon as the engine had stopped, Lucy climbed down from the airplane and ran across the sandy ground to the car. She opened the door and climbed into the back seat beside Frank Roosevelt; they kissed warmly.

Elliott got out of the car and walked over to the Vega—a tall, husky, broad-faced fellow dressed in a khaki flying suit. He was interested in the airplane.

"Any problems?" Jack asked.

The young man shook his head. "Mother knows where we are but not who is with us. No one here recognized him." Elliott knew the whole story of his father and Lucy. His sympathy was with his father.

"Did you get a look at that storm?" Jack asked.

"I got reports on it before I took off from Albany," said Elliott. "Connecticut is taking the brunt of it right now, but it'll be a factor in our sailing before the day is over. In fact, for most of the day it's likely to give us a nice wind astern. When it catches up, we had better get the boat into shelter somewhere."

The Governor of New York was casually dressed, in an open-necked white shirt partly covered by a yellow vest sweater, with wrinkled blue and white seersucker pants. He wore a jaunty, floppy white fishing hat. He sat now, holding Lucy's hand and chatting gaily with her.

"The boat is waiting in the harbor," Jack said. "I saw it from the air."

"Who will be crew?" Elliott asked.

"We will," said Jack. "I've had the hired crew put ashore. You and I and my daughter will work the sheets. I understand you know how. Your father will man the wheel."

An hour later, the crew had *Marietta* under full sail, working their way north toward Great Point. From there they would bear east into the open Atlantic, where they would turn north again and sail up the ocean shore of Cape Cod.

Frank Roosevelt sat behind the wheel, beaming with joy, spinning the wheel with his powerful arms. Marietta once again worked the mizzen sheets, while Jack and Elliott worked the main sheets. Lucy stood behind the Governor.

The day was fine for brisk sailing. The circulation of air around the storm to the west kept a fresh, strong wind blowing from that quarter, and *Marietta* ran ahead of it, making good speed. Jack's intention was to round the north tip of Cape Cod and anchor for the night in Provincetown Harbor. Frank was an experienced sailor, too. He kept an eye constantly on the storm, which was moving steadily northeast; and when they reached the last opening on the Cape, the last point where they could shelter inside an inlet, he agreed with Jack that they could run for Provincetown. And so they sailed north, as the weather behind them gradually deteriorated, exhilarated by the knowledge that they would be in the middle of a heavy blow before they could turn into Cape Cod Bay and then into Provincetown Harbor.

"Daddy brought a trophy home from Chicago," Marietta said mischievously to the Governor. "Ask him what it is."

With the ketch running before the wind, Jack and Elliott could walk back and take hot coffee and chat. This gave the Governor a chance to ask Jack what Marietta had meant.

Jack grinned. "A girl," he said. "A girl who took a painful beating in the cause. Do you want to talk about any of that? Nothing has happened that has to be discussed this weekend."

Frank Roosevelt glanced over his shoulder at Lucy. "This is going to be tough talk, about something not very nice. Do you want to hear it?"

Lucy tightened her grip on his shoulder. "I want to know," she said.

"He didn't let Felicia know," said Marietta mischievously.

Jack scowled at her. "This weekend is highly confidential, as you damn well know, my darling daughter. Take it as a compliment that I trust you enough to bring you along and not have to fear your gossip."

Governor Roosevelt looked up at Elliott with a frown fiercer than Jack's. "Not to be discussed," he said firmly. "Take it as a compliment that I do not ask you to go forward and not hear this."

Elliott was a tall young man. He was muscular and had skillfully helped his father make his way from the car to the runabout that had brought them out to *Marietta,* then aboard. In the family there was naturally some discussion as to which of his sons most looked like FDR—which all of them did, really. The contest, if it could be so called, was probably between Elliott and Franklin, Jr.; and in 1932, when Franklin, Jr., had not entirely attained his manhood, Elliott was the winner.

He was newly married. His parents had not disapproved of the marriage, only that Elliott had married so young. He was anxious to please his father, to demonstrate his good judgment. He was delighted that his father had asked him to fly him out to Nantucket, so demonstrating confidence in his ability as a pilot. Elliott was not a somber young man, but on this cruise he was determined to be subdued and earnest. He simply nodded at his father and said nothing.

"Jack . . ." said the Governor. "I can't run for President while refusing to face unpleasant facts, even on a grand weekend cruise. The Republicans will nominate in two weeks. If I am a candidate for President, I have to face reality, however unpleasant."

"Frank," said Jack. He glanced around at Lucy, Elliott, and Marietta. "I think I can say to you that the chiefs of organized crime have accepted the fact that Prohibition is dead. The danger—if in fact there is danger—is from wild men like Dutch Schultz, Waxey Gordon, and maybe, Al Capone."

"Who tried to kill you, Daddy?" Marietta asked.

"I don't know for sure, and I don't know how much threat they are to Frank," said Jack. "I can say this: In the end, the biggest menace from gangsterism will come from the men who don't threaten the Governor, who are too smart to do so. The threat is from the guys who think they can somehow keep the old deal alive."

"And the threat is serious?" asked Frank Roosevelt.

Jack nodded. "Historically, assassins are not men or women with a rational cause. Historically, they are nuts."

"Who are the nuts?" asked Elliott.

"In my limited experience and judgment," said Jack, "I would be afraid of Dutch Schultz, first and foremost; then Al Capone's still-free henchmen; then men like Waxey Gordon, whom I've never met. Anyway, the ones who think they work outside every form of control. Some of them—Schultz impresses me as an example—think they can run everything, that no one can impose limits on them. Dutch Schultz does not just think he's Napoleon; he thinks he's a god."

Frank Roosevelt squinted at the wind, judged the boat's course, then turned the wheel half a turn to the right to adjust the course.

"What danger?" asked Elliott.

Jack glanced at the sails, at the way the

wind filled them. "Real," he said. "Maybe not ominous but real."

"Are you saying," Lucy asked, "that Frank risks murder if he runs for President?"

"Everyone does, my dear," said the Governor. "Everyone. It is an inescapable element of the job. And Jack is helping me avoid one possible threat."

Lucy Mercer Rutherfurd bent down over Frank Roosevelt and clasped him in her arms. "My God, my darling! Give it up! You don't need it. President of the United States . . . To give your life for it, my darling . . . No. What does it mean? What difference does it mean, in the very long run, who is President of the United States?"

He turned and looked up at her. "Of course, it makes a difference, Lucy," he said. "It does, really, and you know it does. Dear God, think of how many people it does make a difference to!"

"In my judgment," said Marietta, "there's really no alternative to Governor Roosevelt. I can't bear the *thought* of President Al Smith . . . or President Cactus Jack Garner."

"Or another four years of President Hoover," said Elliott. "Running for President is a painful sacrifice for any man, for my father more than most; but I can't think of anyone more able to do what has to be done."

"Thank you, Elliott," said the Governor quietly.

A little after noon the barometer began to fall rapidly, the wind freshened, and the seas rose. Frank Roosevelt agreed to be lashed to a cleat, by a line around his waist. Spray began to whip across the deck. Marietta brought up yellow slickers, and everyone buckled into them. The ketch mounted peaks and slid down into valleys, plowing deep into the water. They were making good speed, but obviously the storm was coming faster.

Astern now they could see tall gray thunderclouds with dark sheets of rain hanging beneath.

Governor Roosevelt clung to the wheel, spinning it to keep *Marietta* on compass course, ten degrees magnetic. His face drenched with salt spray, he could not smoke, and the water soon poured into his coffee; but his enthusiasm remained high and obvious, his strength entirely sufficient to the task.

Crossing the line forty-two degrees north

latitude, the course turned northwest, following the westward curve of the north tip of the Cape. About the same time the wind shifted and came from the south. Sailing became tricky, and the crew was put to hard work. Lucy hovered over Frank, trying to protect him from the spray by interposing her body between him and the wind; but he had to motion her aside so he could see the working of the sheets and call out orders. Shortly, as the course was due west, the wind was abeam, requiring constant adjustment of sails and rudder.

Jack worked with Elliott, cranking the winches. He left command of the ketch to the Governor, who was a skilled and experienced sailor.

At last they reached Race Point, the tip of the Cape. There they had to turn south, tacking into the face of the wind; but they had only four or five miles to tack before they could turn east and then north into the shelter of Provincetown Harbor. They arrived in driving rain and gusting winds, into a harbor where small-craft warning flags flapped and cracked, with lightning and thunder adding drama to their arrival.

The big thunderstorm passed over Cape

Cod Bay while *Marietta* lay at anchor in Provincetown Harbor. It was not of hurricane force. In fact, it was just a late-spring storm. Though it was filled with driving winds, contrary gusts, and hard rain, they could have weathered it at sea if they'd had to.

In the harbor, the ketch rolled and creaked all night. The kerosene lamps swung in their gimbals. Coffee sloshed out of cups. Jack or Elliott was out on deck every quarter hour or oftener, making sure the boat was not dragging its anchor. Marietta ate sandwiches and drank gin, urging Elliott to keep up with her at the gin. Frank and Lucy sat close, taking part in the conversation but sharing quiet comments whispered in each other's ear. Jack drank soup from a cup, and Scotch from a glass. They could not call themselves comfortable, yet every one of them was glad to be in the snug, dry cabin, sharing a sense of adventure and achievement.

"It's like flying," Elliott said. "When you're up there in the murk, being tossed around by the wind, trying to sight the field, you sure aren't having any fun; but when you've landed and can look back on it, you're glad you did it."

"So what are you going to do with Tiffany?" Marietta asked Jack.

"Yes, tell us about this girl, Jack," said Frank. "Where is she now?"

"She's in my house in Boston," said Jack. "I couldn't leave her in Chicago. I wasn't sure the men who hurt her wouldn't come looking for her."

"She's a prostitute," said Marietta.

"Really?" asked Lucy.

"Yes," said Jack. "Calls herself a Hoovergirl."

"But what are you going to do with her?" Marietta asked again.

"She may have saved my life," said Jack. "I'm going to do something for her, that's for sure."

"The way she looks at you, I suspect she's in love with you," said Marietta.

"Marietta . . ."

"Well. That's the way she looks at you."

"Women have always looked at Blackjack Endicott that way, Marietta," said Frank.

"My father is a handsome man," said Marietta simply.

Jack cast his eyes upward. "I'm going out on deck and throw up," he said. He grabbed up his glass of Scotch and climbed the gangway.

Marietta followed him. "Sorry," she said. She had a glass of gin in her hand, and she braced herself on deck and stared toward the shore. "You'll have to make peace with Felicia when we get home. I'll make you a little wager. What do you want to bet she doesn't stop by the house to find out if Tiffany's there and not sailing with us?"

"I won't take that bet," said Jack. "I know she will."

"Why was it so important she not come with us?"

"The relationship between Frank Roosevelt and Lucy Mercer Rutherfurd is so secret,' said Jack, "that I brought the absolute minimum number of people we need to work the boat. I trust Felicia, really; but having her aboard would just mean one more person knowing about Frank and Lucy. The choice was between you and Felicia. You already knew. Frank and Lucy are comfortable with you."

"Felicia was upset. I wouldn't be surprised to see her being rowed out from Provincetown in the morning—having rented a plane and had herself flown out here."

Jack chuckled. "I'll bet you on that," he said. "It wouldn't surprise me at all if she comes looking for us. But I told her we were going to Block Island, Montauk, and Newport. If she flies out looking for us, she'll look in the wrong places."

Marietta laughed. "You have no conscience at all, do you?"

"Odd you should ask," he said.

Elliott came out to join them. "You think we'll have clear sailing tomorrow?" he asked.

Jack nodded. "I'd say so. The storm has moved on up the coast."

"Did you ever think of installing a radio on board?" Elliott asked.

"No," said Jack. "If I did, someone would call me."

"Felicia!" laughed Marietta.

"Father tells me there have been three attempts to harm you, Jack," said Elliott. "I'm going to stay with him until after the nominating convention—and go with him to Chicago if he decides to go. I don't know what good I'll be to him, but—"

"I think he will appreciate having you beside him," said Jack. "Do you know how to use a biscuit?"

"A what?"

"A biscuit. A Roscoe. A gat," said Jack with a sly grin. "A pistol."

Elliott nodded somberly. "I know how to

shoot," he said. "I spent some time on a ranch, you know."

"If I were you," said Jack, "I'd get a small revolver and carry it in a holster under my jacket. And be damned sure nobody knows you have it. Not even your father."

"Things are that serious?"

"Things are that serious."

Their first day's sailing had been challenging and strenuous. They hoped the second day would be easier. It was. In the wake of the storm, the skies were blue, the winds fresh but workable; and they left Provincetown under hard skies, into choppy but not threatening water. They sailed across Cape Cod Bay and into Plymouth Bay. After a circuit of Plymouth Bay, they anchored off Plymouth Rock and ate lunch. In the afternoon they worked their way down the Massachusetts coast, until early in the evening they anchored in Barnstable Harbor.

Their plan was to spend a second night aboard the ketch. Jack and Marietta would row the peapod to town and buy a shore dinner that they would carry back to *Marietta*. In the morning they would be met by cars that would take them to the Hyannis airfield, and the hired crew would board the ketch and sail it back to its home port, Yarmouth.

While Marietta saw to the assembling of the dinner in covered baskets, Jack made telephone calls to be sure the two airplanes would be ready in the morning and that his crew would be available when he wanted them. He picked up a *Boston Globe* and tucked it into one of the baskets.

Back aboard *Marietta,* Jack sat down in a deck chair astern. Frank Roosevelt sat beside him. The Governor worked from a table of bottles and glasses and began to mix cocktails. Elliott went below with Marietta and Lucy to help them unpack the dinner.

Jack unfolded the newspaper. "My God!" he exclaimed and began to read the headline story:

RUM RUNNERS WAR AT SEA!
BOAT, LIVES LOST,
CARGO OF BOOZE SUNK

Yachters Terrified by Gunfire at Sea

"Like Pirate Fight!" Says Witness

An expensive sailing yacht was attacked

and sunk in Rhode Island Sound last evening. Witnesses say two speedboats attacked the ketch with what sounded like submachine gun fire, killing the people on board, and blasting holes in the hull. At least three lives are believed to have been lost, and a cargo of imported liquor went down with the yacht.

The attack occurred early in the evening, about an hour before sundown. Relatively few boats were at sea, owing to the thunderstorm that had passed over the Sound a few hours earlier. All witnesses were aboard boats in the vicinity, none of them nearer than a mile from the firing. Though accounts differ, all witnesses concur that two fast seagoing boats raced out from somewhere on the Rhode Island shore, perhaps from Narragansett Bay, attacked the sailing yacht with heavy bursts of gunfire, likely from submachine guns, then sped north again. Witnesses differ as to how much return fire came from the yacht.

By the time yachtsmen dared approach the big white ketch, it had sunk to its gunwales, and shortly after the first boat drew alongside the sailing yacht sank. No bodies were retrieved from the water, but yatchsmen say at least three people, more likely four, had to be on board. No fewer people could work the sails of a twin-masted sailboat.

A score of bullet-smashed liquor crates were found among the debris, some with broken bottles inside, some with an intact bottle or two. The crates were painted with the markings of famous English and Scottish distillers, and the bottles were of the brands of those same distillers.

Prohibition agents and Coast Guard officers were on the scene within half an hour. The Prohibition agents speculated that the yacht had been carrying liquor from a rendezvous with a ship at sea or from a Canadian port and was sunk by rival bootleggers.

The investigation is continuing.

Jack stood. "I've got to go ashore," he said. "If I'm not back in time, have dinner without me."

He went over the side into the peapod, which they had not hoisted back on deck yet; and in a minute he was rowing strongly away from *Marietta,* while an astonished Frank Roosevelt glanced between him and the newspaper.

At the first telephone he reached, Jack placed a call to Commodore Haliburton at the Yarmouth Yacht Club. After some delay, he reached him.

"Phil? Jack Endicott here. I'm across the way at Barnstable. Tell me about the ketch that was sunk in Rhode Island Sound."

"It was Edward, I'm afraid," said the voice coming through the candlestick telephone. "Dolly and Bart were with him. We're not yet sure who else. The *Georgiana* went down."

"M'*God!* Ed Otis! Ed and his *whole family!* Murdered! In the name of God, why?"

"We've no idea," said the commodore solemnly.

"Well, he wasn't running rum on *Georgiana,*" said Jack. "That's for damned sure."

"Of course not. Prohibition agents are certifiable lunatics, to a man, and these are stupider than most. Coast Guard has corrected the story, already."

"So what really happened?"

"No one knows. Ed had no guns aboard, certainly, and no more liquor than he could drink, surely. The boats circled him, firing what must have been Tommy guns into the hull. Some of the boatmen at sea report seeing clouds of wood chips flying. He—"

"Where did the liquor boxes come from?"

"God knows," said Commodore Haliburton.

Jack's face was dark red. "Want to hear a guess?" he asked, then spoke without waiting for an answer. "The boxes and bottles were thrown overboard from the speedboats. Someone wanted to make it *look* as if Ed were running liquor—to cover the real reason for those murders and that sinking."

"My God, why?"

"I don't know," said Jack grimly. "I'd like to. I'd very damned well like to."

8

Although Marietta had taken Tiffany out and bought her two dresses and other clothes, the striking blonde trollop did not manage to look anything but conspicuously out of place in Jack's home. Wearing black silk decorated with white flowers and green foliage, cut in the height of fashion, she looked handsome but awkward. The bruises on her face were rapidly disappearing but were still evident. She was unhappy. It was plain that she felt out of place.

Marietta had driven back out to Yarmouth, where she intended to devote some time to the club pool and beach, so they were three for dinner: Jack, Tiffany, and Felicia.

Felicia was bright and brittle. She made no effort at all to conceal her resentment over having been excluded from the cruise to Provincetown. Her curiosity about Tiffany did not overcome or conceal her contempt—nor her annoyance at finding the girl installed in residence in Jack's home, however temporary that might be.

Tiffany watched Jack and Felicia and ate nothing until she saw what fork or spoon they used and how they manipulated each utensil. Then she mimicked skillfully. Thus she had eaten soup from a soup plate, salad with a salad fork, and now was cutting a bit of roast beef with precisely the movements she watched Felicia using. Though the wine bottle was within her reach, she did not touch it when her glass was empty but waited for Jack's manservant to pour. She dabbed at her upper lip with her white linen napkin, exactly as she saw Jack dab his mustache.

The truth was, he knew now, Tiffany was a skilled mimic with a good memory, who could talk of Aristotle because she had overheard someone talk about Aristotle. The trouble, of course, was that she could say nothing of Aristotle except what she had heard someone say; and she really didn't understand the significance of what she repeated.

Well, he'd heard young men do the same in Harvard classes—and older men do it twenty years after graduation: mimic their professors, without the remotest understanding of why the professor had said what he'd said (if indeed the professor himself had known.)

"They recovered the body of Edward Otis," he said to Felicia. "None of the others, but—"

Felicia shook her head. "That is the most horrible thing I can imagine," she said. "Ed never carried liquor on that boat! Why in the world would anyone want to—"

Jack nodded. "Why, indeed?"

"If he was any way mixed up with the mobs," said Tiffany, "it doesn't need much why. Those guys don't wait for why. They just *do it.*"

Felicia's chin shot up, whether from indignation at Tiffany's daring to interject a word into the conversation or from dismay at what Tiffany had said, was not clear. "But why a man like that?" she asked. "Ed Otis—"

"I read all about it in the newspapers," said Tiffany. "I'd guess maybe they *wanted* him to carry booze on his boat, and he wouldn't, and—"

"It could have been you," Felicia said to Jack. "When I heard it was a ketch sailing off the Rhode Island coast, I went into hysteria. You . . . Where *were* you, Jack?"

"Changed our minds," he said. "There was a storm to the west, so we decided to sail to Provincetown instead."

"God, I wish I'd known."

"Could have been you," said Tiffany. "Like the guys in Chicago. If they thought you were sailing that kind of a boat down that way—"

"I'd like to drop the subject, ladies," said Jack, raising a glass of rich red wine in salute. "Let's not speculate about what might have happened. What did is bad enough. You see, Tiffany, Felicia and I knew the Otises. And—To their mem'ry!" He drank. "To the memory of as fine people as ever walked or sailed a boat in this mixed-up world."

Felicia left not longer after dinner, commenting archly to Jack at the door that she could hardly stay the night when *Tiffany* was in the house. "So long as *she's* in the house, I don't see how we can—"

"P'raps we can't my dear," said Jack. "In any event, she won't be here long. I owe her a debt, and I'm going to pay it. But she'll be gone soon."

Tiffany ran her hand over the thick white linen of Jack's bed. "I'd rather sleep on

207

threadbare cotton," she said. "Y' know what? You've got calluses on your knees, from doing it on rough sheets like this. You're used to it. I'm not. Look . . . I've got places rubbed raw, just from the one night that we—"

"B'God!" Jack laughed. "You've invented a new index of social status: whether or not men and women have calluses on their knees and elbows!"

"I suppose it's all in what a person's used to," she said ruefully.

"We're adaptable, aren't we, Tiffany?" he asked. "I can become adapted to the soft cotton sheets you like, I imagine; and you can adapt to my rough linen ones."

"No," she said. "Neither way."

He saw that her mood was different from his. He tried to adjust.

"I can't live with you," she said. "Sooner or later I've got to go back to Chicago."

"Back to—"

"Back to being what I am," she said. She was naked, and she rose on her haunches and sat above him, giving him a good view of her. "You've kept me around longer than you should have. How do you explain me? Who does Mrs. Cushing think I am? I know you told

Marietta who I am, but who does Mrs. Cushing—"

"I told her exactly who you are. You called yourself a Hoover-girl. She understands that. She's sympathetic."

"I don't want her goddamn sympathy. Or yours. I'm not your inferior."

"I haven't suggested you are. I have wondered, though, if I could find you some kind of job."

Tiffany tossed her head and laughed. "What could I do?" she asked. "You could hire me as a maid, to help Drake. But no, thank you. I'd rather be what I am than a housemaid. Hey, I'm not going to put on a black dress and little white apron and learn to serve gracefully. Jack . . . I decided what I am, a long time ago.

"I don't want you to be that anymore. I can—"

"You don't want me to be—Who the hell are you? Look, Mister, I did you a favor, you did me a favor, but that doesn't give you the right to—"

"You want to be a whore?"

"I *am* a whore! You could use a politer word . . ."

"Tiffany—"

"I'm not going to work at Woolworth's, either. I could've done that."

Jack blew out a loud, impatient breath. "Well, what *do* you want?"

"Give me a few bucks and let me go."

"Back to Chicago? Where some people may want you dead?"

"Well . . ."

He sighed again. "I've got a friend. You ever hear the name Polly Adler?"

"Is there anybody in the world who hasn't heard of Polly Adler?"

"She might take you in. If I asked her. But I'd rather—"

"Don't tell me what *you'd* rather! Me, I'd rather work at the top of my profession, not start off at the bottom in some other kind of work."

"You want me to talk to Polly?"

Tiffany scrambled off the bed and went to his dresser, where she picked up a bottle and poured herself a splash of Scotch. She tossed it back. "You're no kind of saint, Blackjack Endicott, no goddam social worker," she said. "You be what you are and let me be what I am. You want to do me a favor? You want to help me? Introduce me to Polly Adler. I mean, as soon as the bruises are gone. Introduce me to Polly!"

Charlie Lucky was comfortable. Wearing a maroon silk robe, he lounged in a great soft leather-upholstered chair, smoking a cigar, and sharing with Jack Endicott a bottle of musty old Bordeaux. Polly Adler sat with them, sparingly sipping wine. She wore a flowered black dress that did not flatter her and smoked a cigarette now burned down almost to her amber holder. Polly was as coarse and drab as her girls were delicate and beautiful. According to her reputation she chose girls to look as little like herself as possible. She was a tough, shrewd businesswoman, who did not give away what she sold.

She clapped her hands, and a tall redhead in a violet dressing gown opened the door. Polly pointed at the empty wine bottle. The girl hurried in to pick it up. Her dressing gown was untied and swept back with her stride to show her black underwear.

"Another bottle," said Polly.

The girl nodded. She did not leave the room without pausing to smile at the two men.

Jack was not as comfortable as Charlie Lucky Luciano but had decided he might as well be. Charlie Lucky was not in a mood to talk business—not, anyway, without preliminary sociability—and they had been sitting together in this private room at Polly's for half an hour, while the mobster chatted amiably about his boyhood home in Italy, sipped wine, ate popcorn, and watched Polly's girls come in and out—each in a kimono or scanty outfit that gave the two men a little show of her charms.

"So . . ." said Charlie Lucky insouciantly. "You've made the circle. Who do you want to talk to now?"

Jack shook his head. "I want," he said, "to talk to the men who sank the ketch *Georgiana* in Rhode Island Sound. An innocent man and all his family went down with that boat. Somebody—"

"Rum runners," sneered Charlie Lucky.

Jack shook his head sternly. "No. Even the Prohibition agents don't think so now. And I imagine you can guess why Edward Otis and his family were killed. You can guess, can't you, Charlie?"

Charlie Lucky frowned at Jack, his droopy right eye glinting with menace. "You think I go out and slaughter citizens on their yachts?" he asked.

"No. Not at all. But what we've talked about is out of control, isn't it?"

"Be specific, Mr. Endicott," said Charlie Lucky.

Polly Adler stared fearfully at what she saw as a developing confrontation, as Jack faced Charlie Lucky's threatening expression and did not flinch. She glanced around at three of her girls who were sitting apart, waiting for these gentlemen's pleasure—far enough that they could not hear the conversation, as they weren't meant to. She spotted the redhead returning with the wine and summoned her forward with a sweep of her arm.

"I know you didn't sink *Georgiana* and kill the Otis family," said Jack. "And I concede you don't know who did. But whoever did—" He glanced at Polly. "Can we have a moment of absolute privacy?" he asked.

Charlie Lucky didn't need to toss his head to order the notorious madam to retreat. She was on her feet and moving.

"In confidence," he said firmly to Charlie Lucky Luciano. "The *Georgiana* could easily have been mistaken for my boat, *Marietta*. They are—were—twin-masted ketches, very much alike. If those two speedboats had attacked *Marietta,* instead of *Georgiana,* they would have killed Governor Roosevelt. He was on board *Marietta.*"

"Kee-*rist!*" said Charlie Lucky.

"The men who attacked *Georgiana* threw some liquor boxes overboard, to make it look like the yacht had been a rum runner. But it wasn't. I can promise you Edward Otis never used his boat to smuggle liquor into the States. Pretty damned crude, in. fact—don't you think, Charlie?"

The dark expression on the face of Charlie Lucky Luciano showed he had noticed that this Boston Brahmin was calling him Charlie—a sudden and surely significant change of protocol. At first he shrugged. Then he nodded. "Dumb," he said.

"My daughter and a crew took my boat out of Yarmouth that morning and sailed it to Nantucket. Ed Otis took his boat out within an hour or two of the same time. He went into Edgartown to wait out the storm, then sailed on west. I have a terrible suspicion that Ed Otis and his family were killed—"

"I get ya," said Charlie Lucky. "I see what you suspect."

"They tried to kill me in Chicago, or at least to—"

"I can tell you something about that," said Charlie Lucky. "The two guys who came to your suite at the Palmer House

214

won't ever do anything that dumb again. You can send your Chicago chippie back to Chi."

"Oh . . . Well, somebody in this part of the country doesn't seem to have gotten the message. And I don't want to send . . . to send Tiffany back to Chicago. There may be others who don't have the word."

Charlie Lucky shrugged. "I'll take her in here. The word is she's first class."

"With Polly," said Jack. "Agreed?"

Charlie Lucky picked up the bottle of Bordeaux the redhead had brought from the kitchen. He grinned. "Know what you want, don't you?" His grin broadened. "Mr. . . . Jack. You've got a lot smarter in a little time. Fine Louie learned a lesson the hard way. You carrying a biscuit right now?"

"Are *you?*" Jack asked.

Charlie Lucky shook his head. "If I do and the cops pick me up for double parking, I get time for carrying a concealed weapon. You do it—" He chuckled and shrugged. "Jack—You got standing guys like me can never get, no matter how hard we try. You oughta think about getting into our line. You got money. You could have more than J. P. Morgan in one year. A guy like you—"

"Could act as a front," said Jack.

Charlie Lucky laughed. "A partnership between me and you . . ."

"Charlie . . . Thanks. It's not that I think I'm too good for it. But you take risks I don't have to."

"So you don't much care about the way guys like me make a living, right?"

Jack shook his head. "To the contrary," he said. "I have to care. For right now, we share an interest. And that's as far as we can go with each other, Charlie."

Charlie Lucky frowned and yet at the same time smiled. "The Governor won't appoint that bastard Dewey?"

"You have his word on that. He won't appoint Tom Dewey to the office of United States District Attorney."

Charlie Lucky Luciano picked up the new bottle and poured wine into their glasses. The Bordeaux hadn't had time to breathe, but it would breathe faster in their glasses, and Jack watched without any expression as the in-this-instance-well-meaning mobster smiled over the big glasses he had poured and raised his and saluted Jack.

"Your girl has my protection," he said. "And with Polly. A girl can't do better."

"She knows that."

Charlie Lucky frowned over the wine in his glass and sipped it a second time, to be sure if it was good. "Good?" he asked Jack.

Jack nodded. "This kind of wine tastes better after it is open a few minutes."

"Ah . . . The Italian wine is ready when you open it," said Charlie Lucky, revealing his accent more than Jack had ever heard before. "French wine tastes a little funny anyway, don't you think:? Like . . . like it's stale."

"Bordeaux is what is called an acquired taste," said Jack.

"Yeah. That's the kind of stuff guys like you understand, that guys like me never will. So, okay. No way guys like you and me are gonna be partners. Right? But we got a certain understanding. Right?"

"That is correct."

Polly Adler and her girls returned, cautiously crossing the room and approaching the two men. Jack had not seen the signal Charlie Lucky had given them—probably a lift of the eye or chin—but plainly he had given it, since they would not have dared come close again without some sign of his consent. The girls opened their kimonos to display their underwear and their figures.

Charlie Lucky tipped his head and stared

at them. They amused him, obviously, but not enough to monopolize his attention. "If I was you, Jack," he said, "I'd be interested in who knew you were out sailing last week-end—and who knew where you were gonna be."

"Plenty of people had to know I was taking the boat out," said Jack. "People could have been watching, maybe with binoculars. And people could easily have gotten *Georgiana* confused for *Marietta.*"

"How many knew the Gov was aboard? Maybe he's not so easy a guy to hide as you think. How'd he get to where you picked him up? How secret was it that Governor Roosevelt went aboard your boat? Anybody who saw him would know him."

Jack stood up and walked across the room. He picked up a handful of popcorn from a bowl on a table and began to munch on it as he came back to his chair.

"Charlie," he said. "I'm glad to have met you. I'm glad we see eye to eye on certain things. On the other hand, since I met you people keep trying to kill me."

"Not me," said Charlie Lucky sullenly.

"Of course not you. If you had wanted to do it, you've had plenty of chances, and you wouldn't have botched it. But let's talk

218

about it. The night you and I met, somebody tried to kill me. I thought they were after Hammer Pete, which is who they in fact killed. But now I suspect I was the target. The next time . . . outside the hotel in Brooklyn. Let's talk about those two times. How did somebody know who I was? How do you call that? What's the word for it?"

"You think somebody fingered you," said Charlie Lucky.

"Yes. Yes, uh . . . fingered me. Somebody likely did that."

"Let's talk about the night when we met at Billingsley's joint," said Charlie Lucky. "How many people knew where we were meeting?"

"Hammer Pete called you from the hotel," said Jack. "We were sharing a suite, and I'm almost certain he didn't telephone anyone else before we left for the Stork Club."

"Which means you think somebody on my side talked," said Charlie Lucky with a scowl.

Jack shook his head. "Not necessarily," he said. "The Stork Club is a public place. Someone saw us meeting and made a telephone call."

"No." What Jack heard in Charlie's husky voice explained why people feared the man: a note that was at the same time conniving and sinister. "No. We weren't there that long. How long did we sit and talk together? Twenty minutes? Half an hour? Who in thirty minutes could get a call, get his gunsels together, and get to the right street at the right time to open fire on two guys walking from the Stork Club to their hotel? No—"

"Someone knew in advance, then," said Jack.

"Somebody knew damn well in advance," growled Luciano. "When you walked out of Billingsley's speak, somebody put in a call to somebody not far away. That's how they come bust-ass into the street at just the right time. They were there. Waitin.

"Who?"

"One guy knows," said Charlie Lucky. "Or ought to know. Has got a way to know."

"Who?"

"Billingsley."

When, half an hour later, Sherman Billingsley walked nervously into the private room at Polly's, most of the second bottle of Bordeaux was gone but a third was breathing on a table, with an assortment of hors d'oeuvres.

Polly had announced the arrival of Billingsley, and Charlie Lucky had said to Jack, "You don't wanta see what's gonna happen, now's the time to get out of here. You don't care if you see it, sit over there in the corner and turn off the lamp. He's not goin' to be lookin' at you."

"I'll stay," Jack had said grimly.

Charlie Lucky had dropped his robe and stood in the middle of the room, glass of wine in his left hand, dressed in a white shirt with collar open and a pair of black trousers held up by suspenders.

Billingsley, in evening clothes, black tie, could not conceal his apprehension. He had been summoned away from a table at his speakeasy and told he was wanted by Charlie Lucky, for an immediate conversation. He extended his hand.

The mobster's fist shot past Billingsley's hand and pounded hard into his stomach. Billingsley grunted and tottered back, and Charlie Lucky threw a long punch to his nose. Billingsley staggered and fell.

"Char-lee!"

Charlie Lucky had not spilled a drop of his wine. He stood poised above the fallen bootlegger, obviously ready to kick him. Billingsley clutched both hands to his bleeding nose.

"Char-lee!"

"You're a dead man, you lying son of a bitch," said Charlie Lucky.

Jack, sitting apart, with Polly Adler standing beside him—actually partly in front of him, to prevent Billingsley from seeing him if he looked that way—profoundly hoped Charlie Lucky would not make him the witness to a murder. He started to rise to say so, but Polly gave him a gentle push that for a moment kept him in his seat.

Sherman Billingsley began to weep. "Char-lee, puh-*lease!* Whatever it is, I—"

"Shut up," he said coldly—as coldly as Jack had ever heard a man speak. "You've got one chance, you cheap little liar. You fingered a guy, and I want to know who for."

Billingsley stared at the blood on his hands. He blinked and shook his head. "I never fingered nobody, Charlie," he said. "God—a guy like me . . . Christ, I've done

222

time. More than once. I'm *in*, Charlie. I know better than to—"

"You did or you know who did," said Charlie Lucky.

"For God's sake!" Billingsley whimpered. "I'd finger a guy? *Me?* You know me. I've done time in bad places. I'm with *you*, Charlie. I'm an *in* guy! Finger . . . ?"

"Tell me about it, you piece of shit."

Billingsley began to sob. "Who'm I s'posed to have fingered?" he blubbered.

"You tell me," said Charlie Lucky. "Only chance you got. You tell me the whole story."

"Where'm I s'posed to start? If I don't know what you're talkin' 'bout, where'm I goin' to start?"

"Why don't you try tellin' the truth for once in your rotten little life?"

"'Bout who, Char-leee?" Billingsley wept.

"Oh. You fingered more than one guy?"

"*No!* I'm no rat!"

Charlie Lucky kicked him in the ribs. "The cheapest little rat I know," he said. "So, who'd you finger, Billingsley? Who's the last guy you fingered?"

"Nobody! Never! I swear!"

Charlie Lucky reached out with his foot

and prodded Billingsley's broken nose with the toe of his shoe. The bootlegger cringed but did not dare to retreat.

"I swear, Char-lee! As God is my witness—"

"*Billingsley!* I believe in God. My mother believes in God. I don't want to hear you blaspheme anymore!"

"I'm sorry! I'm sorry! Hey, I believe in God!"

"Talk to me about who you fingered," said Charlie Lucky with lethal menace in his voice.

Sherman Billingsley glanced toward Polly Adler, maybe trying to see who was sitting in the shadows behind her. Possibly he thought it was a man who was going to kill him.

"Char-lee . . . I guess I did sort of put the finger on a guy. But . . . hey, it wasn't because I wanted to. I was *pushed,* Charlie. I was threatened. I mean, threatened with death. And, anyway, the guy I was supposed to finger wasn't anybody that counted. I mean . . . Charlie, I didn't know the guy was connected! I swear! I had no idea he was anybody."

"*Who?*"

"Hey, listen! They didn't get him. The

guy walked away! It was okay. Nothin' bad happened."

Charlie Lucky reached out with the toe of his shoe and gave Billingsley's broken nose another prod, loosing a gout of blood. "Talk!" he barked.

Billingsley nodded. "Hey, it wasn't *nobody*. You remember that hoity-toity creep from Boston? The one you talked to for ten minutes one night in the joint? Him! I made a call after he left. Some guys wanted his ass. God Almighty, Charlie, don't tell me that fancy dude was *somebody!*"

Charlie Lucky swung around, turned his chair to face Billingsley on the floor, and refilled his wine glass before he sat down. He took a sip of wine. "Must have been somebody to me," he said quietly. "The only way you could have fingered him is that you knew he was meeting me. Hey, shit-butt, the only reason a gentleman like that came into your two-bit rotten speak was because I asked him to meet me there. Right? So he was somebody to *me!* Somebody to me, you loathsome little pile of it!"

"I didn't know," Billingsley sobbed. "I didn't think of it like that."

"Because thinking is beyond you," growled Charlie Lucky. "So . . ." The Sicilian blew a loud sigh. "So . . . You got one chance to escape a pair of cement boots, Billingsley. And I mean tonight. Deep six, little man. Tonight! Deep . . . six."

Billingsley nodded. "Charlie, I'd do anything in the world for you. You know that. Even if we didn't have a big problem tonight. Honest, kid! I mean, you know me, Charlie! Don't you know me?"

"I'm gettin' so I do."

"Who's gonna say no to Bo Weinberg?"

Charlie Lucky stared at Billingsley for a long moment, then glanced at Jack. The scarred eyelid had fallen almost entirely across his right eye.

"Bo . . ." Billingsley whispered. "For God's sake, you know Bo! Who's gonna say no to him?"

"He bust your nose like I just did?"

"I'd be lucky if that was all he'd do," Billingsley whispered hoarsely.

"Okay, Sherm," said Charlie Lucky. "You got the speech started. Now finish it. Every detail."

Billingsley pulled the handkerchief from his breast pocket and dabbed at his nose. "Bo called before you did," he said. "He told me to call him if you brought in a guy that night. He *ordered* me, Charlie.

He said he'd . . . use a knife on me if I didn't. H—"

"So, when I called, why didn't you tell me about this?" asked Charlie Lucky.

"Scared, Charlie," Billingsley grunted.

"Yeah. Keep talkin'."

Billingsley sighed as he stared for a moment at the blood soaking his handkerchief. "I . . . called Bo and told him you were bringing this guy to the club that night. He said he'd get back to me. That night he called again and gave me a phone number. He said to call that number when the guy from Boston left the joint."

"And you did," said Charlie Lucky coldly. "You made the call that fingered the guy."

Billingsley nodded. "Yeah, I did, Charlie. I was scared not to. But it came out all right! They didn't get the guy."

"Why did Bo Weinberg want to hit the guy from Boston?"

"He didn't tell me. I swear he didn't! Why would Bo tell *me?*"

"All right," said Charlie Lucky. "Get your ass up."

One of Polly's girls led Sherman Billingsley away to a bathroom where he could clean himself up. Charlie Lucky Luciano told Polly to call in the house doctor and have Billingsley's nose set.

"Bo Weinberg," he said to Jack when they were alone.

"Dutch Schultz," said Jack.

"Right. Actually, Bo's a well-thought-of guy. He's got connections besides the Dutchman. He's also what we call a stone killer. You know what that means?"

Jack shook his head.

"It means he don't care who he kills or how he does it. You're lucky you're alive. You thinkin' of backin' away from this deal? Don't think about it. You can't. If Dutch Schultz has sicced Bo Weinberg on you, you can't yell 'Ally ally outs in free!' Bo plays the game till it's over."

"Till when?" Jack asked.

"Till one of you—Well . . . No, you're lucky another way. With Bo, it's nothin' personal. If the Dutchman calls him off, he's called off. He won't be mad at you 'cause you got away from him once or twice."

"Then—"

Jack was interrupted by Polly Adler, who opened the door and said, "There's a man out here wants to say hello, Charlie. The

Mayor. Care to step out and speak to him a second?"

"Send 'im in," said Charlie Lucky with a sweep of his arm. He turned to Jack and smiled. "Watch how I introduce you," he said. "The guy's a crook, but he's also a boob."

Jimmy Walker, Mayor of New York City, came through the door, beaming, hand extended to the Sicilian mobster. "Charlie!" he bubbled. "Nice to see you!"

Handsome Jimmy Walker. He *was* handsome, with a strong cleft chin and a pleasant smile. He wore white tie. He was a conspicuously affable man, but when his glance stopped on Jack his eyes narrowed and his smile ebbed.

"Say hello to the Mayor," said Charlie Lucky to Jack. "Jimmy, shake the hand of Chickie Collici. Chickie's in from Chicago. Anybody givin' you a hard time, Chickie's the guy to see."

Flustered, Jimmy Walker shook Jack's hand and said he was glad to meet him. Then he said, "Well, nice to . . . nice to see you, gentlemen. I'll be on my way."

"Polly's probably got somethin' special waiting for you, Mayor," said Charlie Lucky.

"Uh . . . yeah, yeah. So . . . nice to see you."

As soon as the door was closed, Charlie Lucky laughed. So did Jack.

Then Charlie Lucky frowned. "I've done about all I can for you, Mr. Endicott," he said. "About all I can. I think you know where the problem is."

Jack nodded. "And you know what will happen if anyone kills Governor Roosevelt," he said.

"I'll keep puttin' the word around," said Charlie Lucky. "I'm not sure the Dutchman will listen."

9

Maury's place remained open. With the death of Hammer Pete O'Malley it had undoubtedly passed under the control of someone else, but Jack didn't ask who. He went there looking for Luigi Loparco, not knowing how else to reach him. He had to leave word with Maury and return a second night.

Felicia insisted on being with him, particularly when she heard that Cab Calloway and his orchestra were playing at the Leedo. She sighed rhapsodic over their music. And she was not the only one. The appearance of Cab Calloway attracted Bostonians who otherwise never went near Maury's speakeasy. Even John and Hester Cabot were there; and when Felicia spotted them, she urged Jack to move to their table.

That proved convenient. When Maury came to say that Luigi Loparco had come in, Jack was able to excuse himself and leave Felicia with the Cabots, not alone.

"What can I do for you?" asked the small, dark gangster as soon as Jack sat down with him.

"In my experience," said Jack, "when a person requires information, he is best advised to talk to the man who probably has it. "

"Meaning?"

Jack folded his hands on the table and leaned forward, an uncharacteristic posture for him but one that let him speak to Loparco without being heard. "I know who killed Hammer Pete," he said.

Loparco's chin jerked up. "I wanna hear it."

Jack glanced around the speakeasy, not because he suspected anyone was trying to overhear—though several people were staring curiously at the intent conversation between John Lowell Endicott and this weasely man whose close-shaven chin was dark with black whiskers—but because he sensed the little man's fondness for striking conspiratorial attitudes.

Maury's pathetic bare-breasted girls ran off the stage, and stagehands bustled to prepare the little stage for the band.

"Who?" asked Loparco.

"Bo Weinberg," Jack said quietly.

Luigi Loparco's eyes widened then narrowed to slits. "What makes you think so?" he asked.

"Charlie Lucky," said Jack. "He found out for me. A man in New York fingered me. Pete was just unlucky enough to be walking beside me."

"Who'd want to knock *you* off?"

"Whoever knows I've been trying to protect Governor Roosevelt."

"Pete bought your idea that Prohibition is dead, no matter who's President," said Loparco thoughtfully.

"Well, apparently Dutch Schultz doesn't believe it," said Jack.

"Dutch Schultz is a crazy man," said Loparco.

Jack nodded. "That's the impression I got when I met him," he said.

"You met the Dutchman?"

"Yes. He is a crazy man. I went to Atlanta and talked to Al Capone, too. Another crazy man. The people who murdered Edward Otis and his family were trying to murder me. The Otis yacht, *Georgiana,* looked very much like my boat."

"Are you sure about all this?"

"I'm sure about all this."

"Jee-zus!"

"I didn't ask to meet with you just so I could tell you all this," said Jack. "The night when Pete and I left the Stork Club in New York, we'd been fingered. I know who did it in New York. What I don't know is how the word got from Boston to New York that Pete and I were going down there."

Loparco shrugged unhappily. "God knows," he said. "Could've been anybody."

"No," said Jack. "Whoever it was sent the word to Dutch Schultz. Maybe directly to Bo Weinberg himself, actually, now that I think of it."

"No," said Loparco. "There's no percentage for Bo in trying to kill you . . . unless the Dutchman wanted you killed."

"I think that's true," Jack agreed. "Or the word could have gone to Dixie Davis. The question is: Who in Boston would send word to Dutch Schultz? Somebody must have a connection with Schultz. Otherwise, what's—As Pete would have said, where's the percentage?"

Loparco nodded. "You're right. You weren't fingered on no rumor. Somebody knew you were coming to New York."

"Somebody knew I was meeting Charlie Lucky."

"And called the Dutchman and told him . . ." muttered Loparco pensively. "Called the goddam Dutchman . . . Who?" He shook his head. "You and Pete were workin' together, so it wasn't anybody that worked for Pete. And you were going to meet Charlie Lucky, so it wasn't the Sicilians, I don't think. That leaves . . ."

Loparco drew a deep breath. "Let me ask around. There are guys who want somebody's ass because of what happened to Pete. Maybe I can find out."

"You can call me," said Jack. "Anytime. I don't have a number for you."

"Do like you did this time," said Loparco. "Tell Maury. He'll get the word to me."

Jack returned to the table where Felicia and the Cabots were drinking and watching the orchestra take the stand.

"You do have a wide variety of acquaintances, Jack," said Cabot. "That O'Malley fellow you brought to the club was murdered in New York the same week. And this one—My, what a menacing sort!"

"That one kills people for a living," said Felicia.

"My word!" laughed Hester Cabot, too

skeptical to take Felicia seriously. "Are you having someone killed, Jack?"

"I'm thinking of Felicia," he said.

Applause rose, and Cab Calloway walked out on the stage. He wore white tie and tails—different in that the suit itself, including the waistcoat, was gleaming white. Only his high silk hat was black, and as he bowed to the room he swept it off and tossed it aside. He was carrying a long white baton, which he raised to signal his musicians to lift their instruments. He brought the baton down, and the band launched into a jazz number in the distinctive Calloway style. Felicia squeezed Jack's leg.

Cab Calloway was a vocalist, and shortly he squeezed the microphone between both his hands and bawled his signature phrase: "Hi-De-Hi! Ho-De-Ho!" The crowd in the Leedo shrieked and clapped their hands.

In the Common Club, Jack sat at the bar, sipping a Scotch with John Cabot and George Saltonstall while they listened to a radio broadcast of the Republican National Convention. No one had the least doubt the party would nominate Herbert Hoover for another term, so the convention was slow and dull. It had no fire. Only today, during the adoption of the platform, was there any promise of excitement. Today an effort would be made to persuade the convention to adopt a plank calling for the repeal of Prohibition. The wets and drys were poised to go at each other's throats.

From the horn speaker on top of the radio came the flat Midwestern voice of the aged James Garfield, son of the assassinated President.

"The present generation of youth," he declared, "does not know the taste of liquor!"

"Well, I'll be . . . *damned!*" exclaimed John Cabot, slapping the bar. "Doesn't know the taste of liquor! That man has to be a goddamned fool!"

"Apparently the convention thinks so," said Jack.

They could hear the faint sound of guffaws and hooting, picked up by the microphone in the convention hall in Chicago.

A few minutes later the telephone rang, and the bartender told Jack the call was for him, from his daughter. Marietta was calling from Yarmouth.

"Daddy! A couple of federal agents are out here, and they've seized *Marietta!*"

The Bugatti was a fast car, and two fed-

237

eral agents were still at the Yarmouth Yacht Club when Jack arrived. He strode out on the dock, wearing a gray single-breasted suit, a gray homburg, and carrying a stick. Marietta trotted after him, pointing out the big yellow notice tacked to the mainmast of the ketch. The two Prohibition agents hurried after him, followed by Caleb Pepperidge, the town constable: a rawboned Yankee in shirtsleeves, wearing a visored black cap with a badge on it and round gold eyeglasses.

Jack did not hesitate. He crossed the plank onto *Marietta,* grabbed off the notice that the yacht had been seized and was in custody of the Federal Prohibition Bureau, crumpled the paper into a ball, and tossed it overboard.

"Here, here! Who do you think you are?" yelled one of the Prohibition agents, a flushed, tubby little man in a wrinkled suit and a crushed and stained brown fedora. He trotted onto the gangplank just as Jack was about to walk back to the dock, and they confronted each other in the middle of the plank.

"My name is John Lowell Endicott, and I am the owner of this boat. By what insanity do you purport to seize it?"

The agent smiled condescendingly. "So . . . So you're the bootlegger. You've been using this boat to haul illegal liquor, so it's seized by the authority of—"

"What evidence have you that this ketch has ever been used to smuggle liquor?" Jack demanded.

"When they sank the other one, down in the Sound, they mistook it for this one, which is its twin," said the agent. "There's only one reason for such a murderous attack on a yacht, and that is the boat has been carrying cargoes of booze. That's all the evidence *I* need."

"You are," said Jack coldly, "more different kinds of damned fool than any other man I ever saw. Get off my gangplank and out of my way."

"Out of *your* way? I'm a federal officer! I—"

Jack raised his walking stick, planted the tip firmly in the middle of the agent's chest, and gave him a sharp push. The man toppled backward off the gangplank and into the water between *Marietta* and the dock.

As he spluttered and yelled, Marietta tossed him a life ring. A gathering crowd of members of the yacht club applauded and laughed.

"You are in very great trouble," growled the second agent, a young man, taller, thinner, who wore a gray tweed cap and a shiny black suit that was too small for him. "You've assaulted a federal officer!"

Caleb Pepperidge grabbed the agent by the arm. "No," he said. "It's you two hoodlums that are in trouble. I saw you assault this gentleman. Both of you. Two on one. You are under arrest."

"*He—*" the agent screamed, jerking his arm away from the constable.

"I witnessed the entire incident," said Pepperidge calmly. "As did these ladies and gentlemen here. Didn't you, ladies and gentlemen?"

A dozen members nodded gravely, trying to suppress their laughter. Several spoke up. Commodore Haliburton said the attack on Mr. Endicott had been unprovoked and cowardly.

"Now," said Caleb Pepperidge with the same slow Yankee calm, "will you come with me peacefully, or do I have to handcuff you?"

Jack studied the tip of his stick, frowning as if he suspected he had dirtied it or bent it in giving the agent a shove. "Shall my lawyers call on you at the town jail?" he asked the agent. "Or would you rather they visit your office in Boston?"

Maury telephoned from the Leedo: Luigi Loparco wanted to see Jack.

When Jack appeared, Loparco was eating a thick steak. Jack had not eaten and agreed to Maury's suggestion that he too have a steak. Prohibition had been bad for the restaurant business. Most of the profit, for most restaurants, had been in liquor, wine, and beer. Without that source of revenue, they'd had to raise prices, and even so, many could not afford to offer the good food they had served before. Besides, many Americans, particularly in the East, did not care to dine in restaurants where they could not have wine with their meals. The speakeasies had none of these problems. They made immense profits on the drinks they served, and they attracted many of their customers by serving excellent meals at low prices. Many people ate in their favorite speaks. Jack ate often at the Leedo.

"The Dutchman's got a friend in Boston," said Loparco as he cut a bite of steak.

"I imagine he would," said Jack.

"Ever hear of Morris Goldish, better known as Moe Goldish?"

Jack nodded. "I've heard the name. Maury's competition."

"Well . . . Not exactly. Moe's an old-timer, like Pete was. He and Pete had their differences in the old days, then decided to divide the town up. Moe's got a brewery. He sells a lot of beer. He controls the policy racket in Southie and a lot of other places. He's got girls and a finger in the waterfront unions. He's a powerful guy. Not as powerful as Hammer Pete was, but powerful."

"He has a club, as I recall," said Jack. "The Avalon."

Loparco nodded. "It's a casino. There's a little action downstairs, not much. I mean, you can drink, pick out a girl, listen to a band. But upstairs . . . He's got a gambling layout that would make Monte Carlo jealous."

"What's his connection with Dutch Schultz?"

"Birds of a feather flock together," said Loparco. "Morris Goldish, Arthur Flegenheimer, Bo Weinberg, Meyer Lansky, Bugsy Siegel, Lepke Buchalter . . . And on the other hand, Charlie Luciano, Frank Costello, Albert Anastasia, Johnny Torrio, Joe Profaci—"

"Alphonse Capone," Jack suggested.

"No. And I'll tell you why. But wait a minute. You also got guys like O'Malley, Bill Duffy, Bill Dwyer, Dion O'Banion . . . and a whole bunch of others. Okay. You get the point?"

"I see what you mean," said Jack. "It doesn't explain—"

"It doesn't explain why a Sicilian named Loparco was in with an Irishman named O'Malley," said Luigi Loparco, vigorously chewing steak. "Business deals and friendships go beyond these other things. Like, Meyer Lansky is never gonna turn against Charlie Luciano. And so on. On the other hand, all things bein' equal, birds of a feather . . . Huh?"

"I understand," said Jack. "So you think Dutch Schultz and Moe Goldish are—"

"Birds of a feather," Loparco interjected. "But there's more to it than that. The birds don't flock together unless there's a percentage in it for 'em."

"So I hear," said Jack dryly. "It seems the percentage is everything."

Loparco shook his head. "Not everything. But important. Hey! Ain't it in your business? Banks and like that? You play the percentages, don't you? What's wrong with workin' the percentages?"

"It depends on what you have to do to make the percentages work out to your advantage," said Jack dryly. "Some of my ancestors were in the slave trade. Some smuggled rum. Some were outright thieves, and some preached from pulpits."

Loparco laughed. "An' you think we do different. Okay. It don't make a crap of difference. We all gotta live. But anyway, I'm tellin' you about the connection between Dutch Schultz and Moe Goldish."

"The connection you've suggested is not very strong," said Jack.

Luigi Loparco swilled beer and shoved another bite of steak into his mouth. He chewed and spoke. "Hammer Pete was the old deal in Boston. Irish. The Irish moved on to better stuff, most of 'em. Next comes the Jews, then the Sicilians. Maybe someday the niggers. You get the idea?"

"I follow you."

"Hammer Pete and his guys are on their way out," Loparco went on. "Gone before long. Hey, I loved the old guy! But he's the past. So what's next? It's gonna be *my* people. I'm not sure who it's gonna be, exactly, but the Patriarca family looks as good as any, and maybe I'm gonna have to move over to them. I'll be doin' a favor to the

Patriarcas, that they'll appreciate, if I put a block in the way of Moe Goldish—which means in the way of the Dutchman."

"We still don't know how word got to Moe Goldish that Pete and I were going down to New York to meet Charlie Lucky."

Loparco chuckled quietly. "I got ways to find out," he said.

"Let's get this all down straight," said Jack. "If we can. Dutch Schultz didn't like my meeting with Charlie Lucky. So he decided to have Bo Weinberg kill me. To do that, he had to know that Pete and I were going to New York to meet with Charlie Lucky. So somebody told Moe, directly or indirectly."

"Hey, you got it all figured out!" said Loparco. "Which is pretty good. Mostly, guys like me don't figure on citizens like you bein' able to figure nothin' out. That's pretty *good*, Mr. Endicott! That's damn good."

"How confident do you feel that Hammer Pete himself didn't let the word out?" Jack asked.

Loparco shrugged. "It'd break a lifetime record," he said. "Pete was known for bein' close-mouthed."

"I didn't tell anybody," said Jack.

Loparco shoved a big bite of steak into his mouth. "I'd think hard on that one, friend," he said.

Frank Roosevelt didn't have to be told that the shots fired at *Georgiana* were meant for *Marietta*. He did have to be told, and personally, that the men who murdered the Otis family and sank their yacht almost certainly did not know that the Governor was on board the boat they thought they were shooting at.

"I was the target," Jack told him.

"Again," said the Governor solemnly. "It seems I've asked a great deal of you, Jack."

Governor Roosevelt was in New York City, making a last effort to recover some of the New York delegates taken from him by Al Smith and his Tammany allies like Jimmy Hines. Although the Governor had as many as six hundred and fifty delegates committed to him, sixty-seven members of the ninety-four-member New York delegation were committed to Smith. It was an irritant and embarrassment. He was sitting in his city office, receiving political leaders and delegates, talking to them, trying to persuade them. He had slotted Jack in for a midafternoon half hour.

Missy was there. The day was too hot for coffee, and she had somewhere obtained a bucket of ice, glasses, and a quart bottle of ginger ale. She looked crisp and fresh in a white summer dress, in contrast to the Governor, whose shirt was damp with sweat and whose khaki suit was wrinkled.

"I have no right to ask so much of you, Jack."

"It's an obligation," said Jack. "You are meeting yours. I shall meet mine."

"Have you read what Walter Lippman has written about me?" the Governor asked. He picked up a newspaper clipping from his desk and read from the column by one of the nation's most widely read pundits. "'He is an amiable man with many philanthropic impulses . . . a pleasant man who, without any important qualifications for the office, would very much like to be President.'" He laid the clipping aside. "You know something? I think you will be able to understand this. The truth is, I don't really much want to be President. If I'm not nominated, I'll have time to catch up on my fishing and swimming and my stamp collection. But its . . ." He paused.

"It's an obligation," said Jack.

Frank Roosevelt nodded. "I think of my father sometimes. He used to say that people like us, who've been endowed with more than our share of the good things in life, have a responsibility to do what we can to help those less fortunate than ourselves. You know very well I'm not one of those ideological fellows who wants to take from the rich and give to the poor. But I think the rich should give, voluntarily, of their substance and of themselves. As you say, Jack, that's an obligation."

"Noblesse oblige," said Jack.

"Oh, let's don't put it that way," said Frank Roosevelt. "Let me tell you what a big manufacturer said to a Senate committee not so long ago. One of the senators pointed out to him that workingmen's families couldn't live on what he was paying men to work in his factories. Now listen to this. He told the committee that wasn't his problem. He bought labor, he said, like any other commodity, for the best price he could get; and workmen sold their services the same way, for the best price *they* could get. What they did, or could do, with their money after they left the factory was none of his business. In other words, he felt no obligation to pay wages sufficient to keep a workingman's family alive. No obligation."

"That's the capitalist system," said Missy.

"Not if the capitalist system is going to survive," said the Governor sharply. "Thank God most businessmen don't think that way."

"Well . . . I'm afraid a great many of them do," said Jack.

"We've got to care," said the Governor. "The government has got to care. The capitalists have got to care. Or some ideology is going to gain so much strength that it destroys everything. And I have to run for President because that's what America has got to have: a caring government, a caring society. We can't just go on ignoring people's suffering, saying we can't do this or that to relieve them because doing this or that is contrary to capitalist principles, or hoary old tradition, or whatever."

"Frank," said Jack, "you are going to make one hell of a President."

Jack left the Governor's office a little after three. He had not made a hotel reservation, had not brought luggage, and meant to take an early-evening train back to Boston. But when he came out on the street he was immediately approached by a dapper man in a light-blue suit, wearing a white hat. It was a moment before Jack recognized Dixie Davis.

"Mr. Endicott," said Davis. "Nice to see you."

"Not a coincidence, I suppose," said Jack.

Davis smiled. "No. I was waiting for you."

"How did you know I was here?"

"Oh . . . A hunch. No. Sorry. You'd never believe that. I got the word. Or rather, Arthur got the word."

"From Moe Goldish," said Jack coldly.

Davis frowned. He hesitated. Then he said, "Arthur got the word. I don't know where it came from."

"What can I do for you?"

"I'd like to buy you a drink," said Davis. "You have a favorite speak?"

"Let's stop into Polly's," said Jack.

Davis's sidelong glance spoke respect for Jack's sagacity in suggesting they repair to Polly Adler's: a place where the Dutchman was not likely to be and ground on which even a crazy man like him would not dare harm a friend of Charlie Lucky.

Fifteen minutes later they were greeted at the door by the famous madam.

"On me, Polly," Jack said. "Private room to talk. A bottle of Scotch. Something to nibble. Okay?"

"Okay," she said.

"Okay except for one thing," said Davis. "It's on me."

She put them in the room where Charlie Lucky had broken Sherman Billingsley's nose—maybe purposefully, maybe not. They sat down facing each other, in two big armchairs, a small table between them.

"Arthur asked me to bring you a word about something," said Davis.

"I'm listening."

"The murder of the Otis family," said Davis. He shook his head. "Arthur had nothing to do with that."

"Then who killed Hammer Pete?" Jack asked.

"You mentioned Morris Goldish," said Davis. "So you know why he would have wanted the death of Peter O'Malley."

"The night I met you," said Jack, "someone tried to kill me. Who was that?"

Davis shook his head. "I didn't even know anyone tried to get you. And I can tell you something more. If Arthur knew

251

somebody tried to kill you when you were in town for a meeting with him, that somebody would be in big trouble with Arthur Flegenheimer."

"Your boss is a dangerous man," said Jack.

They paused in their conversation while one of Polly's girls carried in a tray with Scotch, ice, seltzer, and glasses. Another brought a tray of crackers, cheese, and ripe olives.

Dixie Davis watched until the door was closed after the two girls. Then he said to Jack, "I welcome the chance to meet with you. I wonder if I can speak in confidence?"

Surprised and dubious, Jack shrugged. "A lot of people have been speaking to me in confidence lately," he said. "Not all of them tell the truth."

Davis nodded. "A point well taken. Not everyone tells the truth. Some can't. Some don't dare. But let me drop that point for the moment and go on to something else. You, Mr. Endicott, are either the shrewdest, most courageous man I've ever met, or the greatest fool. Two or three weeks ago, nobody in my walk of life ever heard of you. Now, everyone knows about you. You have a reputation—Oh, thanks."

Jack had poured and was handing him a Scotch and soda.

"You have a sudden new reputation, Mr. Endicott," Davis went on. "You came down from Boston, a 'citizen' as they say, and right off you ingratiated yourself with no less a man than Lucky Luciano. I don't know if you realize this or not, but you are under the protection of Charlie Lucky. He's made it plain that he doesn't want you hurt."

"I don't know if I'm honored or not," said Jack.

"Feel honored," said Davis. "Charlie Lucky bought your idea. Frankly, he'd come to the same conclusion: that Prohibition is dead. He agrees with you, one hundred percent, that the assassination of Governor Roosevelt would be a worse blow to his interests than was the St. Valentine's Day Massacre. Your problem is, Arthur doesn't buy it. And neither do some others."

Jack lifted his chin and looked coldly down his nose at the little mob lawyer. "Whoever killed the Otis family was trying to kill the Governor," he said.

Dixie Davis shook his head. "Mr. Endicott . . . I said to you that Arthur knows nothing about that. I believe it's true. I will not deceive you, though. Arthur does not always confide in me."

"Or in anybody, I imagine," said Jack. "Paranoids don't usually confide everything, even to their psychiatrists."

Davis lifted his glass, took a swallow of Scotch, and seemed to ponder for a moment. " 'Paranoid' . . . All right. He's insane, whatever you want to call him."

"Your boss? You're saying your boss is insane?"

"Mr. Endicott—you talked with him. Please. My point . . . I am afraid. I am very much afraid that one of these days there is going to be a war between Arthur Flegenheimer and his people, against Charlie Lucky and his. Do you know what could happen?"

"You could get killed," said Jack bluntly.

"I could," said Davis. "Very readily. Yes, very readily. And that is why I want to ask for your help."

Jack sampled a bit of the cheese. It was an excellent Stilton. "All right. What could I do for you?"

Dixie Davis glanced around the small room, as if he thought someone might be hidden somewhere. Jack noticed that drops of Sherman Billingsley's blood still marked the carpet. "I would like," said Davis quietly, "for Charlie Lucky to know I am not his enemy."

"Why can't you tell him that yourself?"

Davis shook his head. "When you associate yourself with a man like Arthur, as I have, you don't dare to make a contact with anyone he might suspect is his enemy. Mr. Endicott . . . Being lawyer to Dutch Schultz has been a good deal for me. I have more than I ever dreamed of having. But I have no options. I can't quit." He sighed. "It's not just Arthur. If I worked for Charlie Lucky, I couldn't quit him, either."

"You want a foot in both camps," said Jack.

Davis paused for less than a second, then nodded. "I want the side that's going to win in the end to know I'm not against them."

Jack munched on Stilton and regarded Davis with a wholly unsympathetic eye. "I'm not sure I like you any better than your boss, Mr. Davis," he said.

"It's a question of survival," said Davis, so quickly it was apparent he had anticipated the comment.

Jack let him squirm for a long moment,

savoring the cheese and then the Scotch, which was the real, off-the-boat item. "I've learned a phrase since I've become involved in this," he said. "As some of my new friends might say, 'What's the percentage?'"

"I don't know for sure. What is it?"

Jack put his glass down on the table, with a small slam for emphasis. "All right. When Hammer Pete and I left the Stork Club, who tried to kill us?"

Dixie Davis stared into his glass for a moment. Then he spoke. "Bo Weinberg. Have you heard the name before?"

"You answered the question correctly," said Jack. "I knew it was Bo Weinberg. And Weinberg usually works for Dutch Schultz. Was he working for anybody else that night?"

"No."

"And Hammer Pete was not the target," said Jack. "*I* was."

"Not exactly," said Davis. "Both of you were. Arthur wanted to send a message to the Governor. The message was: Lay off, back off, don't run for President. Arthur thinks he's a big enough man to decide who's going to be President—at least to have a strong influence."

"If he can kill the candidate he doesn't want," said Jack.

"Or scare him off," said Davis. "But Morris Goldish also wanted Peter O'Malley killed. Bo Weinberg attacked you, expecting to get both of you. He never figured Peter O'Malley would stand and return his fire. O'Malley put three shots through the Packard. He killed one of Bo's guys and bloodied another. And you . . . Bo and Arthur were amazed at what you did. You just walked away before the police came. Arthur decided you were a pretty brave fellow. That's why he met with you."

"Okay. Who tried to kill me that night in Brooklyn?"

"I swear I don't know. And I swear I don't know who sent those boats to shoot at that yacht."

"Well . . . Well, Mr. Davis. So far you haven't told me anything I don't know. Why should I talk to Charlie Lucky about you? Where's my percentage?"

"If you tell anybody anything about this conversation, I'm a dead man," said Dixie Davis.

"Understood."

Davis sighed loudly. "I don't think anybody's going to make another attempt to kill you," he said. "I heard Arthur say to Bo Weinberg that Governor Roosevelt has to know somebody has tried to kill you—but it hasn't made him call you off. I could be wrong, but I think you're in the clear."

"Good news if you're right," said Jack.

"Not necessarily. It may mean they're going to switch their attention to the Governor himself."

Jack stopped his glass short of his lips. "Some powerful men have tried to warn the Dutchman not to move against the Governor."

Davis shook his head. "Nobody can frighten Arthur. The more they try, the more it angers him."

"He's a madman," said Jack. "He'll get himself killed."

"He's not alone," said Davis. "Arthur is not the only man toying with the idea of assassinating Governor Roosevelt. Bootleggers . . . But also . . . Uh—"

"Tammany men," said Jack.

"Yes. An alliance. There are politicians who hate the Governor. He's ignored some people who thought no Governor of New York dared ignore them. He's denied them patronage. But there's something worse.

He's launched investigations and prosecutions that threaten to send a number of them to prison. Some of them hate him enough—"

"To kill him," Jack finished the sentence.

"Yes. I'd say Governor Roosevelt is in real danger."

"Where and when?" asked Jack grimly.

"When he goes out campaigning. Not in New York. The Sicilians are clamping down tight there. But . . . Cleveland, Detroit, Chicago. If he goes to the convention. You know there's word he might go out there. I'd advise him to reconsider that idea. It would be hard to protect him in the big crowds he's going to encounter in Chicago."

THE STORK CLUB

Dutch Schultz stared curiously at Sherman Billingsley's grotesquely swollen and taped nose.

"Wha' happen to you, kid?" he asked.

Billingsley frowned. "Damn fool swinging door," he said. "Some idiot in a hurry. Bang! Right in the nose."

Bo Weinberg's expression was not just skeptical; it was contemptuous. He took the explanation for a lie and scorned a man who couldn't come up with a better one than that.

The Dutchman called for beer and a ham sandwich, but Weinberg's tastes were considerably more cultivated. He asked for champagne and caviar. Billingsley hurried away.

Bo Weinberg was a far more refined man than the Dutchman. Handsome and well dressed—and conscious that he was both—he never succeeded in concealing his scorn for the crude and sloppy Arthur Flegenheimer, however much it might have been to his advantage to do so. Dixie Davis could. Bo couldn't. Dutch Schultz saw and bided his time. He still had use for Bo Weinberg.

"Gotta be done," said Dutch Schultz. "The whole damn business depends on it."

"You sure of that, Dutch?"

"Hell, yes, I'm sure. One way or another, it's gotta be done. Guys that count say so."

"Dutch . . . Are you saying Al Smith—"

"My God, no! The ol' Happy Warrior would never go for killing a man! You nuts?"

"Well who, then?" asked Weinberg solemnly. "It's gotta be somebody damn important."

"Bo . . . Bo. What happens to business if Roosevelt puts Jimmy Walker out of the mayor's office? How much depends on that? How much depends on keeping Jimmy Hines where he is? What if the son of a bitch appoints a U.S. District Attorney that decides to launch a crusade against us? What if Lehman is the next Governor of New York? What if a Democrat President goes to Congress and says, 'Hey, guys! Let's repeal Prohibition!'? Bo . . . The whole damned *world* depends on Hoover bein' reelected. And who's gonna beat him?"

"Roosevelt . . ." muttered Bo Weinberg.

"Roosevelt," said Dutch Schultz.

"Who blew that damned boat out of the water?" asked Bo Weinberg.

"An idiot!" Schultz yelled.

"Which idiot?"

"Capone," said Schultz. "His guys."

"Al . . . ? Why would Big Al—"

"Too many dirty little girls," said Dutch Schultz. "Al's got the worst dose any man ever had. It's got to his brain. Hell, ask Nitti. Al's done. Finished. It's a good thing Big Al's in stir. He's no good for nothin' no more."

"But ordered—"

261

"Ordered the attack on the citizen's boat. A dumb trick."

"Or maybe it wasn't," said Weinberg.

"It damn well was! That guy Otis was a *citizen!* A big goddamn citizen! We could've knocked off the Boston citizen for less bad talk."

"So now we go after the Boston citizen again," said Bo.

"Yeah, maybe. One more time, anyway. But not you, Bo. Your assignment is the Man. It's time to quit crappin' around. Your assignment is Franklin D. Roosevelt."

Bo Weinberg shook his head. "Dutch . . . It's not the world's greatest idea."

"If we haven't got the guts, then we just stand back and watch while everything goes to crap," said Schultz. "So, you with me, or not?"

"Hell, I'm always with you."

"Right," said Schultz.

"So where and how do we do it?"

"I've got guys in Chicago that see things the same way I do. And've got the guts to move. Nitti's an old man! Murray the Camel's got no guts. My guys are young and tough. All they need, Bo, is a general."

"Me?"

"You."

"Sounds like a hell of a way to get killed," said Bo Weinberg. "C'mon, Dutch! The Governor of New York! Candidate for President! There'll be a hundred guys around him!"

"Wanta bet?" asked Dutch Schultz.

"G-Men, Dutch! Secret Service! FBI. All like that."

Dutch Schultz shook his head. "No," he said with calm confidence. "The President gets protected by them guys. Not the candidates. There's been talk the candidates ought to be, but they're not. If Roosevelt decides to go to Chicago, from the time he gets off the train till the time he gets in the convention hall, he's out where guys can get to him. My God, man! What's it take to get to a man in a crowd? An' what's it take to escape afterward?"

Bo Weinberg, though his eyes were narrow and calculating, grinned. He nodded. "What's the pay?" he asked.

"Question you don't usually ask," said Schultz.

"Kind of job you don't usually ask," said Weinberg.

"Hundred thou," said the Dutchman.

Bo Weinberg shook his head. "Quarter of a million," he said. "And you're lucky to get a guy to take that kind of risk for any price."

Dutch Schultz nodded. "Payable fifty thou for takin' the contract, the rest when the job is done."

"Okay," said Bo Weinberg. "But I'm gonna need every bit of information I can get."

Dutch Schultz saluted him with his beer bottle, and, even though he was sitting in the Stork Club, took a swig from the bottle. "You'll have it," he said, smacking his lips and grunting his satisfaction. "Like before. We've always known what we needed to, haven't we? We'll know what we need to."

"Like when and if the Gov is going to Chicago."

"We'll know," said Schultz. "Our source of information is good as gold."

"You comin' to Chicago, too, Dutch?"

"Would I miss it?" asked the Dutchman, tipping his bottle for another noisy swig of beer.

10

Jack sat at home alone, in his living room. In front of him on a table was a shallow stone bowl his father had bought many years ago in the belief it was a valuable American Indian artifact. Having learned since his father's death that the bowl was a worthless fake, carved in the Boston jail about 1907 by an Irish pickpocket, Jack used it as an ashtray. Four or five butts lay in it now, and a half-burned Tareyton lay on the edge. He had suddenly lost his taste for cigarettes.

He lifted his glass and took a tiny sip of smoky Scotch. He had a large sheet of paper spread out on the table, and on that paper he had organized notes in boxes and columns.

"I beg your pardon, sir," said Drake. "Mrs. Cushing telephoned once more. I told her you had not returned, as you instructed."

Jack nodded. "I have not returned for

anyone except Marietta and perhaps Governor Roosevelt."

"Yes, sir. Will you require dinner?"

"Uh . . . Thank you, Drake. No, I won't. Either I shall go out or find something for myself in the kitchen later. Please feel free to do whatever you wish. I won't require anything further tonight."

"Thank you, Mr. Endicott. The telephone?"

"I'll let it ring. It's after all for *our* convenience, not that of anyone who wants to intrude on us. Let the damned thing ring."

Drake smiled faintly. "Yes, sir," he said.

Jack stared at his notes. They related to four attempts on his life—first, on Fifty-third Street in New York, when Hammer Pete O'Malley was killed; second, on the street in front of the Metropolitan Hotel in Brooklyn, where he had killed Fine Louie Feinman; third, in the Palmer House in Chicago, where Tiffany had been beaten; and finally, the attack on the Otis family aboard *Georgiana.*

His purpose in organizing notes was to look for any common element in the four incidents.

He did not exclude any possibility. All four of the attacks might have been instigated by Charlie Lucky. It would be foolish to suppose that could not be true—as foolish as it would be to believe anything the man said.

It would have been foolish to believe anything *any* of them said—including the late Hammer Pete, Luigi Loparco, Murray Humphries, and Frank Nitti. All of them were mobsters. Believing any one of them would have been just as big a mistake as believing Dutch Schultz.

Dixie Davis . . . A frightened man, though fear did not necessarily make a man truthful.

In each of the four instances, the would-be killers had known where he, Jack, was going to be, and when.

Except once. And that had been an unhappy coincidence. *Georgiana* looked like *Marietta.* Both ketches had left Yarmouth. When they were out of sight of shore observers, one went west toward Block Island, one north and east along the Cape toward Provincetown.

But the other instances. They had found Jack just where they expected him to be—on Fifty-third Street, in Brooklyn, in the Palmer House.

Palmer House. Nothing much involved

in that, he judged. Sure, they would know where he was staying. Frank Nitti had known, as had Murray the Camel.

Back to the attack in front of the Metropolitan Hotel. Dutch Schultz could have had his cab followed. Charlie Lucky could have fingered him to come out on the street in front of the hotel. Either of them could have arranged the attack there.

So . . . Fifty-third Street. Who knew he and Hammer Pete were at the Stork Club? Bo Weinberg did, because Sherman Billingsley had fingered them. And Bo worked for the Dutchman. The Dutchman had known he, Jack, and Hammer Pete were in New York. How had he known that?

Suddenly it was clear. Suddenly Jack understood how Dutch Schultz had known.

Yes! How he had known Jack and Hammer Pete were in New York. How he had known *Marietta* was at sea. How he had mistaken where *Marietta* would be that Saturday afternoon. Clear! Absolutely clear!

Now all he had to find out was . . . *Why?* Why, in the name of all that was holy . . . Why?

When the telephone rang again, he answered it. As he had expected, Felicia was calling. In the past few weeks the woman had begun to cling to him. They had been friends, even intimate friends, before; but lately she wanted to be with him more than he wanted to be with her, to the point of her becoming pouty and resentful if he went somewhere without her.

"Actually," he said to her, "I just got home." He would not make a liar of Drake. "Believe it or not, I had work to do at the bank."

"Poor baby!" she said. "Have you had dinner?"

"I haven't."

"If you refuse to come over and let me demonstrate my culinary capabilities, I shall be seriously put out with you."

"Very well, Felicia," he said. "I shall be there in twenty minutes."

When he knocked, Felicia herself opened the door. She led him back to the kitchen where she was busily engaged in cutting up a chicken. A radio was playing in the dining room, with the volume turned loud enough so she would hear "Amos 'n' Andy." She said little until the fifteen-minute program ended and she stepped into the dining room and switched off the radio.

"Well," she said. "You think I can't cook?

This will be chicken Florentine, and the only disadvantage of eating my cooking is that you will have to sit here in the kitchen with me. Pour us a drink."

It was indeed chicken Florentine, forty-five minutes later. He helped her carry the dishes to the dining room. She explained she had given her two household people the evening off, in the hope that he would come and they could be alone.

"Tell me, Jack," she said as he poured the wine. "Will Governor Roosevelt go to Chicago for the convention? The rumor is that he might make a personal appearance."

"He hasn't told me. Obviously he won't go unless he's nominated—which is by no means a foregone conclusion."
"In other words, he won't go until the convention's over."

"Yes, essentially. Farley is going out first. Then Howe will go. If things work out, Frank may appear and make a speech. But there's going to be a tough fight over the nomination. He may have no reason to leave Albany."

"In which case, these mobsters will no longer have any reason to want to harm him," she suggested.

"Felicia . . . Frank Roosevelt is my friend. I am involved—quite temporarily, I hope—in this business with the gangsters. But I am not a political confidant of Frank's, and I very much doubt he will tell me anything about his political plans."

"Well, if you asked him—"

"I am not going to ask him. I'd be surprised if he himself knows as yet."

She dropped the subject—maybe because she became conscious of the increasing terseness of Jack's replies to her questions. She switched the radio on again and tuned to a symphony concert. For the time being, conversation stopped as they limited themselves to an occasional comment over the music, about the food or the wine or the concert.

As they finished dinner, the concert gradually faded away behind harsh static. A storm was breaking over Boston. Lightning glared through the windows, and the window panes rattled under the impact of booming thunder. Then the electricity failed, and they were left in darkness except for the light of the four candles burning on the table.

"You'll stay, won't you?" she said. "You can't walk home in this rain anyway, and if you leave me alone in a storm like this I will never forgive you."

She carried a bottle of cognac and glasses to her bedroom. They undressed and sat in the bed, propped up on half a dozen fat pillows, and sipped brandy while the lightning continued to flash and the house shook from the thunder.

"What will you be doing this weekend?" she asked him. "Taking the boat out again?"

He shook his head. "Not this weekend," he said. "I'll be driving the Bugatti in a road race in western Massachusetts. Two hundred miles over twisting, up-hill-and-down roads, some of them unpaved. Sweaty work. I placed fourth in 1929. I'm hoping to better that."

"Don't injure anything important," said Felicia.

Late Friday afternoon Jack arrived at the Purdy Garage where he kept his Bugatti. Durham Purdy came out of his office, wiping his hand with a rag before he offered it for a handshake.

"I did what you said, Mr. Endicott. And damned if you weren't right. Want to see?"

"Yes."

"Well, uh—mebbe y'd better put on a

service coat." Purdy returned to his office and brought out a long white denim coat for Jack to wear over his clothes to protect them from grime. They walked over to the Bugatti.

"We'll move it over the pit," said Purdy.

The Bugatti was a four-passenger sports tourer, Type 44 with a three-liter engine. It was a small open car, painted royal blue and kept spotless and gleaming. The cockpit and rear seat were upholstered in tan glove leather, the steering wheel was wood, as was the instrument panel. The wire wheels were painted yellow. Two of them were mounted on the rear as spares. The free-standing headlights were heavily plated with nickel, as were many other fittings. Overall, the Bugatti was a handsome little car with a distinguished name. Jack need not have raced it to get attention for it; people stared, and some dared run hands gently over its lustrous finish, everywhere he took it.

Jack reached inside and released the hand brake. Then he walked alongside, guiding the car with the steering wheel as Purdy pushed from behind. They moved it over the lube pit. Its wheels straddled the long, narrow, brick-lined hole, so they could climb down and inspect it from beneath.

Jack followed Purdy down the crude ladder into the pit, which was cluttered with drums of oil and grease, grease guns, tools, and even a few automobile parts. He looked up at the undercarriage of his Bugatti.

"I'll get a light up here," said Purdy. He picked up a light off the floor: a long heavy cord and a bulb enclosed in a reflector and cage. He hung it by its hook from a tie rod and directed the glare of the bulb on the inside of the left front wheel. "There. Y' see?"

"No. Not yet."

"Right. Yer not going to. You're not supposed to. But you told me to check *careful,* and I did. Look here."

Purdy put a finger on the fitting that held the tie rod to the wheel. Its chief component was a lock nut. At the edge of the nut, almost invisible, was a deep cut in the rod.

"She's sawed 'bout three-quarters of the way through," said Purdy. "Whoever sawed her tried to hide the cut with grease. Did hide it, too. But you said to look out for stuff that would make the car unsafe, and I figured tie rods, brakes, like that, was most likely. She's sawed on the right wheel, too."

"Devilish," said Jack quietly.

"I'd call it somethin' like that," said Purdy. "I figure that tie rod would hold while you drove on the streets and highway. But you get out in a race someplace, where you'd be whippin' the car through her paces, wrenchin' the wheel back and forth, and maybe goin' at a pretty good clip Well . . . Bingo!"

"Bingo, indeed," muttered Jack. "Do you have any idea who might have done it?"

Purdy shook his head. "I can't think it was any of my boys. They've worked for me for years." He shook his head again. "No. I'd guess somebody broke in here one night. In fact . . . I found some marks on a window. I figure somebody came in and did this."

"There's no way to find out who, is there?"

"Don't figure."

"Well . . . It doesn't make much difference. I have a rather firm idea about who is responsible. And I shall find out. I think I know how I can find out."

"Good. I'll have her fixed yet tonight if you want to drive her tomorrow."

"No. I'd rather you keep it for a week or so, checking everything again. I don't want to drive another race in a car that might kill me. And if you don't mind, I'd like to put a security guard in here at night for a week or two. Is that all right with you?"

"Sure."

"I'll telephone you tomorrow to tell you what agency will be placing the guard with you."

Purdy led the way up the ladder. "Well," he said when they were standing beside the pit, admiring the Bugatti, "it's a good thing there's no race being driven anywhere this weekend, ain't it?"

"Yes," said Jack. "A very good thing."

At ten the next morning, Saturday, Jack walked in off Pearl Street, onto the banking floor of People's Banking & Trust Company. He wore a banker's suit: single-breasted dark-blue pinstripe, with gold watch chain hanging across his vest, a white carnation in his lapel. He went directly to the little swinging gate in the low mahogany rail that separated the marble-floored public room and into the carpeted room where the executives of the bank sat at desks.

Richard Hallowell rose from his desk and came to greet him, hand extended. "Ah, Jack! How very good!"

"Dickie. It's a pleasure to see you."

Richard Hallowell, first vice president of People's Banking & Trust, was fifty years old—paunchy, jowly man with a generous white mustache that contrasted with his flushed face. His hair was white. His gray three-piece suit did not fit him well and hung in wrinkles over his stout body. In greeting Jack, he had followed a habit that was characteristic of him: of cutting his sentences off as soon as he had used enough words to convey what he meant—thus, "How very good!" for "How very good to see you!"

"Do sit," said Hallowell, pointing at a great leather-upholstered armchair that faced his desk. "Coffee?"

Jack sat down. "Yes, thank you."

People's was not Jack's bank, although the Endicott family had funds on deposit here and did own some of its stock. It was a sound, conservatively managed bank that had not failed and was not going to. He and Dickie Hallowell had been friends for more than forty years, though Dickie was two years older than he. They had attended the same schools, were members of the same clubs. Dickie was of a more prosaic turn of mind than Jack, motivated by a vigorously surviving Puritan ethic.

By gesture, Hallowell offered a cigar; and, when Jack declined, lit one for himself. Jack lit a cigarette.

"Well . . . It's good. What can I?"

Jack glanced around the banking floor. What he was about to say to Richard Hallowell was going to shock the lifelong orthodox banker. Jack tried to imagine what it would be like to have spent his life in this atmosphere: among hushed voices doing business at a score of desks, in full view of the people who came in to do their banking business at the teller's windows. It was tradition that even the highest officers of banks sat at desks on the open floor, in view of each other and the public. The old idea apparently had been that bankers, who were suspect, should not do business behind closed doors, where they might stuff money in their pockets. The bank, all banks, had an atmosphere of trust, yet also one of suspicion. It had a characteristic odor, too, of the currency being handled in great quantities at the tellers' windows; and money did not smell good.

"Dickie," said Jack. "I've come in to ask you a favor. I'm going to ask you to violate your personal and professional code of ethics."

"What a way to introduce! Makes it very unlikely I can."

"I know. I am going to try to persuade you by calling it a matter of life and death."

"Whose life?"

"Mine. Dickie . . . Don't think I've become paranoid, but within the past few weeks there have been five separate attempts to murder me."

"Oh, *surely!*"

"I can go into details," said Jack gravely. "I'm not sure you want to hear them. I will give you one, in confidence. When those speedboats sank *Georgiana* and murdered Ed Otis and his family, they thought they were shooting at *Marietta* and at me. I can tell you why if you want to know."

"Perhaps I don't," said the banker.

"I'm trying to save myself from them, Dickie. Unhappily, I have come to believe an important piece of evidence, a piece that is necessary for me to identify my attackers and maybe save myself, is in your hands."

"A banking record," said Hallowell soberly.

"Exactly."

"Can't very well breach my trust.

"You may be serving your client as well," said Jack. "I have reason to believe she is in very big trouble. She needs help."

"Felicia Bowdoin Cushing," said Hallowell.

Jack nodded.

"What kind of trouble?"

"If we can look at her accounts, we can probably tell."

"Can't."

"Dickie . . . B'God—All right, I'll tell you what. You look at them. If you don't find something radically wrong, forget I asked you to let me see them. If you do, come and tell me, and I'll explain. I'll sit here and wait while you look."

"Fair enough."

The banker got up and left his desk. On his way out of the big room he stopped at a secretary's desk and spoke briefly to her. The young woman left her desk and shortly returned, bringing Jack a small silver pot of coffee on a tray with a cup, cream, and sugar.

Jack drank coffee, and in ten minutes Richard Hallowell returned, carrying a heavy ledger book.

"Got a point," he said.

"I thought I might."

"In confidence. Confidence."

"Of course."

Hallowell opened the ledger. "She over-draws," he said. "We cover her from her savings account. She exhausts that. She sells bonds to replenish. Continues . . . Felicia Cushing is going to become insolvent. Broke. Will lose her house."

"Where is all her money going?" Jack asked. "To be honest with you, Dickie, I know. But tell me anyway."

"She writes large checks to an entity called Avalon Enterprises Corporation. Large checks. Do you know what?"

"Yes, I do," said Jack. "The Avalon Club. It's an illegal gambling house."

"Yes . . ." Hallowell muttered. "I know."

"Who endorses her checks?"

"Morris Goldish," said Hallowell sepulchrally. "He is a mobster."

"Dickie . . . This is all highly confidential. That you told me. What we know—"

"Addicted to gambling."

"Yes. And under the thumb of Moe Goldish."

On Thursday afternoon a group of men as-

281

sembled around the big table in the board room of the State Street Bank & Trust Company. They were:

—John Lowell Endicott, sitting at the head of the table and presiding over the meeting.

—Henry Endicott, Jack's uncle.

—George Saltonstall.

—John Cabot.

—Charles Adams.

—Richard Hallowell.

—Philip Haliburton.

They met and talked for an hour, from two until three o'clock; then they opened the doors and invited two others to join their meeting. The two men were:

—James Michael Curley, Mayor of Boston.

—Patrick Coughlin, his Commissioner of Police.

Mayor Curley was a powerful politician, widely popular, in fact a hero to tens of thousands, not just in Boston but in Massachusetts generally. He was a charismatic man, with thick gray hair, bushy black eyebrows, a politician's quick smile, and an open air of sincerity that seemed to challenge anyone who might not extend to him their entire trust.

The police commissioner was a thickset, florid Irishman who would say nothing he was not absolutely certain his boss would approve.

"We appreciate your coming in, Mayor," said Jack.

Mayor Curley smiled. "I am looking at enough financial power to buy Boston, wrap it up in brown paper, and ship it to Texas," he said. "When you gentlemen speak, I listen—and I'd meet you in Iceland if that was where you asked me to come."

"What? Why in the world would we ask you to meet us in Iceland?" asked Charles Adams.

The Mayor smiled gracefully. "A figure of speech," he said.

"Oh."

"Mayor," said Jack. "The men assembled here have constituted ourselves an ad hoc committee on civic improvement."

"Oh, that's good news!" Mayor Curley exclaimed. "With your participation, we can do *so* much to make Boston a better city!"

"We knew you'd welcome our participation," said Jack.

"I do. I most certainly do. Working together, there's almost nothing we can't accomplish," said the Mayor, with happiness more likely feigned than real in his voice.

"Well, we're glad you think so," said Jack, "because we have an initial project on which we solicit your cooperation."

"You have my promise of cooperation before you even tell me what it is," said Mayor Curley expansively.

Jack glanced around the table, with a sly smile. "Good," he said. "Working together, we can accomplish this project in no more than a few days."

The Mayor nodded . . . but his face began to betray a suspicion that he was about to hear bad news. "Uh . . . What is it you want to accomplish, Mr. Endicott?"

"There is a man in Boston by the name of Morris Goldish," said Jack. "Moe Goldish. We want him closed up and run out of town."

The Mayor's jaw dropped. His face glowed pink. "Morris Goldish? But—but *why?* He's a prominent businessman in Boston. I—I've met him. Why would—"

Jack pulled his watch from his vest pocket. "As we speak, Mayor, Prohibition agents are putting the axe to his brewery. Others are breaking up the Avalon Club bar. Internal Revenue agents are at work in four of our banks, poring over the records of Goldish and his corporations. There will be a federal indictment for illegal brewing—and very likely one for income tax evasion. For about an hour now, Goldish has been in federal custody. Now it depends on you and Commissioner Coughlin, to break up his policy banks and close his whorehouses."

The Mayor's lips fluttered. "Pat," he said to Coughlin. "Did you know this Morris fellow was running numbers and—"

Commissioner Coughlin shook his head emphatically. "No! No, I never heard of any such thing."

"Odd," said John Cabot. "Any housewife, any high school kid, who wants to play a number knows where to find a Goldish policy runner—yet the police commissioner himself doesn't know. Do you live in this town, Commissioner?"

Mayor Curley's eyes narrowed as for a moment he considered defying this collection of Brahmin do-gooders. "Why did the feds move so quick?" he asked.

"What chance," asked George Saltonstall, "has President Hoover of carrying Massachusetts in the coming election if he doesn't have the support of men like us?"

The mayor relaxed. His merry smile returned, and he shook his head. "He doesn't have the chance of a snowball in hell with or without your support," he said.

"The charges against Morris Goldish will be tried and sentence imposed whilst the Republican administration is still in office," said Henry Endicott. "Even if not, a *Roosevelt* administration won't drop the charges."

Mayor Curley glanced at his Commissioner of Police, who sat open-mouthed, not really comprehending all of this.

"Think of it another way, Mayor," said Jack. "If you and the Commissioner get to work this afternoon and evening, raiding the Goldish policy banks, grabbing up his runners, closing his houses, and so on . . . If you clamp down hard enough, fast enough, you'll be in a position to prevent his making silly accusations."

The Mayor of Boston clasped his hands before him on the conference table. "You gentlemen have had some days to organize this and think through all its implications. I am faced with it and with a demand for a decision within minutes. However, I will

286

do what you suggest. In the future, though, let's cooperate on a more . . . *cooperative* basis. Okay?"

11

Jack did not employ a chauffeur full time. As often as not he preferred to drive his cars himself and required a chauffeur only when driving was inconvenient for him or when he was attending a play or concert and wanted to be picked up on the street. This morning he had a chauffeur—a young man sent by the agency, who had driven for him before and whom he trusted—because the car was to be returned home and garaged after Jack left it at the airport.

His Lockheed Vega was still at Hyannis, where he had left it in the hangar the day he returned Lucy Mercer Rutherfurd from Nantucket and her weekend's cruise with Frank Roosevelt aboard *Marietta*. It was a long drive out there, though, and Jack took the occasion to relax in the backseat and read the morning newspapers.

The chauffeur was named Ben. Before he backed the Marmon out of the garage, he had dusted it thoroughly, inside and out;

and he had put water and some small flowers in the mounted crystal vases in the back seat. It was a thoughtful touch that always earned him a generous tip. The flowers were fragrant, refreshing. Drake had put a thermos of coffee in the car, too—together with a flask of brandy that Jack would not touch because he was flying.

On the eve of the Democratic National Convention, it looked as if the names of nine candidates for President would be put in nomination. Of those, only three had any serious chance: Governor Franklin D. Roosevelt of New York, former governor Al Smith, and the Speaker of the House of Representatives, John Nance Garner of Texas. Two dark horses waited for their chance in case the convention became deadlocked—Governor Albert Ritchie of Maryland and Newton D. Baker, former Secretary of War.

It appeared that the Roosevelt forces may have made a major mistake already. For more than fifty years Democratic conventions had been bound by the two-thirds rule, that is, nomination required a two-thirds vote. The rule was the means by which the crusty old racists of what H. L. Mencken called the hookworm belt held a veto on nominations. No candidate could be chosen without the consent of the Solid South. During a caucus of Roosevelt leaders, a flamboyant southern radical, the freshman Senator from Louisiana, Huey Long, had proposed abolition of the two-thirds rule and nomination by simple majority. The caucus had enthusiastically adopted the proposal and determined to secure its adoption by the convention. If adopted it would assure a first-ballot nomination for Governor Roosevelt.

But the idea infuriated the other candidates and many conservative Democrats. Al Smith denounced the proposal as "a gambler's trick." The influential Senator Carter Glass of Virginia said he could not support a candidate "who takes a short cut to the nomination." A revolt brewed in the Roosevelt coalition that had been painstakingly put together over the past year.

After conferring with Howe, Governor Roosevelt sent a message to Chicago, asking his friends to drop the proposal. It was a retreat and not an auspicious way to open the convention battle.

Inside the *Globe* but on the front page of *The New York Times* was a story from Germany, describing the growing influence of the Nazi Party and its leader Adolf Hitler since Chancellor von Papen had rescinded his predecessor's ban on the Storm Troops. Each story was accompanied by a picture of the strange Nazi leader who resembled Charlie Chaplin playing the Little Tramp. Jack could not imagine that intelligent Germans took the man seriously. He had, in fact, some friends in Germany, and he knew they didn't.

As they neared Hyannis, Jack changed his clothes in the back of the car. He had decided to fly the Vega to Chicago because it might prove handy in case he had to make a quick trip back to New York. Also, flying in by private plane, he might be able to avoid the attention of some people in Chicago who could take an unfriendly interest in his arrival there.

No longer would his every move be reported to Morris Goldish and from him to Dutch Schultz. Felicia had become wildly hysterical when he confronted her with what he had learned. She confessed that she had been in thrall to Goldish; she had owed him more than she could pay.

She said she loved him and begged him to let her work to regain his respect. He said probably he could have forgiven her, except for the deaths of the Otis family. She shrieked that she knew she had to carry a large share of the responsibility for those murders, and she fell on her knees and begged forgiveness. He walked out of her house and left her on her knees. His final word was that he didn't want to see her again, at least for a while; he would think about maybe forgiving her.

He arranged something for her. His friends who had called themselves the ad hoc committee had to be told what she had done; but they had pledged never to reveal it. They made a condition, however. Felicia would be required to execute a deed of trust, conveying her entire estate to the People's Banking & Trust Company, with Dickie Hallowell as her trustee. If she could not squander her money at gambling tables, she could recoup her fortune in time and would not be reduced to penury. Drunkards' trusts were not uncommon. None of the bankers could recall another case in which a gambler's property was protected by a trust, but this would save Felicia from bankruptcy.

The Vega was fueled and ready to fly. As with the Bugatti, Jack had ordered an exhaustive safety check of the aircraft. It was safe, he was assured. No one had tampered with it.

From Hyannis to Chicago was about eight hundred miles. His air time would be about five and a half hours. He would have to stop twice to refuel, so he hoped to reach Chicago in seven hours, eight at the very most. Taking off about nine, as soon as the mist had cleared, he should reach Chicago well before sunset.

He flew by compass and by watching for landmarks on the ground. He carried neither a radio or any radio-navigation equipment. So long as the weather was reasonably clear, it was not difficult.

His course carried him over Providence, which was easily identifiable by its landmark bay, then past Hartford, which too was not difficult to identify. After that he watched his compass closely, also his maps: highway maps supplied by gasoline companies and a National Geographic map of the northeastern United States. It became apparent after a while that a wind from the southwest was blowing him north of his course, so he adjusted ten degrees south. Also he watched for the signs painted on the roofs of barns and factories, which identified the towns in big yellow letters and pointed big yellow arrows toward them. Flying at about fifteen hundred feet, he could read all these signs easily.

His first refueling stop was on an airfield at Elmira, New York. He wanted to refuel there, because after Elmira his westward course carried him over high mountains, and he didn't want to fly over mountains with a potential fuel problem. He had to fly a couple of wide circles around Elmira before he spotted a sign with an arrow pointed at the landing field. But he wasted only twenty minutes. While the plane was being refueled he used the men's room and bought a sandwich. Twenty minutes after landing he was off again, running about a quarter of an hour behind what he thought should be his schedule.

Winds over the mountains tossed the airplane around, but he stayed on a compass course. Shortly he saw the hazy blue line of Lake Erie on the horizon, and on the lake shore he landed a second time. From here he would fly out over the waters of Lake Erie, and he wanted to do that, too, with a full tank. Taking off from Erie, he was a little more than half way to Chicago.

Somewhere over the greenish-blue waters of the lake he crossed the Canadian border. The Canadian government did not know or care.

This part of the flight was exhilarating. For a short time, he was out of sight of land. Actually . . . maybe not entirely out of sight, since from the air the shoreline was much as it was from a boat on the surface: vague in the haze. But he had never before flown out of sight of land, and the trust it meant he was putting in himself and the Vega generated in him the kind of excitement that had always been important to him and had led him to take many risks other people thought foolish.

Anyway, his navigation was surprisingly good. He made his western landfall over Canada's Pelee Island, with Ohio's Bass Islands clearly in sight to his left. From here it was easy. He needed only to watch his fuel gauge. He flew across southern Michigan, across a tiny stretch of the water of Lake Michigan, crossed over downtown Chicago, and easily found Midway Flying Field. He landed a little ahead of his estimated time.

The downtown hotels were filled with Democrats. He had expected that. He had not even tried to get a room at the Palmer

House—though, truth be known, John Lowell Endicott could probably have taken a room away from some delegate out of Alabama or Arizona, if he wanted to.

"You flew *yer own* airplane?" his cab driver asked. "Jeez!" Jack had confessed his problem with finding a hotel room downtown, and the man went on. "Look, I know where you can have a comf' table room, for not too much."

"Can you suggest a hotel that does cost too much?" Jack asked.

"I can do that," said the driver. He was a light-colored Negro. "I most surely can do that, Boss."

The hotel the driver took him to was called the Cicero Plaza, and it was in Cicero, the suburb Al Capone had made notorious. The driver explained that Capone had often taken rooms there.

"Which means the hotel is *good,* if you know what I mean. Big Al had it all *remod*eled so's to bring it up to his standards. You know that man never used nothin' but what was best. What I hear, his kind of folks don't stay there no more, much. Don' want what you might call the 'den'fication with him. Y' understand? I oftentime take businessmen there. Never had no complaint."

"Well, let me ask you something, then," said Jack. "How much does the management pay you to drop a guest there?"

The driver glanced back over his shoulder. "Boss, Boss," he said. "You wouldn't begrudge a poor man, tryin' to make a livin' for his family his two measly dollars, would ya?"

"What's your name?" Jack asked.

"Oscar Carter," said the driver.

"Oscar . . . You know the town pretty well, I guess. Am I correct in so assuming?"

"I s'pose I do," said Oscar Carter. "My daddy brung us here from Alabama in ought-two."

"How would you like to earn two hundred dollars, Oscar?"

"Who you want me to kill, Boss?"

"I want you to be my driver," said Jack. "For a week. I want this cab waiting for me wherever I am, whenever I want it. You can report your usual runs to the cab company, and I'll pay you the two hundred to be *my* cab only. Are you interested?"

Oscar Carter was a nearly bald man of some fifty years, wearing a bristly gray mustache and a fringe of gray hair. He was slight but wiry. His voice mixed the accent of the Midwest with that of the South and was not clearly of either.

"Boss," he said, "how much you figure a cabby earns in this town, even with the political conventions here? Don' answer. You talkin' five times, maybe ten, what I make this week an nex'. You jus' bought yourself a cab—lock, stock, an' barrel."

"So you still recommend the Cicero Plaza?"

"I do, Boss. I really do."

"Then let's get there," said Jack. "I'll give you something on account, and you hang around. You make yourself always available."

"You raise an eyebrow, Oscar's goin' be there."

The hotel was what Oscar had promised: small, a little obscure, populated by two kinds of guests, and not many of them. The first kind were locals of the class Jack had seen in the Cotton Club during his visit with Murray the Camel. They were what were called wise guys. Others were "citizens"—out-of-town businessmen who had been directed to the Cicero Plaza by God-knew-who and walked about the lobby and ascended and descended in the elevators

298

with a brittle-eyed sense of adventure. It was like the hotels on Bayswater Road in London: potentially comfortable, even luxurious, but off the beaten track and faintly risky.

Jack took a suite. It was small but well appointed. He was pleased with it and accepted it as his headquarters for whatever he had to do in Chicago.

When he came down and entered Oscar's cab, he saw very readily that Cicero had not changed much since Al Capone left. Though the hotel was outwardly respectable, its neighbors were gambling joints, open speakeasies that did not pay so much as a shrug to Prohibition, and bordellos. The streets were alive with traffic. At night, Chicago still came to Cicero.

Jack's destination that first evening was the Congress Hotel, where Jim Farley and Louie Howe were masterminding the Roosevelt campaign.

Raucous conventioneers dominated the downtown streets: yelling, hooting, staggering. They issued from every hotel and wandered around looking for speakeasies and especially for the girly joints they had heard about and looked forward to seeing. They wandered into the middle of traffic.

Drivers honked and swore. The delegates laughed.

On the sidewalk in front of the Stevens Hotel a brass band tooted and banged with far more enthusiasm than musicianship. All the musicians were girls, wearing red jackets and skirts that barely covered their hips.

"That ban' started to play at six o'clock this mawnin," said Oscar Carter. "Six o'clock yesterday mawnin', too. They were brought here by the Governor of Oklahoma, man called Alfalfa Bill Murray. He wants to be President, but I don' think he's gonna make it. His ban' keeps folks awake. A lot of people don' like his language, either. He swears too much, they say."

Guarding the door at the entrance to the Roosevelt headquarters suite in the Congress Hotel was no less a personage than Cornelius Vanderbilt. "Good evening, Neely," said Jack. "What on earth are you doing here?"

"A volunteer," said Vanderbilt. "A hewer of wood and a drawer of water."

A minute later Jack was sitting with Louis Howe, in a bedroom. Howe was eating a sandwich, drinking coffee, and somehow managing to puff on a Sweet Caporal at the same time.

"It's nothing to worry about if he's not going to be nominated,"Jack said to Howe. He was explaining the nature of the danger facing the Governor. "How do you estimate his chances at this point?"

Howe continued to chew on his ham and cheese but spoke anyway. "We'll have six hundred and fifty votes or so on the first ballot," he said. "More than a hundred short of the two-thirds."

"Tell me then, Louie," said Jack. "If Frank is nominated, is he coming to Chicago?"

"That will be a big surprise," said Howe.

"Yes, a very big surprise if an attempt is made to assassinate him in Chicago. Even bigger if the attempt is successful."

"You have to know, don't you?"

"If I'm going to do anything to protect him, I have to know."

Louis Howe shoved another piece of sandwich into his mouth. "In confidence then," he muttered through the bread, ham, and cheese. "Yes. He's coming. You know how the man changes his mind, but as it stands now he's coming."

Jack grimaced. "I'll try to head off trouble somewhere short of his arrival here. It will be up to you to arrange security when he is actually in town."

"What's your pleasure, Boss?" asked Oscar when Jack returned to the cab.

Jack considered. He had flown an airplane all the way from Cape Cod, which was a wearying experience even when things went well. On the other hand, he was not tired, not ready to return to his hotel for a quiet dinner and bed. That was Jack. At forty-eight he retained the sense of adventure, and the enthusiasm for it, he'd had at twenty-eight. He was in Chicago as the Democratic National Convention was about to open. It was not in his nature to return to his hotel and go lethargically to bed.

"What do you suggest?" he asked Oscar.

"'Pends on what you want, Boss. Dinner? Drinks? 'Citement? Girls?"

"Some place exciting," said Jack. "But someplace that maybe won't be packed with conventioneers."

"Got a place in mind," said Oscar. "First-class. You did say you don't mind leavin' a little money behind?"

Like most of the eastern cities, Chicago was not the simple grid of streets that appeared on the map; it was a complex tangle of streets and alleys where a stranger could quickly lose his orientation.

"This here place is what they call the Hot Pepper," said Oscar as he pulled the cab to the curb in a dark narrow street. "It's where—like they say—the elite meet to eat. And do whatever else they got a mind to do."

"Where is it?" Jack asked. He saw nothing, just a forbidding row of doors on a row of brick buildings. "Which door?"

"Forty-eight," said Oscar.

"They'll let me in?"

Oscar chuckled. "Boss, they ain't never been no Prohibition agent wore clothes like you!"

Maybe not in Chicago, Jack reflected as he walked up six steps to the door at Number 48. It was true they dressed differently in the Midwest. Apart from delegates to the Democratic National Convention, many of whom came from parts of the country where correct dress was never seen, even Chicago businessmen were different in appearance from their Boston peers. He had not dressed for evening, was instead still wearing his afternoon clothes; even so, he was more decorously attired than men he saw on the streets in the Loop.

He rapped on the door. The peephole opened. Jack said nothing as dubious eyes looked him up and down. Then the door opened.

"Somebody recommend us?"

"As a matter office, yes. Mr. Oscar Carter, taxi driver. You might want to walk across the street and reward him."

The doorkeeper's face remained rigidly doubtful and otherwise bland. He was a burly gray-haired man, wearing a tuxedo. "Dinner?" he asked.

"If you please."

"With champagne?"

"With Scotch at first. Then maybe with wine. No champagne. No young lady, please."

"We have nice girls."

"I'm sure you do. But I want dinner and drinks, and maybe to see a show if you have one; and I'll run up a tab big enough to justify my table, without a girl to bore me. Is that understood, my friend?"

The man showed a smile at last. "Know what you want, huh? Okay. We got no problem."

Jack slipped a five-dollar bill out of his

pocket and handed it over. "Correct. We've no problem."

Unlike the Cotton Club where he'd gone with Murray the Camel, unlike Maury's big Leedo, unlike Sherman Billingsley's vulgar Stork Club, the Hot Pepper was a small room, accommodating fewer than fifty people at no more than twenty little round tables. It was dark. Except for candles in little lamps on each table, all the light came from the cool white spots that glared down on the stage. The tables were set with linen cloths, crystal, and silver. Before the stage was a small dance floor, parquet, and the rest of the floor was covered with oriental rugs.

In front of a small group of Negro musicians on the stage, an exquisitely beautiful Negro girl danced. She really did dance, to the sinuous music of two clarinets and the rhythm of a muted drum.

The doorkeeper led Jack to a table. The room was so small that no table was particularly better than any other. The doorkeeper had signaled, and a bottle of Scotch—Johnny Walker Black—was brought to the table immediately, with ice and water. The small menu showed Jack he could dine on steak, lamb chop, chicken, or shrimp. The doorkeeper bowed and said a waiter would come to the table soon.

Someone else came sooner. A broad-faced grinning man with an unruly cowlick stared at Jack from a nearby table for a long moment, then rose and stepped over.

"Be danged," he said. "B'lieve I've got the pleasure of sayin' hello to Blackjack Endicott."

Jack stood immediately and took the man's outstretched hand. "Will!" he said.

The man was Will Rogers.

Jack glanced at Will Rogers's table. "Are you alone, Will?" he asked.

Will Rogers showed his trademark boyish grin. "Reckon I've been stood up," he said.

"Then join me," said Jack. "You're here for the convention, I imagine?"

Sitting down, Will Rogers grinned again and said, "Well, you know me. I'm not a member of any organized political party. I'm a Democrat. Anyway, this here convention, even before it gets organized and started, is better than what the Republicans had, which was so boring they had to have men like in old Puritan churches, going up and down the aisles with feathers on sticks and tickling people's noses to wake them up."

"You're for Governor Roosevelt, I suppose?"

"Being from Oklahoma, I'm s'posed to be for Alfalfa Bill." He tipped his head to one side and scratched it. "But that's kinda tough, y' know. I'd really rather vote for a man that kin read and write."

Jack had met Will Rogers on an airport on Long Island. The famous comedian was fascinated with airplanes and was a close friend of Wiley Post. Will Rogers often flew with Post. He said he found it relaxing to go "cruising the sky." Jack had been flying a Jenny that day, and Rogers had asked for a ride. They had not seen each other often since that single day on the airfield, but neither had forgotten the other.

"If your date shows up, she can join us too," said Jack.

Will Rogers chuckled. "Oh, I didn't have no date," he said. "Mama'd never stand for that. No, I was s'posed to meet a politician here. And you know how that is. He probably got a better offer."

"Have a drink," said Jack.

"They were gonna bring me some bourbon. B'lieve I'll pass up the Scotch. It's just bourbon with iodine in it, y'know."

The music stopped, and the girl bowed.

The people at the tables applauded. She trotted off, and half a dozen more musicians, who had been waiting just outside, came in and joined the others on the stage.

"That there was what I call a beautiful girl," said Will Rogers. "Talented, too. It's shameful they don't pay her enough to buy a dress her size 'stead of one so skimpy and tight."

The crowd began to applaud again as a short, stocky black musician strode across the front of the room and mounted the stage. He turned and bowed, showing an ingenuous toothy grin. He was the leader of the band and also the lead trumpet, and when he began to play even Jack, who enjoyed jazz but was no connoisseur of it, recognized he was hearing something special. The man sang, too, in a deep gravelly voice. His style was unique, inimitable. Jack knew enough to identify elements of ragtime, blues, and something else this man had probably invented and given no name.

The crowd didn't talk while he and his band played. Even the waiters took orders by signal. People pointed at the menus to place their orders.

When the band took a break, Will Rogers joined in the hearty applause and said, "How 'bout that!"

"Who is he, do you know?" Jack asked.

"I do know. That is Louis Armstrong. From New Orleans originally, which is where he learned his music, I suppose. He's one of the most famous jazz musicians in the world."

Jack glanced around the room. "Odd that he's playing in a little club like this," he suggested.

Will Rogers shook his head. "Not odd. In the first place, this is the kind of joint where a talent like Louis Armstrong can make a living. Would they hire him for one of your fancy hotel ballrooms? A Negro? Playing that kind of music? The speaks is where jazz lives and prospers. Besides . . . Besides, the kind of guys that own places like this also own management contracts with talents like him."

"Where are musicians like that going to work when Prohibition ends?"

Will Rogers grinned broadly. "I figure in Oklahoma," he said. "'Cause we'll keep Prohibition by state law, so we'll still have bootleggers and speakeasies."

Their waiter returned now to ask if they

wanted to order dinner. Jack asked how the shrimp was cooked.

"This here's Chicago," said Will Rogers. "You eat anythin' here but beef, you're makin' a big mistake. It's almost as bad as Kansas City."

Jack conceded the point, and they ordered steaks and wine.

"Glad I ran into you," Will Rogers said. "Nice place, this, but I wasn't lookin' forward to eating alone."

"Neither was I. There are a few people I *don't* want to see, but it's was a pleasant surprise finding you here, Will."

"I don't know if you have been alone, truth to tell. A fellow over there seems to know you."

Jack turned to see who he meant. He turned just in time to catch the eye of Murray Humphries, Murray the Camel, who smiled cordially.

"I have to do this," Jack said to Will Rogers as he indicated by a gesture that Murray the Camel might like to join them.

He would. "Just for a moment. Just for a drink," he said as he drew back a chair and sat down.

Jack recalled now that Hot Pepper was the club Murray the Camel had mentioned as his favorite. If he'd remembered earlier, he wouldn't have come here. One reason he had taken a hotel suite in Cicero was to avoid encountering Humphries or Nitti or any of the rest of their crowd. He'd hoped to be in town a day or two, anyway, before they discovered him.

"I didn't know you were in town," said Murray the Camel.

"Just got in late this afternoon," said Jack.

"I think I recognized this gentleman," Murray said to Will Rogers. "Murray Humphries, Mr. Rogers. It's a pleasure to meet you."

"Pleasure's mine," said Will Rogers. "Excuse me a minute. Gotta visit the little boys' room. Be right back."

Murray nodded and smiled. "Your tabs tonight are on our friend in Atlanta," he said.

"Let's be frank about that," said Jack.

Murray's smile broadened. "Sure. It's on some friends."

"I've heard some bad things about our friend in Atlanta," said Jack. "That he's sick."

Murray the Camel shrugged. "Rumor," he said. "There were always rumors about him."

"Another rumor," said Jack, "is that he might be one of the sources of my problem."

Murray's smile disappeared in an instant. "I wouldn't give credence to that rumor," he said crisply.

"It would be helpful if I didn't have to."

"The source of your problem blew into town this morning. He's got a suite at the Palmer House."

"Who's that?"

"The Dutchman's in Chicago. And he's seeing people. He's a loose cannon. There's your problem."

"Can anyone in Chicago help me with that problem?" Jack asked.

Murray the Camel shrugged. "What can we do?"

12

A little past midnight Jack left the Hot Pepper, leaving Will Rogers, who said he wanted to see another performance by the dancer. Murray the Camel was still there, too, and he returned to Jack's table and sat down again with the famous comedian.

Oscar Carter was waiting outside as he had promised he would.

"Wanta go home now?" Oscar asked.

"Yes, definitely," Jack said. The day had at last caught up with him, and he suspected he might sleep a little on the drive out to Cicero. "Definitely."

Oscar started the cab and pulled away from the curb. He knew his streets, and Jack quickly ceased trying to orient himself as the cab turned left and right and left.

"Boss, we may have ourselves a little problem," Oscar said just as Jack closed his eyes.

"What?"

"Whilst I was sittin' there waitin' for you,

I noticed how a couple of tough-lookin' fellas was waitin' too. I said to myself, 'I wouldn't wanna be whoever them two are waitin' for.' Well . . . Seems like they was waitin' for *you*. They took off when we left, and they're right back there, right now."

Jack looked out the back window. The car following them was a black LaSalle, a formidable car that could outrun Oscar's taxi, a Chevrolet.

"Following . . . I don't want them to know where I'm staying. Do you think you can lose them?"

"Might could," said Oscar laconically as he shoved the taxi into second gear and accelerated through a right turn, then sped north on a street Jack thought was named Franklin. He couldn't read the street signs, and it wouldn't have made much difference if he could; he didn't know Chicago, which was as exotic to him as Tokyo.

Somebody in the club had—as the term was—fingered him. He couldn't believe it was Murray the Camel, though the most obvious finger man was Murray. But if Murray the Camel or Frank Nitti wanted him killed, they'd had their opportunity, easily and smoothly, the last time he was in town. And the story from Charlie

Lucky—which could of course be a lie—was that the two men who had beaten up Tiffany in the Palmer House had been—What? Killed? Charlie Lucky's word had been that the pair wouldn't do anything like that again. If not them . . . *who?*

The LaSalle had fallen back but quickly made up the distance and was directly behind them again.

"I don' think they just followin'," said Oscar. "This here's a Chicago kind of deal, Boss. I think we got *big* trouble."

"Make a couple of turns, then stop when we have a little distance on them," said Jack. "I'll jump out. There is no point in your getting hurt, Oscar."

"B'lieve I won't do it that way," said Oscar. "You ain' paid me yet."

"I'll pay you now—"

"Nevah mind that. Here they come!"

The LaSalle had pulled out to the left and was rapidly moving up alongside. Oscar deftly whipped the cab to the right and turned into an eastbound street. The LaSalle fell back but accelerated and caught up. Once more it edged out and raced alongside the Chevrolet.

Jack was carrying his biscuit, his .38 Smith & Wesson revolver. The window was down beside him, and he crouched on the floor of the Chevrolet and steadied the gun on the steel body. All three right-hand windows of the LaSalle were open. He saw two men inside, peering at the taxi, looking for the man in the back seat and for the moment mystified because he had dropped to his knees on the floor and they could not immediately spot him. One of those men had what Jack recognized as a Thompson submachine gun.

His thought had been to put a bullet through the hood of the big LaSalle, hoping to burst its carburetor or something else vital and so stop it. But not with a Tommy gun pointed skyward at the moment but ready to be lowered and leveled on the taxi. Apart from his own life, Oscar Carter's was at stake. Jack took aim on the man with the gun.

From a speeding, swerving car he had almost no chance of hitting the gunman, especially not with the snub-nosed .38. He took the best aim he could and fired.

The bullet punched a hole in the rear door of the LaSalle. It hit no one. But it scared the driver, who for a moment veered away. He had not been told their quarry would be a man with a gun.

Oscar Carter turned and for a brief moment stared into the backseat. "Oh-ho!" he yelled. "So! No wondah you wanta pay me two hundred bucks."

"Drive!" Jack bellowed. "We'll talk about money later. That bastard with the Tommy gun is just as likely to kill you as me."

"Got a point there, Boss," said Oscar somberly.

Oscar swerved right and accelerated south on a narrow street in the Loop, all but deserted at this time of night. The LaSalle roared into the same street and again came up alongside on the left.

The man with the Tommy gun didn't wait to be shot at. He loosed a burst at the Chevrolet. But Oscar was whipping right and left, and the Chevrolet was not an easy target from a speeding, careening car. The stream of slugs missed and whined off the pavement.

They were racing into the middle of the Loop. Pedestrians saw them coming and ducked behind parked cars. Drivers ahead ran their cars to the curb.

The LaSalle moved closer. Jack found himself staring into the muzzle of the Tommy gun. He had only four shots left in the Smith & Wesson and dared not waste one. He dared not wait too long, either. Taking the best aim he could, he fired again.

Luck: good luck, bad luck. Later he would wonder which it had been. His shot seemed to have hit the gunman in the face. Jack was not sure but thought he had seen an explosion of flesh and blood from the man's cheek and jaw. Anyway, the man dropped his gun out the window and fell back inside the LaSalle.

"Now—" Jack yelled at Oscar, meaning to say step on it and get out of here. But Oscar interrupted him by doing no such thing. Instead, he jammed on the brakes, took his hands off the steering wheel, and shoved a revolver of his own out the window.

Oscar fired. Oscar emptied his revolver: six quick shots into the LaSalle. Maybe he didn't hit anybody, but when he threw his hands onto his steering wheel again and shoved his accelerator to the floor, the LaSalle did not accelerate to follow. It drifted to the curb and slammed into a parked Chrysler.

They sat at a table in a Negro night club.

Jack was conscious that he was the only white man there. He was conscious, too, that Oscar Carter was well known and well thought of here and that, being brought by Oscar, he was accepted—just for tonight, just as long as Oscar wanted him. He was a curiosity, but they would tolerate him if he was a guest.

The room was big and smoky and crowded. People drank shots of whiskey, chased with glasses of beer. Men sat at their tables in clothes ranging from vest under-shirts and slacks to double-breasted suits and snap-brim fedoras. The women, too, were variously and colorfully dressed. They danced on a wooden floor made slick for dancing by the application of wax chips. Jack saw in the crowd a special zest, a sort of animation engendered maybe in despair momentarily set aside. Poverty was the companion of their zest but not its con-queror.

Across the room, heard over the murmur of conversation, low, throaty saxophones moaned out a kind of music he did not know.

Oscar had said they should come here, said he needed a drink, said it was some-place where they could talk. "Not many places, Boss, where a black man and a white man can sit down together and talk. Can here."

Jack sensed a comfortable security about the place, too. Prohibition agents would not dare come in here. Neither would many Chicago cops. Neither would . . . Well, neither would whoever they were. The club was a refuge, against all kinds of things. Violation would be resisted.

"I'm in or I'm out," said Oscar. "Ain' no man drives a man for two hundred or whatever and takes the kind of chance like I took tonight."

"I swear I had no idea that was going to happen," said Jack. "Which makes no difference. You have a point."

"Who is you, Boss? Time to level."

Jack spent ten minutes explaining why he was in Chicago. He omitted little.

"What's Governor Roosevelt gonna do for my people?" Oscar asked.

Jack glanced around. He was conscious that people at nearby tables were watching them, and he hoped nothing he had said had been overheard.

"I don't know, Oscar. I really don't know what the Governor will do for your people, if anything. I can tell you one thing only:

that Governor Roosevelt will do whatever he has to do to relieve the suffering of people in this country, and when he does that, you won't be left out. Whether he'll do anything special for you, I don't know."

Oscar sighed loudly. "Better than we've got from anybody else."

"Anyway," said Jack, "I'm not another mobster looking for what they call a 'wheel man.' I didn't intentionally put your life at risk tonight. I'm sorry I did, and I'm grateful for what you did, and I agree that my two hundred dollars is not enough."

Oscar tipped a small glass and gulped all the whiskey in it. He grabbed up his beer and gulped that to clear his mouth of the taste of the whiskey. Jack, who had tasted the whiskey in their glasses, could understand his need to chase it. The beer was nauseating, too. This was what Prohibition imposed on the common people. They were its victims. He wasn't. These people were the victims of the hookworm-belt yahoos, as Mencken would have it. Mencken was right.

"Big Al is a sick man," said Oscar. "That word is around. The sickness is at two ends, if you know what I mean."

"I've heard about it," said Jack. "Paresis."

"Figure him out," said Oscar. "Figure some of his old guys in. They don' like the new order of things."

"I've heard that," said Jack.

Oscar glanced around the room. Some of the women, even in the close, smoky summer heat, wore cloth coats with fur collars, and hats trimmed with fur. They swayed back and forth in rhythm with the saxophones. Their sweat gleamed on their brown cheeks and foreheads. Some of them noticed his glance and returned glances of their own: unambiguously provocative.

"They is some . . ." said Oscar. "Maybe even some of my people . . . who want to move in where the legitimate heirs of Big Al are leavin' a hole to be filled."

"I understand that."

"Not in our interest for Governor Roosevelt to be murdered in Chicago. Don't you agree?"

"That's in *nobody's* interest, Oscar."

Oscar paused for a moment and seemed to ponder his options. "Okay, I'll be your driver. What you gonna pay me?"

"A thousand dollars," said Jack.

Oscar's grin spread wide under his white

mustache. "For a thousand I'm *willin'* to get killed," he said.

Jack's thoughts had already moved on. "What we have to do is find out who those men were. And who they work for."

"I figure the mornin' newspapers goin' to tell you that," said Oscar. "Meanwhile, if this is the way it is, you gotta have somethin' better than that popgun. I'll get you a real piece. An' we'll start takin' certain precautions."

The morning newspapers did tell who the gunmen were:

GANGLAND SHOOTOUT
IN LOOP!

In a high-speed running gun battle that terrified pedestrians and motorists in several blocks, rival hands of gangsters traded murderous fire that resulted in the death of one man and critical injury to another.

Dead is Robert Blaustein, alias Bobby Blue, a New York hoodlum supposedly imported by "Three-Fingers Jack" White as an "enforcer." A man with a long record of arrests and prison terms, he is also the principal suspect in the April shooting death of Simon Lasky. Struck in the face by a .38 caliber slug, Blaustein died almost instantly.

Critically wounded with a bullet in his abdomen that had not been removed by surgeons more than four hours after the shooting was Frank DeChristoforo, identified by police as a "soldier" for the imprisoned Al Capone.

"You see this?" Oscar asked as Jack entered the cab in the morning. He handed the newspaper over the back of the front seat. "Said it'd tell us. Looks like each of us got one."

Jack nodded. The newspaper story went on to tell how a Thompson submachine gun, magazine three-quarters exhausted, had been found on the street a block from the point where the LaSalle had crashed into a parked car.

"We were lucky," said Oscar. "I got rid of my piece, an' now you gotta ditch that popgun. You know, what they call ballistics. If we used one of them guns again, that might link us up with what happened last night. I don' know 'bout you, but I don' wanta be known as a shoot-'em-up gangster. You give me the little revolver, and I'll get rid of it for you, same as I got rid of mine."

Jack was reluctant to surrender the little old Smith & Wesson that had been his father's, but he knew Oscar Carter was right; there was risk in keeping it. He pulled it from its holster and handed it to Oscar.

"What'll you do with it?"

"Wipe off the fingerprints, then toss her in the sanitary canal. There's enough guns in there to outfit an army. Even if somebody dredges her up sometime, it wouldn't mean nothin'. It'd jus' be one of the thousands."

"Capone's man," said Jack, pointing at the newspaper. "I suspected that's where the problem came from."

"Boss," said Oscar. "Like I told you, ol' Al is a sick man. They ain't nobody takin' orders from him no more."

"Maybe not taking orders," said Jack, "but I doubt he's without influence. He sent word to some people in Chicago that they should see me the last time I was here, and they saw me—people who were not likely to have seen me otherwise."

"Lots of the Capone mob are at loose ends," said Oscar. "Nitti has cut 'em off the payroll. They're for hire."

"Well, I know who's hiring them," Jack said.

"Then we either run from 'em or go get 'em," said Oscar Carter. "You got other ideas?"

"I know who their chief and their enforcer probably are."

"Boss, I thought you said you're not one of that kind."

"I'm not," said Jack. "I'm a great deal more intelligent and resourceful than they are."

"I can b'lieve it. So what we do now?"

"The first thing we do," said Jack, "is understand something. I will pay you a thousand dollars to be my driver, plus a source of whatever you know about things in Chicago. Not to risk your life getting involved in my problem."

Oscar Carter nodded gravely. "First thing I'm gonna do, Boss, is work on savin' my skin. Maybe in the course of doin', I accidentally save yours, too. First thing— Here's a gun to replace the cute little Smith & Wesson."

Jack had fired the kind of pistol Oscar now handed him: a Colt .45 automatic, the standard-issue officer's sidearm most army officers had been handed in 1917. He himself had been issued a .45 caliber Colt revolver in 1917 and had used it throughout his war service; but most officers had carried the automatic. It had a reputation for being a fearsome weapon, firing a huge slug that would blow a man apart. If it hit him. The second element of its reputation was that only a practiced marksman could hit a barn with it—from inside. It would not fit into his soft-leather holster. Fortunately, double-breasted jackets—currently styled—were roomy under the arms, and he could shove it down in the waistband of his trousers and so conceal it from any but a keen-eyed observer.

Oscar also turned over a handful of extra cartridges. "Like I said, Boss . . . What we do now?"

"I've been considering that," said Jack. "I think we beard the lion in his den."

Half an hour later, Jack stepped up to the desk at the Palmer House. "Mr. Flegenheimer's suite, please," he said briskly to the clerk.

"I don't think we have a Mr. Flegenheimer among our guests," said the oily young man. "In any event, if we did, his suite number would be confidential."

Jack handed him half a twenty-dollar bill.

"Twelve-thirty-four."

"Thank you," said Jack with a little smile. He turned and walked away.

"Uh, sir . . ."

Jack showed him the other half of the twenty. "When I come back down," he said. *"If* you didn't call him and tell him I was coming."

The elevator operator stopped the car smoothly at the twelfth floor, and Jack walked down the hall to Room 1234. He knocked. The door opened a crack, held by a chain. He handed a card to the man who was peering out.

"Tell Arthur that Mr. Endicott is here to see him," he said. In a moment the door opened wide and there stood Dutch Schultz, his arms spread apart, a great grin splitting his face, laughing with the look of a man happy to see a friend. He grabbed Jack's hand and shook it warmly.

"Jack Endicott! Come in! Come on in, buddy! Glad to see ya!"

Jack walked into the suite. "Odd," he said to Dutch Schultz, "but this is the suite I had the last time I was in Chicago. A poor little girl got beaten up here. The men who

328

did it are on the bottom of the Lake, as I understand."

"Oh . . . Jesus!" said Schultz. "Maybe the place has got bad luck. Anyway, come in and have a seat. You know Dixie. But I guess you haven't met Bo Weinberg."

Weinberg stood and walked toward Jack, hand extended. "I'm glad to meet you, Mr. Endicott," he said. "Dutch had mentioned you."

"There are some who think we've met before, Mr. Weinberg," said Jack smoothly.

Weinberg frowned. "I don't—"

Jack smiled. "Some people have tried to make me believe you tried to kill me one night in New York."

Dutch Schultz guffawed. "Haw! That's rich! Hey, Jack! If Bo'd tried to kill you, you'd be dead, I guarantee you."

Jack shook Bo Weinberg's hand, holding it in a firm grip even after he felt Weinberg nervously trying to pull back. "Rumors," he said. His eyes met Weinberg's and held on them as he kept his grip tight. "There are always rumors. That's why I came to see you gentlemen. There are ugly rumors around."

He released Bo Weinberg's hand then and walked over to shake hands with the patently miserable Dixie Davis whose eyes silently implored Jack not to say anything from which the other two could possibly infer the conversation he'd had with Jack at Polly Adler's.

"We're havin' coffee," said Schultz. "Cup?"

Jack nodded. Schultz himself poured coffee from a silver pot into a china cup. He was awkward; he would have been more at ease pouring from an aluminum pot into a mug.

Dutch Schultz wore a white shirt and a gaudy maroon-and-red necktie in a pattern that suggested snakeskin. He also wore an unbuttoned vest and a thin gold watch chain that looped through a buttonhole. A thick orange fountain pen was clipped to his vest pocket. As had been the case when Jack saw him before, the Dutchman's barber had done him no favor. His haircut would have embarrassed a prairie farmer.

Not so Bo Weinberg who, though in his shirtsleeves, was not sloppy like Schultz. And Davis was of course carefully tailored and barbered, apparently a specialty with him.

"I told you when we met in New York," Jack said to Schultz, "that people were doing nasty things and attributing them to you. We talked about that. Remember?"

Schultz nodded. "I remember. Guys are always tellin' dumb stories about me. What's it called, counselor?"

"Slander," said Dixie Davis hoarsely.

"Yeah. Guys are always making slander about me. It goes with the line of business, I guess."

"I suppose it does," said Jack dryly. "And slander can be a very harmful thing, can't it, Mr. Davis?"

"Oh—oh, yes," Davis chirped. "It can be damaging."

"For example," said Jack, "a businessman in Boston named Morris 'Moe' Goldish became the subject of some rumors. Now he's in jail. His business has been destroyed. Slander. It can hurt a man badly."

"I never doubted it," said Schultz. "The lies told about a mad—Hey, even Abraham Lincoln was lied about. Right, Dixie? Right. They lied about Honest Abe. I often think about that. What's the word? Slander. Yeah. They even slandered Abraham Lincoln. So what can I hope for?"

"Who is accusing us of what?" asked Bo Weinberg coldly.

Jack turned toward Weinberg, whose face, amiable enough at first, was now hard and icy. "It's still the problem with Governor Roosevelt," he said. "Somebody has threatened him. At first, nobody had any great reason for taking the threat seriously. Since then . . . Well, people have tried to kill me. People have tried to kill the Governor. The Edward Otis family died off Rhode Island in shooting meant for Governor Roosevelt."

"Why Roosevelt?" asked Dutch Schultz. "What's somebody shooting at this guy Otis got to do with anybody trying to hurt Governor Roosevelt?"

"Whoever fired on the Otis yacht thought they were firing on mine," said Jack caustically. "Governor Roosevelt was my guest aboard my boat that weekend."

"Jesus Christ!" muttered Schultz.

"Whoever meant to kill me," said Jack with cold calm, "only failed to kill the Governor of New York because of a stupid error. And, Mr. Flegenheimer . . . you are being accused."

"By who?"

Jack shrugged. "Various people," he said. "Shall we say, some people of Mediterranean origin."

Schultz frowned hard at Dixie Davis. "Who?"

"The Sicilians," said the lawyer dolefully.

"Lies!"

"I am glad to hear you say so," said Jack. "I knew when we talked before that you could not possibly be the man who was interested in assassinating Governor Roosevelt."

Dutch Schultz nodded. He nodded again. "Right," he said. "Sure. Of course, right. Mr. Endicott. Jack. What possible interest could I have in harming Governor Roosevelt?"

"Or me," said Jack. "You couldn't have had anything to do with trying to kill me."

"No," said Schultz. "Actually . . . I've thought about you a lot since that night we first met. You know—some ways, you're something like that guy Talleyrand. You know what I mean? I mean, if Governor Roosevelt is like Napoleon, then you're like Talleyrand. If I'm like Napoleon, then Dixie here's my Talleyrand. Don't that make sense?"

Jack nodded, but he recalled that Talleyrand had betrayed Napoleon, and he wondered if Schultz knew that and was suggesting that Dixie Davis might be double-crossing him. Or was he suggesting that he, Jack, might be tempted to betray Frank Roosevelt?

Bo Weinberg's thought was on an entirely different line. "Rumors I hear about you," he said to Jack, "say the man that tries to take you out had better be damn careful, 'cause you're a dead shot."

Jack smiled and nodded at Weinberg. "Dead is what I almost have been two or three times," he said.

"We understand each other, though, don't we?" said Dutch Schultz. "I'm bein' slandered. I mean, the last thing in the world I've got in mind is to do somethin' to hurt you or to hurt Governor Roosevelt."

"I'm pleased to hear it," said Jack.

"Back to the hotel, Oscar," Jack said when he was again in the taxi. "I've some telephone calls to make."

Actually he was hoping he could complete his business with one telephone call. He had to place six long-distance calls to Massachusetts before he finally reached Representative Joseph Martin, the prominent Republican from North Attleboro. He reached him at a Rotary Club luncheon.

"Joe?"

"Yes. Yes, this is Joe Martin. Who's calling?"

"Jack Endicott, How are you, Joe?"

"Fine. But astonished. They said you are telephoning from Chicago."

"Yes. From Cicero, actually. I need to ask you a favor, Joe."

"You know I'm always at your service, Jack. Even if I do guess you're out there promoting the candidacy of Governor Roosevelt."

"Well, that's not exactly what I'm doing, Joe. Sometime I'll explain it to you. Sometime I'll explain the strange request I'm about to make. What I'm asking you to do is telephone Director Hoover at FBI headquarters in Washington and ask him to give you all the information he can about three men: Robert Blaustein, alias Bobby Blue, Frank DeChristoforo, and Simon Lasky. Please tell the Director I'm interested in any connection between these men and Dutch Schultz. I'd be most grateful to you and to the Director for any information he can come up with. Also— and I'm sorry to have to say this—I am in urgent need of the information as quickly as I can get it."

"Gangsters," said Congressman Martin.

"What in the world is your interest in gangsters?"

"In confidence, Joe, I have reason to think there may be a conspiracy to assassinate Frank Roosevelt. You can tell Director Hoover that, but I'd appreciate it if you didn't mention it to anyone else."

"All right, Jack. I'll try to reach Hoover. Where can you be reached?"

Jack stayed at the Cicero Plaza Hotel, impatiently waiting for Martin to call him back, hoping he would hear from him before the end of the day. He did not. Instead, he received a telegram:

AT REQUEST REPRESENTATIVE MARTIN I AM PLEASED TO SUPPLY FOLLOWING INFORMATION FROM BUREAU FILES STOP FRANK DECHISTOFORO A LONGTIME CHICAGO HOODLUM WITH CONVICTIONS FOR EXTORTION BURGLARY AND ARSON STOP BLAUSTEIN FORMERLY OF NEW YORK HAS CONVICTIONS FOR HIJACKING AND ROBBERY STOP BLAUSTIEN SUSPECTED IN SEVERAL MURDERS INCLUDING SIMON LASKY STOP LASKY FORMERLY ASSOCIATED WITH SCHULTZ IN BRONX NUMBERS BANK STOP RUMOR HE WAS SUSPECTED OF SKIMMING MONEY AND WAS BANISHED TO CHICAGO

BY SCHULTZ STOP POSSIBLE BLAUSTEIN HIRED BY SCHULTZ TO ELIMINATE LASKY BUT NO DIRECT EVIDENCE OF SAME STOP HOOVER, DIRECTOR, FEDERAL BUREAU OF INVESTIGATION

Jack, carrying a walking stick and wearing a white carnation in his lapel, rode the elevator to the top floor of the Palmer House. That left him alone in the car with the white-gloved operator. He showed the man a folded twenty-dollar bill.

"That's for the man who can tell me what floor this man got off the elevator yesterday," he said to the wary Negro. He showed him the newspaper photograph, from the evening paper, of the late Robert Blaustein. "Get the floor right, you get the money."

The man shook his head. "I see the picture, sir," he said. "I know where you got it. But I never see that man, sir. I swear I never see that man."

"So you don't win twenty dollars," said Jack as the car began to descend. "But you can win five, and one of your friends can win the twenty, if you bring me the right answer. I'll be sitting in the lobby reading my newspaper, for the next half hour. Ask around."

"Yes, sir. I will, sir."

Toward the end of the half hour a bellboy approached Jack. "Excuse me, sir. One of the elevator operators has found something you lost. Or so he believes."

Jack rose, tipped the bellboy a quarter, and returned to the elevator bank. His operator, running car four, was on a floor far above, but Jack watched the indicator arrow and saw he was coming down.

The man stepped out of the elevator for a moment, glancing around and apparently hoping no supervisor was watching. "How would the twelfth floor suit you, sir?" he asked.

"When?"

"A little after noon, sir. And the boy says there's no question about who it was. He's sure about it, sir."

13

"I'm tired of being set up like a target to be shot at," Jack said to Oscar Carter. "Sooner or later, they're going to hit me. Besides, if I'm to do anything to protect Governor Roosevelt, I must do something better than just sit and wait for them to make an attempt on him."

"So long's he don't *come* to Chicago—" said Oscar.

"I can't tell him not to. I'd like to take positive action before he makes his decision to come or not to come."

"Tall order," said Oscar.

"I've got an idea," said Jack. "I'll explain it to you in about an hour."

He took that hour to place a telephone call to Frank Roosevelt from his room at the Cicero Plaza. While he waited for the operator to put the call through from Chicago to the governor's mansion in Albany, a process that could take from fifteen minutes to half an hour, he switched on the radio in his room and worked the tuning dial until he found a station broadcasting news from the convention.

Among the comments about doings there was one to the effect that "a burgeoning 'stop Roosevelt' movement is hourly growing in strength here at Chicago Stadium. The new Governor of New York may have more votes than any other candidate, but clearly it is the old Governor of that state, the ebullient Alfred E. Smith, who is the sentimental favorite and the key man in the dramatic crusade to prevent the personable but shallow Roosevelt from capturing the leadership of this party."

The telephone rang, and Jack turned off the radio. The operator reported that she had reached Albany and Mr. Roosevelt was on the line.

"It's grand to hear from you, Jack," said the familiar cadenced voice of the Governor, thinned by its journey across hundreds of miles of copper wire. "It's grand in fact to hear from someone who isn't weeping in his beer."

"I don't have any beer to weep in, Frank."

"Do you mean you would be weeping if you could?"

"No. I've identified our problem. It's Dutch Schultz, as we supposed all along. He's allied with some remnants of the old Capone mob, but the Dutchman is the moving force."

"I'm informed he's come to Chicago."

"He's here. I met with him this morning."

Frank Roosevelt laughed. "You met with him! You're irrepressible, Jack Endicott!"

"Do you know how I handled the Moe Goldish threat in Boston?" Jack asked.

"I'm like Will Rogers. I only know what I read in the papers."

"Well, why can't we do something of the like to Dutch Schultz? If he had big trouble back home, he'd leave Chicago; and he might even bring Bo Weinberg home with him. Why can't the State of New York come down on him, hard?"

"We'd have problems with that, Jack," said the Governor of New York. "Tammany prosecutors. Tammany judges. The forces that made a Dutch Schultz possible in the first place would protect him against an assault from Albany. Tammany has always hated me, you know. My determination to free the city from the abomination of Jimmy Walker has rekindled their hate."

"Walker is out here," said Jack. "Swaggering around Chicago."

"He'll be swaggering around a penitentiary when Sam Seabury's investigation is complete."

"Anyway, you're saying you can't initiate a crackdown on Dutch Schultz that would bring him back to New York in a hurry?"

"I could, but he wouldn't worry. He'd be taken care of. We might get him in the end, but not this week."

"All right, Frank. I'll take care of it out here."

"How, Jack? What are you going to do?"

"I'm not quite sure; don't worry about it. But I will ask you to do one thing."

"What is that?"

"Don't come to Chicago until you check with me. This city could be damned dangerous for you, Frank. Unless I can make some progress against what I'm sure Dutch Schultz is planning, you might be much better advised to make your acceptance speech from Albany."

The voice of Frank Roosevelt came across the line, chuckling. "All right, my friend," he said. "I will talk to you again before I reach any decision. Uh . . . You realize, of course, I may have no decision to worry about. They're making the nominating speeches today. I'm told mine is weak. And the convention is packed to the rafters with Al's claque. It's my men who are crying in their beer."

"When will they vote, Frank?"

"When they've nominated men like Alfalfa Bill Murray and Governor George White of Ohio, when every favorite son has had his moment of glory. Maybe by dawn tomorrow morning."

"Frank . . . I wish you success. I'll do what I can to protect you out here. I won't go near the convention, though. You know . . . Hell, Frank, I'm a Republican! I asked Joe Martin to help you out this afternoon, and—and, you might want to remember, he did what I asked."

"Joe Martin!"

"He doesn't want to see you elected. But, more than that, he doesn't want to see you assassinated. He's a decent man, Frank."

"I never doubted it," said Frank Roosevelt. "Politics is politics. Joe Martin understands that. It's the Tammany warriors who don't."

"All right, Frank. The pregnant night, huh? Give me a telephone number I can use to reach you if all your lines are tied up."

"Yes, of course. And—Jack . . . One thing more. If I am privileged to come to Chicago and accept the nomination in a speech to the convention, I—Jack. You know who I'd like to have there."

"I understand."

"There aren't many people I can ask to help with that."

"You can ask me."

"She's in Indianapolis," said Frank Roosevelt quietly, his voice not quite succeeding in containing his emotions. "She has a friend there—a college friend—she has gone to visit. You understand. If you could meet her at the railroad station and—"

"Frank. I can do better than that. I flew my airplane out here. I can fly to Indianapolis in an hour or so, have her in the hall when you make your triumphal speech—and, my dear old friend, I know it is going to be a triumph for you—and have her back to Indianapolis that same night."

To Jack's surprise, though not entirely so, Frank Roosevelt's voice failed him. "Yes . . ." was all he managed to say.

"Oscar," said Jack. "Here's the way it is.

That attack last night. Somebody in the Hot Pepper recognized me and fingered me. If you hadn't damned near got killed and then damned near killed that man DeChristoforo, I'd suspect it was you. But . . . But, my friend, I don't think it was you. I mean—hell, I *know* it wasn't you."

Oscar Carter's grave face wrinkled with a hard frown. "What that word you use, Boss? You call me 'friend?' Ain' no white man ever called me a friend before."

"Well, this goddam world is screwed up, Oscar," said Jack crisply. "So far as I am concerned, no money I could pay you as an employee would compensate for what you're doing for me. We only met each other yesterday, but so far as I am concerned, you are my friend. I hope you think I'm yours."

"Not an easy idea, Boss," said Oscar, "but I think you mean what you say."

"To start with," said Jack, "let's drop the word 'Boss,' Call me Jack. "

"Don' know if I can," said Oscar. "But I drop the 'Boss.' "

"Okay," said Jack. "So here's my idea . . ."

Oscar dropped Jack in the Loop. He hailed

a cab and was driven to the Hot Pepper, Oscar following at a distance. Oscar parked a block away, where he could see Jack come out but where he would not—they hoped—be recognized as the cab that had carried him last night.

Jack had chosen tonight to dress in evening clothes. At the checkroom he left his top hat and stick. The Colt .45 rode heavily in the waistband of his trousers, outside his waistcoat, requiring him constantly to reach for and adjust it. The maître d' recognized him as the man whose tab last night had been taken by Murray the Camel and asked if he would like to have his "usual" table. Jack said he would and sat down again where he had chatted last night with Will Rogers.

Louis Armstrong was playing the Hot Pepper again that night. Two exotic dancers worked between sets by the band. The crowd tonight was smaller—the delegates to the convention were in their uncomfortable seats on the floor now, anticipating a vote sometime during the night. Few of them would miss that.

But some Democrats in Chicago for the convention did not sit on the convention floor and cast votes. Not all were delegates. And Jack recognized two men sitting at a table to one side and mostly out of the light. One was Jimmy Walker, pensively smoking a cigarette and nodding as he listened to whatever Jimmy Hines had to say to him. At another table, on the far side of the room, the comedian Jimmy Durante sat with a man and woman and talked with happy animation. "Hot-cha-chaa!" Jack heard him say.

Murray the Camel Humphries came to Jack's table. "Can't join you for dinner this evening," he said, "but I'll have a drink with you if you don't mind."

"By all means," Jack said.

"Was that you they were shooting at last night?" Humphries asked.

"I'm afraid it was."

"You've got one hell of a set of body-guards," said Humphries.

Jack smiled. "Yes, the fellows are rather good," he said. "Fortunately."

Humphries nodded. "Blaustein and De-Christoforo were working for the Dutch-man. I can't prove it, but I've got no doubt about it."

"Don't turn and look now, but there's someone in this room who also works for the Dutchman. You noticed Mayor Walker?"

"I thought that's who that fellow might be."

"The other man, the heavier one, is Jimmy Hines. He's a Tammany district leader, and he and Schultz are hand-in-glove. He's another man who'd like to see something bad happen to Governor Roosevelt."

"Tammany district leader . . . That make him a powerful man?"

"Very powerful, so long as Tammany controls New York City," said Jack. "He oversees the appointment of district attorneys, which is why Dutch Schultz has never been prosecuted."

"What about this fellow Dewey?"

"He's a *United States* district attorney. Federal."

Murray the Camel turned and glanced at Jimmy Hines, as if his eyes were drawn to a man who exercised the kind of power Jack had described. His eyebrows rose as he stared at the smoothly fat, loose-jowled man who was at the moment apparently telling a joke to the impassive, meditative Jimmy Walker.

"All I can say to you, my friend, is be

careful. Where Dutch Schultz got Blaustein and DeChristoforo, he can get others like them. What's more, Bo Weinberg is in town."

"I know. I met him this morning. At the Palmer House."

"You met—! That means you saw the Dutchman, too. They're in the same suite."

"And Dixie Davis," said Jack, letting a little smile spread under his thin black mustache. "Old friends of mine."

"Why am I telling *you* to be careful?" Humphries asked. "Either you know exactly what you are doing or you're the damnedest fool I ever met."

Jack ate a steak at the Hot Pepper, and when his waiter brought the check he asked him to call a taxi. Subtlety was not an element of what waited on the street. The taxi was at the door. A few yards up the street a sleek Graham with distinctive gull-wing fenders sat at the curb. A block away Oscar Carter's taxi sat in the dark, also waiting.

"Chicago Stadium," Jack said to the driver. "I want to see what's going on at the Democrats' convention."

The driver said nothing, nodded, and shoved the car into gear. As they pulled away from the Hot Pepper, the Graham pulled away too and followed them. Jack pretended not to look. He would have liked to have checked to see if Oscar were following, and he tried to see by moving from side to side and staring at the rearview mirror. He couldn't catch sight of Oscar's cab and had to rely on his confidence in the man for his assurance.

Four blocks away from the Hot Pepper the driver stopped in the middle of a block. A man got out of a parked Ford and slipped into the front seat.

"What's this?" Jack asked.

"My brother," said the driver. "He needs a ride." The hefty man who had gotten in glanced back at him once then stared stolidly ahead. He did not see Jack furtively draw the .45 Colt automatic from under his clothes.

He didn't know much about the layout of Chicago streets, but it was apparent even to him that the cab was not going toward the Chicago Stadium. It was going north.

"Gentlemen," said Jack, "I hate to mention it, but we are not going where I said I wanted to go."

The burly passenger glanced back once

350

more. "That's smart," he said. "You got it figured out. So relax."

Jack engaged the safety on the massive pistol in his right hand, then raised it above his right shoulder and struck. The heavy steel frame of the Colt crunched into the man's skull, and he collapsed silently against the dashboard and did not move.

Jack pressed the muzzle of the pistol against the driver's ear. "Now," he said quietly, firmly. "He was right. I did have it figured out. So what about you? Do you have it figured out?"

"Yeah," said the driver fearfully. "Yeah . . . So where do you want me to go?"

"Where were you supposed to take me?"

"Well . . . Just a place. Just a road along the lake."

"I understand. Very well. Let's go there."

"You—hey, you don't wanta go there!"

"What? Not go there? And miss the chance of meeting the gentlemen in the Graham?"

"You know what they got in mind?"

"I understand perfectly. I also know that I shall have the advantage of surprise—that is, I shall have that advantage unless you do something foolish to try to warn them. Of course, if you do that, you will get a surprise like the one your 'brother' received."

The driver fell silent, obviously thinking, weighing his options and chances. He drove, continuing north, then east—Jack judged the direction they were taking.

Jack, too, weighed his chances. Much depended on Oscar Carter. It was not too late to order the driver to turn back. But what would the men in the Graham do then? As it was, he and Oscar were following a plan. They had guessed that the taxi driver who picked him up at the Hot Pepper might be a hostile. Oscar had warned him not to get in the cab if there were another man in it. Picking up the "brother" a few blocks away had been the only element they had not anticipated.

Surprise . . . Maybe it was overvalued. In the trenches, the idea had always been that you could maybe overcome barbed wire, machine-gun fire, shells, and even gas . . . if only you surprised the enemy. A lot of good men had been sacrificed to that theory. "Brother," now slumped in the front seat with blood running down his back, had trusted surprise.

Jack leaned over the back of the seat and began to feel the driver for a weapon.

"Relax," he said. "I'm only looking for—this." He pulled a short-barreled revolver out of the man's jacket. Feeling further, he found a knife.

Chicago was spreading north along the lake front. Even so, they reached shortly a dark stretch of road with vacant fields to the left and waterfront to the right.

"This is it," said the driver, and he pulled off the road and onto a narrow, rutted lane that led toward the water. "Where I was told to bring you."

"Lie down on the floor," said Jack. "I need hardly tell you what will happen if I see you move."

"Brother" moaned, but it was not the sound of a man likely to get up.

The Graham had followed the taxi off the road and was bumping over the ruts toward . . . toward what could not be called a beach so much as a stretch of muddy waterfront, thinly overgrown with willow scrub and weeds.

Jack slipped out of the back seat of the taxi, on the right side. For a brief moment he considered using it as a shield. Then he decided he would be better off if the men in the Graham did not know where he was. He trotted away into the cover of the bushy

353

willows that clung to the water's edge. There he knelt and watched.

The Graham stopped with its headlights beaming on the taxi. A man opened the door on its right side and stepped out. As he walked forward and the gleam from the headlights fell on him, Jack could see he was carrying a submachine gun.

"Lou?"

The terrified taxi driver kept his silence, and "brother" remained silent too.

The man with the Tommy gun walked forward. He was a snappy dresser, in an overstyled double-breasted suit with wide and tall lapels, as well as a white fedora. He leveled the submachine gun and peered at the taxi and into the darkness beyond.

Jack decided he would not be safe if this man fired a burst. He had given up the taxi as a shield, so even a wildly aimed burst of fire might catch him. Kneeling, he took aim with the Colt .45. He squeezed the trigger. The big gun roared and flashed.

He missed the gunman, his bullet smashing through the radiator of the Graham. Scalding water erupted from the exploded radiator, and one thick stream of it soaked the gunman's legs. He leaped up and down, yelling, dropped his Tommy gun, and used both hands to slap at his steaming trousers.

Two men jumped from the back seat of the Graham. One of them ran toward the water, brandishing a sawed-off shotgun. He had abandoned the shelter of the Graham just in time to be struck and knocked into lake Michigan by Oscar Carter's Chevrolet, which had come down the rutted lane without lights. The one who ran forward, ignoring the scalded man but sweeping the muzzle of another Thompson submachine gun back and forth, was struck in the left leg by Jack's second shot. He flopped on the ground, shrieking.

Oscar shot the driver of the Graham.

Jack walked forward, holding the Colt ahead of him, glancing back and forth, looking for the least sign of aggressive action by anyone. Oscar ran to the man with the scalded legs, roughly turned him over and pulled a revolver from inside his jacket. He grabbed the submachine gun the man had dropped and threw it as far as he could into the lake. Then he threw the man's revolver.

Jack followed that idea. In a minute he and Oscar threw all the mobsters' weapons into the water. Then Oscar opened the hoods of the taxi and the Graham and disabled their engines. He fired a shot through the carburetor of the big car but only tore all the wires off the taxi's engine.

Jack stood in the glare from the headlights of the Graham. The man with scalded legs was on his hands and knees, groaning. Jack stared at him for a moment, to be sure his earlier identification was correct. It was. He'd thought he recognized him when he first came into the headlights' glow. The man on his hands and knees was Bo Weinberg.

Oscar stepped up and kicked him in the teeth. "Figure this'n's the chief," he said. Bo Weinberg had rolled over on his back and stared up fearfully at Oscar Carter. Oscar stepped on his nose and ground his heel on it.

CHICAGO

July 1, 1932

Bedlam reigned in the Chicago Stadium. After the Roosevelt nominating speech, the organist began to play "Anchors Aweigh," a song supposed to refer to Governor Roosevelt's service as Assistant Secretary of the

Navy in the Wilson administration. The Al Smith claque rose in the galleries and began to boo and jeer raucously, until they all but drowned out the organ and the floor demonstration for Roosevelt. One of the Roosevelt managers got word to the organist to switch songs, and the organist switched to a currently popular tune—"Happy Days Are Here Again." The paid Smith claque went on booing.

Not until almost dawn, 4:28 A.M., could the chairman of the convention gavel the hoarse and sweating and exhausted delegates into their seats and initiate the first call of the states.

The vote was 661 for Roosevelt to 202 for Smith and 90 for Garner, with scattered votes for favorite sons and others—more than a hundred votes short of nomination under the two-thirds rule.

An hour later the convention took a second ballot. The Roosevelt campaign managers had withheld a few votes so as to be certain their candidate would have more votes on the second ballot than the first, but the gain was only sixteen votes, nothing near the hundred needed. At 9:30 A.M. the convention tried a third time. No change. It appeared as though what everyone dreaded may have occurred—a deadlock.

Under the influence of deadening fatigue and more than a thousand cases of "ginger ale" imported to Chicago to slake Democratic thirsts, most of the delegates were all but unconscious. When at 9:30 A.M. the Roosevelt managers signaled the chairman to adjourn until evening, everyone was glad.

In the Roosevelt suite in the Congress Hotel, Louis McHenry Howe lay on his back on the floor, his head propped up with pillows, gasping for breath under an attack of asthma. James Farley fell asleep with the telephone in his hand while he waited for a call from Albany. John Lowell Endicott, looking bizarre in evening clothes stained with mud, pushed his way into the suite, knelt beside Howe, and told him he thought the Governor could safely come to Chicago. Howe nodded and whispered weakly that there was no reason yet for the Governor to think about coming to Chicago.

In the Smith camp, weary men were elated. Their nemesis Roosevelt had been stopped! All that remained now was to put together a firm anti-Roosevelt coalition and capture the nomination for the Happy Warrior.

In another hotel suite, anger reigned. Dutch Schultz stalked back and forth in his parlor, swigging beer. Bo Weinberg lay on a couch while a doctor applied unguent to his red and swollen legs. His face was half covered by the fat bandage on his bloody broken nose.

"Nigger . . ." he kept muttering. "Goddamn nigger stepped on my face!"

"Shut up!" yelled Schultz. "What do I care about your goddamn face? That ain't the half . . . Cops figure out who that car belonged to, who those guys are . . . Dixie, you asshole! You got them train tickets?"

Dixie Davis nodded. "Yes, Arthur," he said. "An hour from now, we're on our way to New York."

"Where there's some sanity, anyway," said Schultz. "Get my stuff tossed in my bags! Isn't that part of a lawyer's job?"

"Yes, Arthur."

"You talked to Jimmy Hines?"

"I did," said Davis. "He's going to stay till he sees Al nominated."

"*Al!* It's going to be Roosevelt! Which is the end of everything. You get back on that phone to Hines and tell him I want him on this train with us. We may need a smart-ass politician with us in case of trouble."

"Yes, Arthur."

"Napoleon!" Schultz yelled. "Why'd you have to give me that goddam book about Napoleon? So's I'd see how traitors and incompetents were going to do me in? Well— I can see it all too well. It ain't Waterloo yet, but Chicago is one of the battles on the road. Isn't there *nobody* can do any damn thing right?"

The key was John Nance Garner, "Cactus Jack," Texan, the Speaker of the House of Representatives. Or maybe it was Congressman Sam Rayburn, another Texan. Or possibly the egomaniacal boss of the Hearst newspaper chain, William Randolph Hearst, who hated Franklin D. Roosevelt but hated Al Smith more. Or maybe the key was the simple fact that the Democrats were tired of losing elections and would very likely lose still another if their convention nominated a lackluster compromise candidate.

Late in the afternoon, Cactus Jack Garner telephoned Sam Raybum. "Sam," he said, "it's plain this man Roosevelt is the choice of the convention. It's time to break it up. I don't want a deadlock. Release my delegates."

Garner had more than the Texas delegates. The California delegates were also pledged to him. Texas plus California would put Roosevelt over.

When the convention convened again that evening for the fourth roll call, California switched, and the bandwagon rolled. Governor Roosevelt was nominated, 945 to 190½. The angry, bitter Al Smith refused to concede the winning candidate the traditional courtesy of a unanimous vote and kept his votes.

The next morning Governor Roosevelt, with Mrs. Roosevelt, and Elliott, took off from Albany in a Ford Tri-Motor, heading for Chicago and history.

EPILOGUE

On the evening of October 23, 1935, Dutch Schultz was murdered in the Palace Tavern in Newark, New Jersey, apparently by gunmen in the employ of Lepke Buchalter and Albert Anastasia, chiefs of a shady organization sometimes called Murder, Incorporated, killers for the Syndicate. Their gunmen shot down the Dutchman as he returned from a visit to the men's room. He lived for twenty-four hours in a Newark hospital, part of the time raving incoherently, part of the time begging the doctors to save him. He was thirty-three years old.

With two exceptions, all his chief lieutenants were killed the same evening, some there in the tavern, others elsewhere. The exceptions were:

—Bo Weinberg. The Dutchman himself had murdered Bo not long before, by binding him and holding his feet in a tub of concrete until it set, then toppling Bo over the rail of a boat at sea off Coney Island. It was a classic gangland murder, one of the few ever really carried out in that legendary way.

—Dixie Davis. He was spared on orders of Charlie Lucky. Davis was summoned to a meeting where Luciano grilled him about the Schultz enterprises and assets, which he wanted to take over. Then, to Davis's astonishment, Charlie Lucky let him go—with a sort of blessing. Later Davis was disbarred, then served three years in prison for his role in the Dutchman's numbers operations. Released in 1939, he married his showgirl sweetheart.

He was in the public eye twice more, then never again. In the year he was released he wrote a series of articles for *Collier's* magazine, recounting his experiences as lawyer for the Dutch Schultz mob. That same year he was called by Thomas E. Dewey as a prosecution witness in the trial that resulted in a prison sentence for Jimmy Hines. He died in California in 1970, his criminal activities all but forgotten.

—Lucky Luciano consolidated control of the New York rackets in his own hands and by 1936 was widely regarded as the most powerful mobster in America. He was careful to insulate himself from his rackets, and it proved nearly impossible to prosecute him. In 1936 Thomas E. Dewey brought him to trial on charges of forcing girls into prostitution. Luciano was convicted and sentenced to serve fifty years in prison. Many people believe Dewey framed Luciano. Unable to break the power of the top mob boss, he may have manufactured a phony case against him.

Among the people who thought so was Polly Adler, who probably knew more than anyone else in the world about prostitution in New York. In 1954 she published a best-selling account of her life as a famous madam. The book was called *A House Is Not a Home,* and in it she expressed her doubts about the charges against Luciano. Why, she wondered, would so powerful a man risk such a heavy sentence for so little possible profit?

Luciano served ten years. In 1946, Dewey, then Governor of New York, commuted his sentence. His stated reason was the Luciano, from prison, had made a significant contribution to the nation's effort to win World War II by ordering the waterfront unions not to strike but to keep their members hard at work loading the ships that carried men and material to Europe. To many people that didn't ring true, either. In any event, Luciano was released, deported to Italy, and spent the rest of his life chafing in forced retirement—though many believe he was instrumental in inducing the American Mafia to enter the narcotics trade. He died of a heart attack in 1961, at age sixty- seven.

—Al Capone was transferred from the Atlanta Penitentiary to Alcatraz, where he served what convicts call hard time. He was released in 1939, a disease-ravaged man who didn't always know who or where he was. He retired to an estate in Florida and died in 1947, at age forty-eight.

—Frank Nitti and Murray Humphries, with others, took control of the rackets in Chicago. Eventually, facing indictment for labor racketeering, Nitti shot himself. Murray the Camel lived on in prosperity and comfort and died in bed in the 1960s.

—Albert Anastasia, whom Jack met in Charlie Lucky's suite in the Metropolitan Hotel, was murdered in 1957. Joe Profaci, who shook Jack's hand the same night, lived to be arrested a few weeks after Anastasia's death, at the Appalachin Meeting—the biggest conference of American mob leaders ever assembled—and died in 1962. Mayor

Curley went to federal prison shortly after World War II. He remained popular in Boston, just the same. Mayor Jimmy Walker was forced to resign, but he was never prosecuted.

Frank Roosevelt was of course elected President of the United States. From time to time throughout his presidency he would call on his good friend Jack Endicott to help him with particularly touchy problems.